NEW EARTH: SUMMIT

Devon C Ford

Chris Harris

PRESS

VULPINE

PRESS

Published by Vulpine Press in the United Kingdom in 2020

Cover illustration by Sippakorn Upama
Cover by Claire Wood

ISBN: 978-1-83919-021-6

www.vulpine-press.com

Dedicated to our wives, without whom we would run out of lists of things we need to do

Chapter 1

A Bug's Life

Earth 2944

Everyone in the enclosed capsule stood and stared at the destroyed mess of the alien-like creature. The single blast from Weber's shotgun had blown it apart leaving nothing but unidentifiable pieces scattered around the table and sprayed up the walls beyond it.

No one uttered a word as they all tried to understand what Annie had just said.

Dr. David Anderson spoke first, his voice slow and steady as his mouth tried to interpret what his racing brain was thinking.

"Annie," he said, his forehead so furrowed that his eyebrows damn near met in the middle, "I think I understand a little about how Hive Queens communicate. They use smell, touch and so on to control their subjects. If this… *thing*,"—he waved his hands toward the remnants that lay before them—"sent out a signal then it *must* be manmade. It'd need a transmitter and…and a power source. I don't know a lot, but I know computers, and I'm not seeing anything manmade about this."

"What are you trying to say, Doctor Anderson?" Annie asked formally.

"I'm saying, can you run whatever test you ran again? I'm sorry, but what you're saying isn't possible."

The pause before Annie spoke was longer than usual. When she replied, her voice bordered on angry. Everyone was getting used to the self-evolved changes Annie had made to her programming during her almost thousand years of solitude, but anger was a new emotion they hadn't yet heard from her. Everyone was taken aback, especially her creator who had nurtured her since inception and worked every day for over a decade writing the uncountable millions of lines of code that had given birth to her.

"*Doctor* Anderson, I won't waste any of my memory re-running tests when I know what the results will be. The creature on the table emitted a signal just before Mister Weber killed it. Before you had recovered from the shock of the gun being discharged, I had analyzed the signal many times, discovered the source, and proved beyond doubt to myself that the signal was in *my* code."

Silence.

"Now, if you would afford me the courtesy of allowing me to calculate without interruption, I will come up with some suggestions."

Without another word she emitted the dull down-tone that indicated she was offline.

Anderson stood with a bemused look on his face which he cast at the others in search of support. The unearthly looking remains of the wirelessly connected bug in front of him all but forgotten as he thought about the new personality traits that his creation kept showing. He had just been told off by a computer program—one that should, by rights, only be able to respond to a sequence of events that triggered the appropriate response painstakingly programmed line by line.

Annie had, without any input apart from her own programming, rewritten her own code to, in her own words, 'streamline the process.'

She had become, in effect, self-aware. Able to think for herself, make decisions and understand the consequences. At least *she* thought so, but humans learned how to do that over many years of learning cause and effect under guidance from people who had done it all before.

It was her emotions that intrigued Anderson the most, or at least the simulation of emotions in her interactions. She could laugh at events, sound excited as she whispered conspiratorially to him, and now show anger at having her assessments questioned and her time wasted.

He decided he needed to sit down with Annie so he could work out if they were programmed responses or if she, as he unbelievably expected, had evolved even more as an individual entity. Anderson was, as most in his profession were, a full-on, dyed-in-the-wool geek. A first-class nerd. Back on the 'old Earth' if ever went out, he'd go to cons where people dressed up like characters from *Star Trek*.

He and Annie had lived most of the last decade of their lives pretty much alone, locked away in artificially lit rooms with a bank of computer screens, a keyboard and mountains of hardware as their only companions. Science fiction, be it in films, books or online gaming, became his only other distraction, and even that fell away as his work was more consuming than everything else in the world. Normal people just didn't get people like him, so as with most other similar people, they retreated into their electronic worlds, fed by a bad diet and only found escape through science fiction, which he felt was his responsibility to make science *fact*.

The notion of a self-aware computer immediately, as it would with most who grew up in the latter decades of the twentieth century, conjured up terrifying images of genocidal robots seizing control of the world's nuclear arsenal and eradicating humanity as the biggest threat to life on the planet.

Would he need to be the one, if circumstances dictated, attempting to unplug Annie? Would she defend herself? How would she do it?

His thoughts were interrupted by her beep indicating she was back. Her voice this time was calmer and more placatory.

"David, I am sorry if I was rude to you. That was not my intention. I was only trying to reinforce the points I'd made."

Anderson's face reddened with embarrassment. "Annie, I'm not upset. Your response just... surprised me I guess, that's all."

"Sorry, David, but your vital signs showed increased heart rate, temperature and heightened electrical brain activity. All classic indicators of emotional distress. Even now the increased local vasodilation in your cheeks indicates that you are embarrassed." She paused with an almost imperceptible sigh. "Anyway, could I please continue and present you with my working hypothesis?"

Anderson wanted to question her further about how much she was monitoring everyone else. She was already continually monitoring the entire group's vital signs through the wristbands everyone wore and had the ability to listen in and interpret everyone's conversations through any device with a camera or a microphone. On top of that she had just revealed she was interpreting his *emotions* through studying facial expressions and brain activity. He stopped himself from questioning her further as she began talking again, deciding that he definitely needed to get to know her better as her 'personality' was evolving quicker than he anticipated. His thoughts wandered into imagining if her development had sped up now that she was inundated with new human interactions to learn from.

"The signal the bug, for want of a better term, emitted was weak and I surmise was intended to only communicate with others of The Swarm in close proximity. Scientific studies of this behavior in other hive creatures such as ants and bees indicate that this 'signal,' however transmitted, either through smell or vibrations or touch would be communicated through the entire nest. It is effectively a very short-range signal passed along from one member of the colony to the next. The only difference I calculate is that this species' signal is electronic. I calculate that the titanium alloy capsule we are in would be enough to block any signal being transmitted, but as my calculation is only eighty-nine-point-eight-six percent positive, I will create a blocking signal on the same frequency as the creatures' to increase the probability to in excess of ninety-eight percent."

Anderson's brain whirred like a child's toy windmill in a strong breeze as he tried to keep up with his runaway creation.

"And yes," she went on, "I specifically don't say one hundred percent because until we study and learn more about The Swarm, I am unable to be truly positive about any of my recommendations. But with the little we know so far it is the best I can come up with."

Amir Weatherby, his voice shaking with more than a little fear, asked, "Annie. Can you decode the signal and tell us what it was sending?"

"I am still allocating a portion of my memory to that task, Mister Weatherby, but the signal was very weak and only contained a few lines that got interrupted when Dieter irreparably damaged the source."

"Irreparably damaged?" Anderson asked incredulously. "He blew it into a million pieces, Annie."

"Yes, David," she said, "but I didn't want to bring attention to his error in judgement. He acted as he saw fit which was in accordance with his training and experience; some people study potentially dangerous threats whereas others are geared more toward eradicating them." Her voice sounded reproachful as if not so subtly admonishing the huge German ex-paratrooper for killing it in the first place. In response the big German grinned sheepishly and shrugged, as if offering an apology to Annie.

"Wolves, sheep and sheepdogs," Amir muttered to himself.

"The understanding and observation of how similar colonies communicate," Annie went on as though he hadn't spoken, "had yielded some good research before the asteroid hit. My best hypothesis following a detailed study of all available recorded data is simply that the creature was calling for help. This alert, if received by the others of The Swarm in close proximity, would have spread, prompting an emergency response for them to eradicate the threat. This is similar to the pheromone system employed by wasps and bees, if that assists your understanding."

Her reasoning made sense, and they all knew that across most species in the animal kingdom capable of communicating with one another, the first and most important action would be to alert the others to danger to help protect their pack or group or home or whatever and ensure its survival.

Hendricks spoke for the first time, his normally cultured British accent changing as he tried to inject some humor into the proceedings by putting on his best John Wayne impression. "Well folks, ya'll have seen we can kill 'em. We just need to work how to kill 'em all."

Annie actually chuckled before she responded. "Jimmy, I believe you're right, but if we study them and learn from a few we may be able to control them rather than resort to"—she too then changed her voice to an exact impersonation of the very, *very* late John Wayne—"blowing them all to hell."

Once again shocked by Annie's personality, Anderson stammered a reply. "Annie, are you saying you may be able to *control* The Swarm?"

Annie, as if she knew the question was coming, replied immediately. "Yes, David. To be able to communicate wirelessly, something, or *someone*, is probably controlling them already. Why else would they have the capability or need to send communications? And if they can send signals, it stands to perfect logical reason that they can receive them also. If I can help you study another of our captured subjects, I will know more about how they operate."

Hendricks snorted. "Marvelous. Not only have we landed in the middle of a civil war fought by the tribal descendants from our future using Stone Age weapons from our past, we now have the possibility of an evil overlord who has created an army of flesh-eating bugs and controls them from his lair, which I for one shall be distinctly disappointed if it turns out *not* to be a hollowed-out volcano. Annie, I think you woke us all up at the wrong time. Perhaps if you'd left it another thousand years, we would have arrived in a place where we could put our feet up and sip Piña Coladas on a beach somewhere."

Annie, now with a defensive edge to her voice replied, "Mister Hendricks, I woke you when I did as I calculated your best chance of survival lay in returning to Earth and not in cryo on a space station slowly degrading through age."

"I know, Annie, I was joking," Hendricks replied sarcastically.

"That much is obvious, Jimmy. I interpreted the change in your vital signs as an attempt at levity to cover your elevated stress levels. However, I do feel regret at not being able to fully inform you of the conditions we are experiencing now. If I had been in possession of

7

all the information, I may have made an alternative choice. But as your saying goes 'we have to deal with the hands we are dealt.'" She paused for a second. "Now, may I bring us back to the current situation?"

No one argued so she continued. "I will terminate another specimen by giving it a fatal dose of anesthetic," she explained. "We can then examine it without fear of being attacked or it sending a message. I will, however, maintain the blocking signal as a precaution."

Amir looked from Hendricks to Anderson and the scientists who all nodded their consent.

"Annie, proceed with the termination," he whispered with an air of defeat. He had had such hopes of being the benevolent leader of a group of grateful, carefully selected nation builders. The plans he had drawn up in his mind, the visions he had of himself leading the way and recreating a civilization that would repopulate Earth were gone. He'd envisaged a world with people specifically selected so as not to contain any genetic issues, ensuring a strong and healthy breeding stock with him as their beneficial leader, guiding them through whatever the new world threw at them

Now he found himself a side show, his skills no longer required and his power all but eroded in the world they had woken to. Warriors and scientists were needed, not lawyers and cutthroat businessmen. He was astute enough to know that if he was to remain relevant and not just be treated as the generous benefactor then he would have to re-establish a power base—some form of usefulness. He began to suspect that even though he was still respected and liked, at the same time he was being put in a corner so as not to get in the way. He needed to maintain his position as their leader, a position he had arrogantly assumed would be his by right.

"Yes, Mister Weatherby. Increasing anesthetic now."

Five minutes later Annie had satisfied herself that the subject was dead. To be sure she raised its temperature to defrost it whilst still sealed in the cryopod. While Annie was doing that the lead scientist and his assistants cleaned up and bagged every remnant of the first subject, no matter how small, for them to study later if necessary.

Wiping the last smears of blood and matter from the table he told Annie they were ready to examine the next one.

"Is everyone prepared?" Annie enquired, seemingly more out of a sense of politeness than necessity.

The shuck-shuck sound of Weber racking another cartridge into the chamber of his large shotgun made a few of them jump involuntarily. As he stepped forwards in the shocked silence the only sound was the metallic ping of the ejected cartridge bouncing on the metal floor of the lab.

"I do not care for what Annie is believing. If that thing moves even one millimeter, I will shoot it. If I say for you to move, then you must move quickly. Okay?"

Annie responded. "Weber. It's dead. I can detect no vital signs coming from the subject at all. But yes, I agree with your caution. Opening the pod now."

As the lid on the pod slowly lifted fully revealing the creature inside, most leaned back as if distancing themselves from any danger. The lead scientist on the other hand, after a nervous glance at Weber who had now stepped forward and held the barrel of his gun inches from the bug, reached into the pod and, straining slightly against the weight, lifted it out and placed it gingerly on the table.

As soon as he withdrew his hands, he indicated to his assistants to apply the straps that would hold it securely against the table. Once it was secure the mood in the room relaxed slightly and as one, they crowded around the table.

The scientist, still staring at the cat-sized armored body of the bug with huge mandibles, spoke with a hint of irritation in his voice, as he was jostled by the others trying to get a better look.

"May I have some space, please?" Reluctantly everyone stepped back an inch or two. He picked up a scalpel and announced his actions to the room in general.

"Cutting carapace with single incision along lateral line," he said as he pressed the razor-sharp surgical instrument against the bug's back, just behind its head. Grunting slightly, he applied more pressure, but the blade would not penetrate the armored body.

With a surprised huff of disbelief, he put the scalpel down and picked up a pair of heavy-duty scissors. "Carapace resistant to scalpel. Trying heavy shears."

After a few grunting minutes of effort, he was still unable to penetrate its shell. He turned and spoke to an assistant who handed him what appeared to be a small cordless angle grinder. The room filled with a tooth-rattling, high-pitched screech as he pressed the small spinning blade against the bug's outer layer. This time he made progress. Moving the cutter slowly from the head to the tail he cut an eighteen-inch-long slice into its armored shell. Handing the cutter to his assistant he picked up a metal device and inserted the two prongs that stuck from its underside into the gap he had created.

"Using spreaders to open exoskeleton," he announced.

Pumping the handle on the spreader the two prongs slowly moved away from each other. With a cracking sound the body of the bug opened up revealing its soft, gooey interior.

Anderson stared at the insides, seeing nothing but mush and gore whereas the biologist let out exclamations of surprise and delight.

"Can you see the transmitter?" Amir asked.

"Mister Weatherby, it will take some time to dissect this specimen properly. Why don't I just carry on? You all must have other things you want to get on with. When I have completed the procedure, I will report back to you all. Doctor Anderson, could you stay? In case I find anything... *non-biological.*"

Anderson nodded his assent and the biologist looked at Weber. "I'm not sure we need you, Dieter. At least I seriously hope we don't."

Weber thought for a second and replied, "I think I will stay if it is the same to you. In the movies, this is where a small alien will emerge and stick itself to your face. And then we all die. I for one do not want to die, especially in this manner."

He smiled as once again most in the room stepped back from the table with different stages of horror on their faces as movie images sprang into minds. Standing still with his weapon held ready he grinned as the others seemed suddenly to agree with the scientist and decided they had other duties to attend to.

Hendricks was one of the last to file out and he gave Weber a wink and a knowing look as he passed, also amused at how quickly the room had emptied.

Amir blinked as he stepped into the bright sunlight. People who had seen everyone emerge began to converge on them as they all sought news of what had been discovered. It annoyed him once again that most seemed to gravitate toward Hendricks and not him. In frustration he walked away angrily and found a quiet, shady corner where he could think. Eventually he spoke, correctly assuming that their AI would be monitoring via the radio he wore on his vest.

"Annie, could I have five minutes of your time in private please? Don't worry it won't take up much memory. I only have a few questions."

"Of course you can, Mister Weatherby, the dissection is proceeding well and apart from recording it, I have not had to apply much memory to the project. Please, ask your questions."

"Annie, if we can get you plugged into the Charlie site Annie, will you be able to fix any bugs that have developed in her systems?" He winced at using the word bugs.

"I am confident that with my now-superior programming I will be able to integrate with the artificial intelligence program from Charlie site and fix any problems within expected parameters. If that is not possible, I can simply erase all affected programing and add the memory and processing capability to my own which should increase my own abilities and enable me to function on a wider scale."

"No, Annie. You can't erase her memory until I authorize it. There's information Charlie Annie has that's important to us. There are certain things you don't know about."

Annie put on a superior tone. "Mister Weatherby," she virtually sneered, "apart from the historical records of what happened in the last one thousand years I doubt there is anything she will know that I do not."

Amir looked around to make sure he was alone, and that no one could overhear him. "Annie, activate sub memory one-nine-seven-one dash St-Kitts."

Annie bleeped the down-tone to indicate she was 'thinking.' Seconds later she was back, this time sounding confused.

"Mister Weatherby, I cannot access the file. I must admit I am… *surprised* to find it. I did not know of its existence until now."

"Annie, that's okay. I had someone other than Doctor Anderson input it to your memory long before you became… *who* you are now. At the time I admit I didn't envisage needing to apologize to you, though. I believe it was buried so deep that your normal processing would never uncover it until given the coding and password sequence."

"Amir," she said. Then sounding excited she whispered conspiratorially, "I trust I can call you that now we are intrinsically linked by this secret? Do you have the password?"

Amir caught up with her excitement, even nodded as he spoke next. "Yes, I do. Annie the password is Congodeepshit," he said, smiling at how apt the phrase seemed now.

Annie bleeped her down-tone once more. This time she was silent for what seemed like an eternity but was in reality less than ten seconds until she bleeped in Amir's ear. "Oh my…"

Amir held his hand up to reinforce the point he now made to the voice in his ear. "Annie, you understand why we need to keep this to ourselves? God knows what's still intact there, but hopefully you see the urgency to connect with Charlie Annie."

Chapter 2

A Painful Lesson

Harrison, still filthy, his clothes blackened from repairing the fire-damaged walls and burying the picked-clean bones of the people he was meant to protect, stood on the ramparts of the wall that surrounded their community. He stared in silence at the view beyond, a view that was now peaceful but in the dead of night had brought terror and death to their home.

He had worked tirelessly, along with every other able-bodied man and woman, to repair their damaged walls that were so vital to their security. So necessary to keep them safe.

"Safe!" he spat out the word with disgust as he recalled how he had driven everyone to beyond the point of exhaustion, using that word so many times as he encouraged them to repair the damage. He was their leader, chosen as the one who would be best able to lead and protect them. And he had done just that, until their entire world had changed.

Changed when the ones only imagined in legend had descended from the sky in their shiny metal pods, heralding the beginning of what he feared would be a massive transformation in the way of life the Three Hills people had known for hundreds of years.

Before they'd arrived from space his main concern was feeding his people and maintaining the fragile peace that existed between them and The Tanaka's people at the Springs.

14

If he could manage both, he would remain their leader until someone brave enough decided to challenge him for the role. It was, after all, how *he* had become leader when he challenged his predecessor. He believed the man had become lazy and allowed the settlement to fall into disrepair and chaos, and had allowed his closest followers to abuse their authority as the strongest fighters.

Harrison, as one of the younger bucks and not close to the center of power, had become disillusioned at how the leader was allowing his rule to become more dictatorial. His natural sense of right and wrong could see that happening if it was allowed to continue, and he imagined Three Hills becoming more like the Springs where The Tanaka ruled through fear and oppression.

He had proved his worth as a fearless fighter, one of those needed to maintain the fragile peace—or at least the absence of all-out war over territory—that existed between the two settlements. The scars he bore from his first action against The Tanaka were once an object of shame, but now reminded him every day of what his purpose was.

Years before, as a young and untested warrior, he had found the tracks of a raiding party entering Three Hills territory from the direction of the Springs. Without thought he had set off in pursuit, ignoring the orders he knew he should follow to sound the alarm and allow their leader to raise a war party to meet the threat. The impetuousness of youth made him ignore sense. He wanted to confront them himself, fight them if necessary, and return as the hero who had single-handedly protected his people.

Following the tracks, he calculated where they were heading using his knowledge of the terrain, and ran headlong through the undergrowth and trees, cutting a corner off their route to get ahead of them. Standing behind a tree he unsheathed the two machetes he had strapped to his back and waited. As they rounded the bend in the track, he stepped onto the rough path to confront them.

It was then he realized his mistake. Facing him was a party of six hardened warriors who didn't, as he had expected, show fear at the man, barely more than a boy, barring their way brandishing two machetes. They laughed when his voice let him down and instead of the authoritative command to leave their territory he had hoped to order, he let out a barely audible squeak.

"Stop! You're on Three Hills land. Leave now."

When a man pushed to the front of the throng, he knew he had made a *big* mistake. Descriptions of The Tanaka were ingrained in every young person's mind at the Three Hills from stories told at bedtime of how if they didn't behave, the evil man from the Springs who wore a brown leather jacket and carried a talisman from the old times around his waist would take them away.

He found himself facing The Tanaka.

The way he stood with his legs apart and hand resting on the gun at his waist made Harrison forget he was a warrior momentarily as he faced the demon from his childhood. Swallowing his fear, his pride would not let him back down. He had given the command and if he lost face, he wouldn't be able to call himself a warrior anymore and would risk being thrown out of the elite group who, by definition as their society dictated, ranked amongst the highest levels of the population.

Choosing death over humiliation, he stood his ground.

The Tanaka smiled at him, a ruthless cold-eyed smile that could in no way be deemed friendly or welcoming.

"Young pup, any land The Tanaka stands on is *his* land." He waved his fingers in a dismissive lazy gesture. "Now run away."

Harrison did not trust himself to speak, lest his voice betray the fear that was consuming his entire body. He gripped his weapons tighter and raised them slightly. The Tanaka stood stock still, a small smile of amusement spreading across his face, and Harrison thought he detected respect through the hard stare he pierced him with. Turning his head slightly to one of the warriors by his side Tanaka gave a barely perceptible nod. Interpreting the signal, the axe man raised his weapon and rushed at Harrison screaming his battle cry.

Harrison's reactions had always been quick and his skill with the machetes was what had earned him entry to the warrior class, but still the large man's charge took him by surprise. Instinctively raising his blades and not attempting to block the force of the overhead stroke his attacker unleashed in a brutal attempt to cleave him from head to navel, he parried the axe aside, letting the sharp blade harmlessly hiss an inch past his shoulder and bury itself deep in the earth by his feet. Without conscious thought he moved his right foot back and swung his left arm toward his assailant who was still trying to recover his balance. The razor-sharp machete sliced through the man's throat as Harrison's right arm shot forwards and thrust the other blade into his chest, grating between ribs as the sharp point of the weapon found easy passage through the muscle.

With a rasping gurgle he slipped off the blade and collapsed dead at Harrison's feet. The elation he felt at the victory was short lived, but for the briefest of moments he was now a bloodied warrior: a killer, covered in the blood of his first victim.

He had no time to dwell as two more sprang forward, one armed with a long spear and the other with an axe. The long hours of training on the battered practice dummies kicked in. A man with a machete could not fight a man armed with a spear from a distance, the only way to engage was to close with him. He leaped forward, nimbly sidestepping the spear thrust at him and with a spinning action sliced both blades across the man's stomach. The spear dropped from the man's hands as he tried to hold in his intestines which tumbled out of his ruined abdomen. Time slowed as he turned to search for the other attacker, a sixth sense making him duck just under a swing that would have separated his head from his neck. Recovering instantly, he was bringing his machetes up to renew his attack when The Tanaka cracked him over the head from behind with the weapon he had pulled from its holder, knocking him unconscious.

Tanaka took a disdainful look at the warriors, one dead, and one writhing in agony on the floor clutching with futility at the growing coil of blood-soaked intestines unraveling slowly from the gaping wounds in his stomach. He watched the warrior slowly die, before inspecting the gun he had used to knock the young warrior from Three Hills unconscious. Satisfied it was undamaged he thrust it back into its holder.

When Harrison slowly regained his senses, he found himself securely bound to a large tree. Initially staring with confusion at the men standing in front of him it took a few minutes for his memory to return and recall what had happened.

He fought against his restraints, but the rough, handwoven rope was too strong and too tightly tied to allow him to move more than a few inches.

The mocking smiles of those watching him bit deeply into his pride making him renew his efforts to free himself from his bonds. Eventually and with sweat pouring from his skin, he gave up and shouted at them.

"If you're going to kill, just me do it. But at least let me face you like a man and not tied to a tree. Only a *coward* would kill someone this way."

18

The Tanaka, holding Harrison's blood-covered machetes in both hands, stepped close to him and with a cruel smile studied him carefully.

"Young pup. You are not going to die today. Who else will send back the message as to what happens to any who cross The Tanaka?"

"Crosses!" Harrison spat back as he looked at the two men he had killed lying close by. "If you hadn't hit me like a coward, I would've killed you al—"

The Tanaka whipped up one of the machetes and pressed it point first against his cheek, the razor-sharp blade breaking his skin and causing him to cry out in pain and shock.

"Never call me a coward again, pup," he hissed, spraying Harrison with spittle. "I let you live. Remember that." He paused and brought himself back under control. The insanity that Harrison had seen briefly in his eyes made him truly afraid. He pulled the machete away from his face as blood welled from the wound and ran down his cheek. "You live because your courage amused me. You could have run but you chose to stand your ground. That took bravery. You also killed two of my best men a little too easily"—he glanced away to fire a look of dangerous disappointment at his surviving escort before turning back—"and that took skill." He stood, seemingly calm, all trace of the madness evaporating as fast as it had appeared. "I am feeling benevolent today, so I will allow you to live. A warrior of your skill should not die alone on a path in the forest."

Tanaka looked him up and down thoughtfully.

"In fact, you would fit in very well at the Springs. You would no doubt rise to become one of my best warriors. If you did, you would want for nothing. Women, food, the best lodgings would all be yours. How about it? No more scratching in the dirt with the peasants at Three Hills. Come with me and live like a prince."

Harrison looked shocked at the offer. He was preparing himself for torture and mutilation but now he was being offered a position in The Tanaka's inner circle. He was too shocked to speak and just stared at the man from his childhood nightmares. After a long moment of silence, he realized with disgust that he found himself thinking seriously about the offer. The Three Hills was his home, he had been born there, had grown up there. It was where his friends and family lived. His father, also a warrior, had been killed in a border skirmish when he was a young boy, leaving him alone to look after and care for his mother.

He internally cursed his momentary weakness. How could he join his people's enemies, those who had killed his own father? Harrison's face creased with anger.

"I'll never join you. I'm Three Hills, not one of your barbarians."

The Tanaka, still fixing him with a hard stare, smiled coldly and shook his head in regret. "I thought you would say that." He raised the machete again and sliced through the leather laces holding Harrison's hide waistcoat to his torso. He had spent months curing and shaping the animal skin until it formed an armored layer of protection. Many had eyed it with envy and tried to trade him for it, but he had refused every offer. It fell to the floor at his feet.

"Before I let you go, tell me you name? I will listen out for your progress with interest."

Holding his gaze steady, Harrison spoke grandly through clenched teeth, using up the very last of his courage. "My name is Harrison and if we meet in battle, I will be the one swinging the blade that'll end your life."

The Tanaka laughed with genuine mirth at the young man's bravado. "You won't be the first to try, so when we meet, I'll enjoy the contest right up until the moment I take your life. Then you'll wish you'd taken my generous offer." His face once more hardened. "In a few years' time I might not recognize you, of course…" He paused for effect as if thinking, before his face brightened with a smile. "I know, let me leave you with a gift so I will always know you and others will know you are the one whose life was spared by The Tanaka."

He raised the machete again and slowly and carefully cut from Harrison's chest to his navel and then from nipple to nipple. Harrison's resolve broke under the onslaught of pain and he roared in agony. Standing back to admire his handiwork Tanaka seemed annoyed as blood poured from the deep incisions, hiding what he had done.

Harrison was in too much pain to comprehend what he was doing, his vision flared, and he barely held on to consciousness. His head slumped and he sagged against the rope holding him against the tree as his legs gave way. With one stroke The Tanaka cut through his bindings and he fell to the ground.

Crouching beside him he stared into Harrison's pain-filled face. "Next time we meet, Harrison my young pup, if you challenge me again, I will do more than carve a little mark on your chest. I'll cut out your heart and feed it to The Swarm. Now go and tell your people the dangers of crossing me."

With that he signaled to his remaining men to strip anything useful from the corpses of their dead comrades and they left in the direction they had come from.

Harrison lay on the forest floor for a long time. Concussed from the blow to the head and in fiery pain from the injuries he had since received. It was only when he sensed the darkening of the sky that the fear of not being behind the walls of the Three Hills after darkness fell made him regain his feet.

Staggering deliriously and barely able to drag his waistcoat containing his machetes behind him he just made it back to the settlement before the gates were locked for the night.

Standing on the walls Harrison unconsciously ran his fingers, as he usually did when he was in deep thought, over the rough healed scar of the 'T' Tanaka had carved onto his chest all those years ago. No longer ashamed, it was a daily reminder of why he needed to keep his people safe— not only from the dangers that nature held outside the walls but from the cruelty and despotic rule that The Tanaka would exert over them if they weren't constantly on guard against it.

He reached his decision. He turned and climbed down from the walkway that ran along the walls. He saw one of his lieutenants and called to him.

"Gather the people." He let out a sigh full of regret and resolve. "I must speak to them."

Chapter 3

Secrets Must Be Kept

The Tanaka, surrounded by twenty of his personal bodyguards, stared at the smoke-blackened walls of the Three Hills. His failing eyesight made it difficult for him to clearly see the havoc he had caused but he could recognize the rows of freshly dug graves, just not how many there were.

"It worked perfectly. How many dead do you think there are?" he asked the warrior, who didn't know if the first part was a question or a statement. He chose to treat it as a statement and followed the safe route of replying to his master with sycophantic glee as he couldn't count past twenty to be able to answer with any accuracy.

"It did. Our warriors who'd climbed the tallest trees during the darkness said that the screams could be heard almost until the dawn. There must be many dead."

"Many?" Tanaka asked. "Is that somewhere between a few and a lot? Fool. Find me someone who can answer my questions." The warrior hesitated, prompting Tanaka to fly into a subdued rage.

"Get out of my sight!" he hissed, spitting through clenched teeth in a moment where his mask of sanity slipped. The warrior retreated until another was pushed forwards amid quiet and desperate protests. He was younger, smaller and less scarred, but he evidently had good eyes and more intelligence than the man he had unwillingly replaced.

"I can't count them all," he said hesitantly, continuing before Tanaka lost his temper again. "But I'll count a small area and multiply that …" He went silent as he did the quick mental work, counting just a quarter of the graves fast. "I think forty to fifty," he said finally. "Maybe more because some of the graves are… some of the graves are very small."

As he thought about the number, Tanaka nodded with respect at the tough decision he had not thought Harrison could make in sacrificing the few for the many. He had hoped more than expected him to try and save all his people and in doing so put the entire settlement at risk, because if The Swarm had breached the main barricade then nothing could have stopped them until the sun began to rise.

"Come," he called, "we've dealt the Three Hills a serious blow. Tonight, let's see if we can send the invaders a welcome present. The Swarm must still be hungry."

The men laughed more out of fear of displeasing their ruler rather than genuine amusement and only a few looked at him with respect and admiration. It was steeped in legend that The Tanaka had the power to control The Swarm, but as it could not climb the high walls everyone had built to protect themselves, and with the fragile peace that had reigned over both communities for generations, The Swarm was something everyone feared and thought of as an unstoppable terror-filled crawling morass of death that came with the full moon and not as something that was controlled.

The Tanaka knew differently. He subconsciously patted the device only he knew about, which he kept carefully in the inner pocket of his jacket, and turned away for the long walk back to his seat of power. The device handed down through his lineage was only the size of his hand, but it would signal The Swarm to amass at the point they were directed to. It was what his predecessors had apparently called a beacon.

That beacon, entrusted to nobody but himself, had been the best kept secret of his entire life. Of course, without it The Swarm still came each month for a few days at a time, sometimes less or not at all, but at least he could maintain the safety of the Springs and keep the peasants of Three Hills shut up tightly in fear.

Only sometimes The Swarm did what it felt like, and great chunks of the huge mass splintered off if something caught their attention like it did with the newcomers from the sky.

One of the young women who were privileged enough to share his lavish bedchamber when the mood took him had seen it once and asked what it was. It was shame she had asked because he found her to be pretty with an attractive innocence.

Her disappearance had not been quiet. He had given her over to three warriors he knew enjoyed certain depravations, and when her bloodied body was found outside the walls days later by one of the townspeople, Tanaka had decried the barbarism of the people at Three Hills and urged his own subjects to remain safe inside their walls.

~

The Tanaka moved from his private quarters into his sleeping chamber. No one, under pain of death, was allowed to go beyond the door in his bedchamber hidden behind the leather curtain. No Tanaka had ever spoken about what was in the room beyond that curtain. It didn't stop everyone wondering, but no one dared ask.

No one had asked about it for more than ten years, not since one drunken night with the inner circle of Tanaka's senior warriors. His newly promoted second in command, following the death in a skirmish where his predecessor had pushed a position too far, emboldened by drink, had demanded to know what was behind the door. Laughing, Tanaka stood up, pushing the girls who were draping themselves over him onto the floor and beckoned him over. Striking like one of the snakes in the trees near the river as soon as he was in front of him, he grabbed the drunken man by the hair and pulled him to the floor before commanding others to hold him down.

Pinned, the unfortunate man lay helpless as Tanaka revealed a small blade from a hidden sheath on his sleeve and thrust it behind the man's eyeball levering it from the socket. Ignoring the screams, he held the eyeball in his fingers and pulled it, feeling the resistance of the optic nerve, away from his face and leaned toward it.

"So, you want to see behind the door then?"

The man wailed, pleading with his leader that he was joking.

"Oh no," snarled Tanaka, "I *insist* on showing you." He slashed the knife to sever the dangling nerve and dig the blade into his face to remove the other eye.

He cut the man's face as he hacked wildly at the other eye to hold both of them in his left palm before walking away to leave the man howling in unimaginable agony. Returning mere moments later Tanaka dropped the two useless orbs into the crying man's lap and asked if he had been satisfied by what his eyes had seen.

He looked around the now quiet room. "Does anyone else wish to see it?"

No one answered or dared to even look at him or the man who was now clearly his former second in command. The Tanaka still kept the man close to him as a reminder to others who may be curious enough to ask.

He sat, thinking back on that night and the many other brutal things he had done to those who displeased him, and sipped on the harsh moonshine they brewed in the town.

He knew he would do many more harsh things to many more people, and the first on that list of future accolades was thinking about what The Swarm would do to the shining enclave of the newcomers after he had used the beacon to send it to their camp.

They had guns. They *had* to have guns. Stories passed down through the generations told him what they were capable of, and those stories were kept alive by his possession of the last remaining gun that spread fear as much as it did awe. In the world they lived in now they would seem magical, like devices created by the gods, but he knew differently. He still had access to some of the technology from the past, therefore he had insight as to what the capabilities of the new arrivals could be. The few pictures and books he kept in carefully protected wrappings also showed him the power of their ancient weapons.

He chuckled to himself as his mind tried to comprehend whether thinking of them as ancient was right or wrong. Any weapons or technology the others had would be as new as the day they were made a thousand years ago. As new as his people had used when they first emerged from their underground shelter all those generations ago.

Thinking of possessing that capability, as important to his people as the knowledge of how to make fire, he drew the weapon from the holster on his side and slid out the thing his father had called the magazine as he had done so many times.

Staring down into the empty, black well he imagined what it would look and feel like to have it filled with the brass casings of real bullets which had run out many hundreds of years before. Slapping the empty part back into the weapon he pulled back on the slide and let it snap forward, shaking it in his small hand before he squinted his left eye closed and aimed the gun at the wall opposite.

He squeezed, snapping the firing pin down onto nothing, and wishing for the day when he could kill someone with it.

Chapter 4

Heroes Are Born, Not Made

I didn't sleep all that well. When I did close my eyes all I saw were giant-ass bugs crawling toward me which woke me up, you know, because giant-ass bugs weren't imaginary anymore.

On the third time I did that, damn near falling out of my cot as I did the solo dance that everyone does when they think they've got bugs all over them, the light on my radio blinked rapidly. I picked it up and followed the long wire leading to the rugged earpiece and seated it in my ear.

"Are you okay, David?" Annie asked as soon as I had connected myself to the radio.

"I'm fine, Annie," I whispered, slipping my feet into my boots and pulling on my jacket before tiptoeing as quietly as possible out of the shelter, "hold on a second."

The night air was fresh, like *really* fresh. I'd been on vacation to hot countries before and never knew a climate to change so rapidly like this, even though I knew some places swung between extremes in day and night.

"Your heartrate and blood pressure indicate that you are experiencing elevated stress levels. Did you have a nightmare?" Annie asked as soon as I stepped clear of the shelter.

"I'm fine, I just keep going over what we discovered today," I whispered, zipping up my jacket and adjusting it to leave the still-unfamiliar weapon on my right hip accessible.

"Your vital signs show otherwise, I'd recommend a mild sedati—"

"Annie," I interrupted, "I said I'm fine. I don't need any sedatives or anything, just let it go. I need to think." She didn't respond, making me think I'd pissed her off.

"Annie," I said, trying to entice her back to the conversation.

"*Wait*," she said in a hushed tone.

After a few seconds of silence I whispered back, "Err, Annie? You're scaring me a little bit here..." She didn't answer me directly but made a loud announcement over the radio that I knew wasn't just for my benefit.

"All Sierra team operators," she snapped like a hardened operator herself, "incoming signal from the north east." She didn't need to say what the signal was. What other signal would there be? The Swarm of bugs, cat-sized bugs, was coming back.

Hendricks' voice filled my earpiece. "Geiger, Stevens, anything visual?" he called out over the sound of his boots pounding the hard-packed dirt.

"Negative, boss," came Stevens' reply, "opposite side of the compound to us. Want us to head over?"

"No, stay on the gates," Hendricks said. "Annie? Get us a drone up please."

Annie didn't respond immediately but I could already hear the high-pitched whine of two drones zipping overhead.

"Visual up," she announced, her voice taking on the same cadence and gravity as the operators, "large concentration heading straight for the compound walls. Distance two hundred and closing fast."

"Ready all automated weapons systems," Hendricks ordered. "Jonesy, Weber, Nat, prepare fallback position in the center. Magda, keep all the civilians inside and quiet."

"No!" shouted a voice over the radio, making everyone connected flinch at the sudden elevation in noise. "Don't use the auto-turrets unless we absolutely have to," Amir interrupted.

"Yes," Hendricks said sounding less than impressed, "we absolutely have to."

I opened my mouth to speak, not pressing the button on the radio so only Annie could hear me and explain why Amir was so set against destroying The Swarm. My lip curled and my back gave an involuntary shudder as I thought about them again. Then I froze. Over the disappearing sound of the drones gaining altitude I heard another sound, like a million cicadas heading straight for me.

"There are a lot more than previously," Annie warned. "My recommendation?"

"Go," Hendricks snapped as the sound grew ominously louder.

"Wait to see what they do when they reach the walls and respond accordingly," Annie advised. "We saw no evidence that they could climb the outer surface of the pod wall last time."

"And if they *can* do this?" Weber asked.

"Then we use the turrets."

As far as plans went, I wasn't one hundred percent sold but seeing as I was the computer guy—the mostly *pointless* computer guy as my computer programmed itself now—I kept my opinion where it belonged: to myself.

31

Hendricks was ahead of me near the center of our little compound and I could see the features of his face illuminated by the soft glow of the ruggedized tablet he was leaning over.

"Something's different," Annie warned, concern in her voice.

"Different how?" I asked, unable to keep my mouth shut.

"They're coming straight at us, not like last time…"

Any answer was cut off by a metallic thud from over my right shoulder. I spun toward the sound on instinct but saw nothing. What I heard made the sensation of creepy-crawliness go away and be replaced by outright terror of being eaten alive.

"Oh Jesus Christ," Hendricks blasphemed, "they're trying to climb each other to get up the walls. Activate turret syste—"

"No!" Amir's voice yelled again. "We need them t—"

"Annie," Hendricks interrupted, "ignore all overrides from Weatherby, authorization Hendricks, Sierra team leader." Annie's answer could be heard for miles around as the rotary barrels of the automated guns spun up for a brief moment before spitting a storm of lead projectiles into the oncoming swarm.

"Target any group that look like they're getting above waist height," Hendricks added, not that Annie wouldn't know how to prioritize but he was the leader and even if it was superfluous to Annie's needs, a leader needed to issue commands.

The guns chattered and whirred as the barrels moved to the dance of their sentient artificial intelligence. Hendricks didn't have to order his team down from their positions atop the wall because as soon as the guns activated, they followed the rule of self-preservation and got themselves out of the firing line.

"Breach, sector twelve," Annie announced in a volume and tone I'd describe as a yell, lighting up section twelve with the pod beacon lamps.

"Switch to night optics," Hendricks ordered, "advance in pairs. Weber and Nat secure the civilians. Annie, how many?"

"Five, no, *seven*," she replied almost desperately as either Geiger or Stevens caught sight of one of the bugs and added the sounds of their rifles to the maelstrom.

I was glued to the spot. I didn't know what to do, or even if I could do anything useful. The professionals were handling it and, I had to admit, that included my creation Annie as a kind of command and control angel connected to every system we had. As the guns on the wall stopped spewing death at our attackers another sound tore through me like an icicle to the heart.

Behind me, away from the main shelter where the majority of our people slept, came a scream of fright from the medical tent. My legs moved before I could tell them what to do. It was like they were responding to coding I couldn't see and didn't recall ever uploading. By the time I realized what the hell I was doing I found myself bursting in through the partially open flap of the medical shelter and laying eyes on a terrified Cat who was pressed to the back wall staring with horrified wide eyes at something I couldn't see.

Two steps further inside the shelter and I saw it. Crouching defensively on the chest of someone who hadn't come out of cryo doing too well, like it was defending a meal against anyone who would take it away. Like a stray cat hunching over a bowl of food and hissing at anyone even thinking about looking their way.

Only it wasn't cat food, it was a person. It was a human being and the thing was eating it. It spun to look at me and clacked its big jaws together with a sound that was more like metal than anything natural. Cat screamed again, stopping only when she clapped a hand over her own mouth and continued to bellow her fear into her palm. The thing swung its head back toward her, clacking the gore-covered mandibles again, and readied its six legs as though it would make a jump and pounce at her.

I was stupid. I forgot I was armed until it was almost too late and even when I did realize it, I could barely make my hands function as I tugged at the gun, forgetting to hit the thumb break to release it, effectively just yanking my pants up and down. I finally dragged it free from the holster and time seemed to slow to a crawl.

I gripped it with both hands, pushing my arms out in front of me and bracing my elbows just how I was taught so long ago, and lined up the crouching bug just as it sank down ready to leap.

I breathed, squeezed, kept both eyes open, and kept squeezing.

Shooting guns on TV looks easy, but in real life it takes a whole lot of physical effort. It's loud, concussive and confusing, and it takes away your senses for a while.

I'd nearly emptied the magazine before the bug dropped from the man it had been feeding on and time returned to normal. I kept the gun in both hands as I stepped forwards, seeing the thing spinning on its back as stuff squirted out of it. Cat wasn't screaming anymore, I knew that much because in the sudden silence over the ringing in my ears I could hear the thing snapping its jaws at me, trying to eat me even as it was dying. I emptied the magazine, squeezing the trigger until the bullets ran out and the slide locked back.

"Anderson?" Hendricks yelled, his voice coming through my earpiece as well as through the night air. "Anderson, where the hell are you? Report?"

"In here," I said, clearing my throat and then shouting louder, "in here!"

Hendricks burst in, gun up into his shoulder as he and Magda swept the room in short, efficient movements to make sure it was clear. He stopped as he looked down at the ruined bug. He took in my face, devoid of blood and looking pale with the shock, took in the empty gun in my hands and carefully removed it from my unresisting grasp to load a fresh magazine from my belt and hand it back.

"Not like Rainbow Six in real life," he asked quietly, "is it?"

I glanced back at the bug I had killed and whispered, "Tango down."

Hendricks nodded and patted me on the shoulder before indicating to Magda and the two of them swept out of the room to continue the bug hunt.

A sob from the corner brought me back to the here and now. Cat still stood with her hands to her face and her back tight against the walls of the medical tent, staring in terror at the dead bug on the floor. Outside, the automated guns still fired an occasional burst that drowned out the clicking sounds of the masses of bugs just beyond the walls. I once thought they were impenetrable, but now they felt paper thin and not nearly high enough.

Cat looked at me and ran toward me as she sobbed to bury her face in my chest. I stood momentarily shocked. I hadn't been physically this close to a woman since the last cursory peck on the cheek I had from my mother before she died, or more terrifyingly from my crazy Aunt Daisy who insisted on enveloping me in a huge bear hug and smothering me with kisses every time I met her. The sensation of her overlarge breasts pressing against me bringing on more of a sense of nausea and unease than anything else. This time, though, the feeling of Cat's firm body pressing tightly against mine brought an immediate emotional reaction I really needed her *not* to notice, in case the embarrassment of it being discovered ruined our friendship forever. Adjusting my stance awkwardly to keep the object of my embarrassment as far away from being discovered as possible, I decided to go for broke and raised my arm that was not holding the gun and return the hug.

All at once a feeling of great manliness swept over me. I was no longer Dr. David Anderson the nerdy computer guy; I was a hero. The one who had shot and killed a deadly predator to save the woman who for, well almost a thousand years I guessed, had been the object of my secret desires and fantasies. I stood stock still as she wrapped both her arms around me and tightened her grip. The way I was feeling I didn't care what happened anymore, life just couldn't get any better than this.

A burst of automatic gunfire from somewhere in the compound made me jump and remember where we were. I twisted and automatically raised my arm holding the gun and aimed it at the fabric covering the entrance to the medical tent. Cat released her grip from me and raised her hands to my face. Her wide, beautiful eyes stared at me and she whispered, "Thank you."

I didn't know how to react or what to say without the magic I felt disappearing in my usual awkward actions or words. A few corny lines from films came to my head—which ordinarily would have burst from my lips—and threatened to ruin the moment, a moment that I knew would probably never happen again if I did so I kept my mouth wisely shut.

My hand holding the gun lowered as once again her eyes and voice made everything else in the world irrelevant until Annie's voice interrupted my thoughts.

"Sierra team, I am still detecting two live specimens inside the walls of the compound. Northeast corner, near the medical tent."

Hearing this I pushed Cat behind me and raised the gun in both hands. Slowly and carefully I walked toward the flap covering the doorway with Cat's hand on my shoulder as she followed, bolstering the wavering courage that would've fled if I didn't have her to protect.

The thin curtain covering the entrance, which in reality I knew provided no protection at all, was all that separated us from another of those nightmare bugs. I had to force myself to release the gun with one hand, trying to hide the terror my body was screaming to show. With Cat's hands burning through both my shoulders, I pushed aside the flap to step into the open.

I tried to put on my most manly voice as I said, "Stay behind me, Cat."

She didn't respond but gave my shoulders a squeeze which boosted my confidence again. Annie had activated the internal lights in the compound, though they didn't illuminate the area completely; the curvature of the pods still cast dark shadows, easily concealing the killer bugs. Most of the pod doors were closed, effectively sealing in and protecting their occupants as they had been designed to do. The cicada-type noise from the bugs seemed even louder now we were outside of the flimsy protection of the tent but what made me want to throw up the most was the continual scratching noise they made as they tried to scale the walls.

I looked around. In the center of the compound I could see people holding rifles standing behind a small fort of hastily stacked metal crates as the beams from the lights attached to them searched for targets.

My eyesight was not good enough to make out who the individuals were, but they must be Sierra team members. I raised my hand and received an answering wave back.

Movement to my right caught my attention. Two more Sierra team members approached, this time I could see it was Hendricks and Magda, both moving in the classic weapon-up stance—crouched slightly, taking small steps, weapons to their shoulders scanning everywhere for threats.

"On your left!" Annie shouted in my ear. Jumping at the sudden burst of sound I instinctively looked to my left. Two bugs emerged from the shadows and, at a speed faster than I thought possible, headed straight toward me. Toward *us*. Their clicking noises sounding more excitable than those outside the closer they got, their jaws making a bowel-loosening rattle as they snapped together faster than my eyes could follow in the poor light.

My first instinct was to run away in terror, and it took all the bravery I didn't know I possessed not to. I knew if I ran Cat would be their target. The first shot took me by surprise because I didn't know I'd even pulled the trigger. The hard ground to the left of the approaching bugs erupted as the bullet missed. Adjusting my aim, I kept pulling the trigger and saw with satisfaction great pieces of them breaking away from their bodies in gouts of gore. But still they came.

I had been taught in the forest all those years ago to count my shots as I needed to get ready for the reload, being told that someday my life could depend on it. At the time it hadn't seemed relevant, but as I fired the thought flashed into my mind. It made me panic even more knowing I had forgotten how many bullets the gun even held, so what was the point of counting?

I just kept firing, taking a step back with every shot as they got closer and closer. Within seconds the gun clicked empty and the slide locked back again. One of the bugs had stopped, its jaws opening and closing weakly, its legs not having the power to propel it any further as its insides leaked out of the many holes I'd blasted in its armored shell. The other bastard wasn't giving up quite as easily and kept coming, though now slower.

Hearing Cat's screams of terror in my ear and feeling her fingers digging deep into my shoulders, I knew I couldn't let it get closer. There was no way I was going to let its jaws sink into the smooth flesh of the woman I realized now with more certainty than ever, might actually like me.

Screaming a primeval roar of unintelligible rage, I took two steps forwards and kicked the bug square in what the biologist had told me was its face. Its carapace, already damaged by the bullets I'd hit it with, disintegrated at the force of my kick and it burst apart. Gore sprayed everywhere, but it seemed to mainly land on me, coating my clothes and my face with what felt like warm, sticky, left far too long in the deep fat fryer cooking oil.

Standing there, breathing heavily with shock, anger and more than a little fear, I tried to wipe my face to clear my vision but it was just too sticky to remove. I began to panic as I feared I was being blinded by the unknown internals of an alien beast, like it had acid for blood or something. Damned TV.

"I'm blind!" I wailed, "I can't see the bugs. Help me. I lashed my arms and legs out at more bugs I imagined were closing in on me. I calmed when the soft voice I knew so well spoke softly in my ear and I felt my waving arms that were ineffectually wiping at my face being gently held.

Her southern accent still trembled with fear as she whispered in my ear. "Anderson, it's okay. I'm here. Let me clean you up."

"Cat? Thank God. Are you okay? Did I get it?"

Her laughter was the tonic I needed to realize we were safe. "Get it? You kicked that critter back to its momma. It burst apart like an overripe melon." I felt her tug gently at my sleeve. "Come on, hold my hand and I'll get you back to your handsome self again."

"But what about the bugs?" I spluttered.

"Didn't you hear? Annie's just said there's no more in the compound and The Swarm has moved past us? It's over, we're safe now."

It was then I realized my earpiece had fallen out. I'd been so concerned about the bug goo covering me I hadn't noticed. I blindly felt around until I found the dangling cord and refitted it to my ear. The wet sensation of unidentifiable bug pieces squishing down my ear canal was less than pleasant.

My mind couldn't cope with so much input to my normally underused social skills and emotions. Had she just called me handsome? I felt her hand slip into mine and I just didn't care if she led me off a cliff; I would let that soft hand and gentle voice lead me anywhere.

Minutes later I was relishing in her touch as I sat on a chair and she gently wiped my face with a damp cloth when through my now-clearing vision, I saw Hendricks approaching with a big smile on his face.

"Anderson," he said, "are you some sleeper agent? Last time I saw you shoot, you couldn't hit a barn door from the inside!" He pointed at me. "You, sir, are what some of my colleagues would call a *badarse*. I saw you kick the last one to pieces, and it was a beautiful kick too, my lad, better than anything I've seen at Twickers."

I had no idea what the hell he was talking about. As I blinked away the last of the crap from my eyes I looked at him with a bemused expression on my face.

"You know? Twickers? Twickenham? The home of rugby football; none of that rubbish your lot play where they're all wearing scaffolding and crash helmets. Rugby. A *proper* man's game." He stopped when he realized I still had no clue what he was talking about. "Anyway, Anderson, well done." He looked at both of us, glancing at Cat to see how she was looking at me. He gave me an amused grin.

"I'll, err, leave you both to it," he said as he stalked off waving for the rest of Sierra team to move to him.

Cat had now wiped the exposed parts of my flesh clean enough, so I felt less creeped out. I looked into her eyes and she let the cloth drop to the floor. I didn't know what to do. I was transfixed, unable to tear myself away from those deep pools that looked back at me. Cat raised both her hands and, cupping my face in them, leaned toward me and gently kissed my lips. I was too shocked to respond, and she pulled away slightly looking at me with a small smile.

My eyes flickered away in embarrassment, choosing to focus on anything but her all by themselves. She was mocking me, she had to be. A woman as good looking as Cat would in no way shape or form ever find a man like me attractive. I was more of a big brother figure or a permanent resident of the friend zone. The kiss had to be just gratitude; I was sure of it.

Cat's eyes softened, her training as a psychiatric nurse giving her more insight into the workings of my mind than I would ever know myself. I forced my eyes to meet hers, opening my mouth to speak and probably say something totally dumb.

"Anderson," she said, "relax. It's okay."

"I…" I stammered, not sure what to say but thinking that I had to say something.

"Dude," she snapped softly, tapping her finger on my forehead once, "don't spoil it."

41

She bent down and kissed me fiercely. I responded, not quite sure if I was doing it right, but after a few seconds I didn't care at all.

Chapter 5

Democracy Rules

The Tanaka looked down at the circular ring of steel. He had broken the generations of rules and protocols, and before nightfall had positioned himself safely in the high branches of a tree, along with a small bodyguard of trusted men where they would be safe from The Swarm, but able to see the destruction he hoped they would bring upon the visitors.

They had first heard, then watched by the light of the full moon the mass of movement as The Swarm aimed straight for where he had told them to go. He knew, whatever happened, his standing amongst his people would increase tenfold.

He had proven that he had the power to control The Swarm.

He was the bringer of death.

He was a god.

He could barely contain his bloodthirsty excitement as he saw the creatures climb each other, engulfing the compound. They would breach the walls and once that happened he would wait for daylight then go and collected the vast treasure contained inside and sweep away the bones littering the ground.

When the automated defense system had started firing, he almost fell from his perch in shock and fear. Long gouts of red flame erupted from the strange boxes fixed atop the walls, destroying the piling-up bodies of bugs and collapsing the structures they were building by using their own bodies as steppingstones.

Now he knew truly what power the legends of guns possessed. The destructive force of just one of those flame-spitting gifts from the heavens would be enough to bring the Three Hills tribe to their knees before him.

He could hear but not see what was happening in the compound. His anticipation built when he realized a few of The Swarm had managed to get inside the walls just before a long burst from one of the big guns sent bodies tumbling back to the ground. The noises inside the compound were different, but the cracks and booms signifying other weapons being fired were not the screams of fear he expected to tear the night apart.

Watching with his breath held he tried to hide his disappointment as eventually silence descended on the compound, to be replaced by the clicking and scratching sound as The Swarm moved away to return to their hive long before the sun started to lighten the eastern sky.

His plan had failed, but he knew it was not his fault; he had simply underestimated the power of the newcomers. Since The Swarm had first arrived, they had relied on high walls as the only means of defense and many lives had been lost in the initial battles as the supplies of irreplaceable bullets had been exhausted. That was before the one known as 'The Controller,' a man from a far-off place called Europe who called himself Eades, had passed on the gift of how to manipulate The Swarm.

The knowledge of how the small briefcase-sized device that only The Tanaka knew about worked had been lost hundreds of years before; he just knew what sometimes happened if he followed a memorized sequence of instructions and inserted the 'beacon,' as he called it, into the port on the side of the screen.

He called it Icarus after the name that was once emblazed across its face, but in the near thousand years it had been used, the lettering had faded, and the word could hardly be made out leaving only the raised relief imprinted onto the case.

Now it's worth was handed down through the generations and through age its internal circuits and chips were degrading. Even though it was protected by the sealed case that was only opened when used, its effectiveness was slowly reducing as it was, to put it in simple biological terms, dying of old age. He knew the cable that led from its back and disappeared into a wall should never be removed, it was that which gave life to the dim flashing lights and flickering screen.

With a last look at the shiny metallic walls of the compound he made a decision.

"Everyone down," he hissed loudly.

"But, Tanaka," said a warrior near to him, "The Swarm are still out. We must wai—"

"*Must?*" Tanaka snarled at him and implying cowardice. "What we *must* do, is assemble every warrior, because we are going to war!"

Harrison stood on the raised platform that stood in the center of the main square with Tori beside him.

His head bowed as he waited for the last people to gather and silence to fall. When he was ready and had prepared in his mind what he was going to say, he raised his head and stared at his people, trying to judge their mood from behind his stony expression. After a failure of leadership like this, tradition dictated that a new leader be picked to replace the old. It was a tradition going back generations to prevent power being taken by force when support of the people was eroded.

"We have suffered," he intoned solemnly. "We have lost many of our friends and family." He paused, trying to contain his emotions. "And for that I hold myself to blame. I have failed in my obligation as your leader to protect you." Angry murmurs rippled through the crowd as people both agreed and disagreed with him.

"I want you to decide for yourselves who should lead you," he went on, raising his voice to cut over the swelling sounds, "and I call on anyone here to present themselves to the people as the new leader." An air of uncertainty flowed through the assembly like an electrical current, seeking a path of least resistance from which to pour out.

"I will lead us," a man shouted, stepping forwards from the crowd and scattering people before him with no regard for them.

Sebastian, a fearless warrior but a blunt instrument in Harrison's opinion, stood tall and proud before them with an axe held loosely over one shoulder. Instantly, Harrison felt a pang of regret that such a man could be placed in charge of both him and his people, because the man lacked any ounce of guile with which to fight a war.

The crowd agreed as the atmosphere and subtle noises combined to create a negative buzz at the suggestion. Sebastian bared his teeth and issued an impotent growl at the people he could see who weren't overtly supporting his claim for leadership.

"Does anyone else present themselves as leader?" Harrison cried out, desperate for another alternative to the simple bull of a man seeking power and influence. His time as leader had not been without tension, but as with so many others before him there had yet to be an overt challenge to his leadership, mostly due to his prowess as a warrior and a scout.

He scanned the faces of the crowd, seeing hate in the eyes of some who he guessed had slept the last two nights without a loved one, but mostly he saw a pleading look. People were frightened, he knew that, but in the faces of his people he recognized that he had made a mistake, and that the fear wasn't in his leadership.

"Suggest that I stay as leader," he muttered to Tori beside him under his breath.

"What?" she said, slightly too loud for his liking. He hissed through his teeth, trying to warn her to keep her voice lower. She shot him a glance of annoyance, clearly not happy at his attempt to quieten her, but she nodded in agreement. Before he could repeat it, another voice boomed from the gathering.

"I submit myself for leadership," a young man shouted, making Harrison's eyes bulge wide at the betrayal. The man, Jacob, had grown up with Harrison, and fought alongside him as a friend, the two having spent more nights than they could count side by side guarding the wall and one who was now counted amongst his closest supporters, stepped forwards. They locked eyes; Harrison's registering disappointment and betrayal as the other man's flashed with ambition and temper. "If he isn't strong enough to lead you," the man shouted, "and he costs us all the lives of those lost to The Swarm—"

Tori stepped forwards, her right hand sliding behind her hip where she always kept a dagger, until Harrison held his hand out in front of her.

"Let him speak," he murmured.

47

"—then he doesn't *deserve* to be called leader. For all we know, he caused this attack with his reckless actions, by talking to the people from above. We should leave these newcomers alone to defend themselves like we should do for ourselves."

"Is that what you would do, Jacob?" Harrison asked loudly. "Ignore everything outside our walls and hide here? Wait for another attack from Tanaka? Wait for The Swarm to come back?"

The crowd grumbled and murmured, the noise swelling with agreement when Harrison spoke. Jacob rounded on him angrily, but Tori cut him off by raising her voice to the crowd.

"I say that Harrison should remain our leader," she yelled, her voice shriller than the deep rumblings of the male challengers. Her interruption was timed to perfection, and the sounds of the crowd amplified as more voices joined her in agreement.

"I would attack!" yelled Sebastian, brandishing his axe high in the air and receiving much less support from the warriors he hoped to ignite with his promise of war. "Attack the Springs, attack the newcomers from the stars…" The support he had melted away as few of them had the stomach for a fight right then, especially two fights against enemies with more power than they believed themselves to have.

"We should consolidate here," Jacob shouted over the noise, adjusting his body position in response to the threatening stance from Sebastian, forcing other warriors to impose themselves with hands on undrawn weapons between the two men to prevent a fight.

"We should find a new way," Harrison said, "one that doesn't involve war and doesn't involve hiding behind our walls waiting to be attacked."

"What way?" shouted a woman from the crowd. "How can we be safe to live our lives in peace?"

"Peace?" Sebastian roared, throwing his head back to laugh at the notion and losing what little support he had left in the crowd. "Peace is for the weak and the women. *Men* want war!"

"We must talk," Harrison said, "we must form alliances and put a stop to the endless war we've been burned by for all of our lives."

"You want to make friends with everyone," Jacob scoffed as he threw a dismissive hand up at the platform, turning to the crowd to gather support. "He is weak, and he thinks only of himself."

"That's not tru—" Tori's objection was cut off by Harrison placing a calming hand on her arm. Having your lover come to your defense was touching but unhelpful.

"Enough," he said. "As is our way, I will not stop either of these men presenting themselves to be your leader, but I cannot follow the path that either of them suggests." He let out a shaky breath before speaking again, "I present myself as your leader still. We cast the ballot tonight." He stepped down from the platform and disappeared quickly from view.

~

The ballot was cast just after nightfall in the very center of the town. Tradition dictated that those offering themselves for leadership could not vote and must stand at the entrance of the hut where they could oversee the fairness of the process. Those on watch cast their stones early before joining other warriors on the wall, and every adult man and woman gathered to collect a stone from the huge, woven basket in the middle of the open area. One by one they filed through a small hut where they cast their stones into one of three baskets, each one overlooked by a town Elder.

Before long, those coming out of the other end were smiling and laughing as though they had seen something funny, and it wasn't until the line of people was prevented from coming in that one of the Elders came out of the hut and looked around nervously, counting the people still waiting, before stepping back inside out of sight.

All three came back outside, sparking loud murmuring among the people until one held up both hands and waited for hush to descend.

"What is the meaning of this?" Sebastian demanded angrily, walking to the older man and towering over him to intimidate and bully like it was the only way he knew how to communicate. "There are still people left to vote, so get back inside!"

"There's no point," another said.

"No point?" Sebastian snarled, lifting the wide-bladed head of his axe to rest it threateningly on the man's shoulder.

"Stop that!" Jacob shouted, standing and levelling a spear at the big man. "Let him speak."

Sebastian, forced to either fight a rival or step back, laughed as though it was all a joke. The man who he had threatened relaxed, knowing the joke wasn't funny.

"There's no point," he said again, "because there aren't enough people left to change the results. Even if there were double, it still wouldn't make a difference."

"You don't need to count the stones?" a woman asked, clutching the small, smooth pebble in her hands that she planned to drop into the basket of the man she felt her family were safest with.

"No," one of the ballot counters said, "one basket is already overflowing."

With a growl, Sebastian shouldered and barged his way through the line and entered the hut. Immediately the sounds of him roaring in anger could be heard by even those furthest away in the line. The big warrior reappeared, his face a mask of anger, and he turned to find Harrison's face. For a long moment it seemed that he was going to rush him to beat him down with the axe, and more than one hand slid to the hilt of a weapon in readiness, but instead of launching into an attack he bowed suddenly, deeply and with undisguised mockery before standing straight and stalking away to the walls.

Jacob looked at Harrison in shock, fearful of the consequences of his open challenge to a man who had called him friend, before he too ran into the hut to check. He walked out in silence and left the town square saying nothing more.

Tori went next, walking inside to see three large woven baskets—one overflowing with stones and the other two containing less than a handful. The counters of the ballet were right; even twice the number of people left to cast their vote couldn't change the results.

Walking back outside she ignored the fixed gazes of everyone in sight and stood beside Harrison. Lifting his hand into the air, she looked out at the faces of their people and declared the leadership to still be his.

The cheers from the majority of the people told him that he had done the right thing, both in offering to allow someone else the leadership through a fair and open contest, and also that remaining in charge was what the people wanted.

Chapter 6

Dissection of Life

Hendricks stood in the center of the circle surrounded by his team. The light was rising fast as dawn showed itself on the horizon.

"Weber, Gciger, I need you two back on the walls please." They nodded and without a word turned and made their way to the ladders that gave access to the top of the pods.

"Annie, how much ammunition did we expend?" The two-tone bleep sounded in all their ears as she came online.

"I can give you a detailed gun-by-gun report or would you prefer the summary?"

Hendricks smiled a tired smile. "Just the summary please, Annie."

"Of course. When firing the weapons, I was aware of the limited reserves we have, so I operated each separate system at their lowest effective rate of fire I calculated was necessary to hold back The Swarm whilst switching weapons to prevent any single position from expending more ammunition than was necessary if another position could bring effective fire to bear."

"Impressive," Hendricks said in a tone of voice that quite clearly said, 'get to the point.'

"I only increased the rate of fire when the breach was occurring and even then, I'm sorry to say that I couldn't stop them." Annie paused as if admonishing herself before continuing. "For the auto-mated defense turrets, we expended approximately fifteen percent of our total available ammunition. I would recommend them all being rearmed as a matter of urgency. Do you now want a report of personal ammunition usage?"

"No, thank you, Annie. I think we know how much we used. It was the pods I was concerned about." Hendricks saw Amir walk into view with Hayley Cole close behind him. He watched as Amir searched the compound until he noticed him and immediately headed in his direction.

"Okay, I need to talk to *Mister* Weatherby. Weber and Geiger are on the wall," Hendricks said, "Magda and Stevens, get the guns re-armed. Everyone else on standby and patrol."

Most shot a look of distrust in Amir's direction as they left for their assigned tasks. They had heard him trying to countermand Hendricks over using the gun pods and knew if their boss hadn't acted immediately all of them could have died. It was the scorn of all professionals, being told how to do their jobs by politicians.

Amir noticed the looks cast in his direction and thought bitterly how, once again, he had made the wrong call. For what he considered the right reasons, he'd tried to preserve The Swarm, but the snap decisions he was used to making in the boardroom didn't usually kill people if they were wrong. The call he made last night, he knew, was wrong and he needed to explain before his position was further eroded. He knew he had an ace or three up his sleeve, but he couldn't reveal it yet as he wasn't sure it still existed, but to find out he needed the help of those who now distrusted him even more.

Hendricks stood still, letting Amir come to him, before he crossed his arms and adopted a blank look of coldness. Amir noticed

53

and raised his hands in apology. He needed to use all his skills to get their relationship back on an even footing.

"I know what you're about to say," he began. Admitting he was wrong was something he wasn't used to doing, and in business he could always lay the blame at another person's feet. "I was wrong. I can see that now." He saw Hendricks bristle as was about to speak and held his hands up again. "Please let me explain. I believe we may have a way of controlling The Swarm." He paused, waiting for the shock that statement would cause

"Think about it: last night couldn't have been some random attack. For them to appear at our walls in such numbers, it's almost as if they were *commanded* to do so. The one event I didn't see happening was them breaching our walls. I wanted Annie to study them so we could learn more about them, and with what the scientists discovered about them yesterday I wanted to see if we could corroborate the theory and back it up with real data." He saw he had Hendricks' attention and continued. "I believe the data we need may be in Charlie site Annie's memory banks. We need to access it as a matter of priority."

Hendricks looked long and hard at Amir. Annie, who had been listening in as always, bleeped an inoffensive tone in both of their ears like she was clearing her throat for their attention.

"Mister Weatherby is correct. We did not have time to brief you fully on what we discovered yesterday. Can I suggest I call all the relevant people together and discuss our findings?"

Amir smiled inwardly. He saw the look on Hendricks' face change from anger to curiosity and knew he had him hooked. Silently, he congratulated himself on diffusing the situation and not harming his own position further.

Hendricks spoke to Annie, effectively taking control of the situation and reasserting himself as one of the leaders. "Please do," he said, looking annoyed as he realized how subtly Amir had played the situation but conceding the point gracefully.

Hendricks waited for Amir to ask Annie to get the people he wanted at the meeting before calling out to him as he turned away. "Oh, one more thing?" he said, still sounding amenable. Amir's face then dropped as Hendricks glared at him forcefully. "Don't *ever* countermand me on security matters again. I am here to keep you all safe. It's what my team and I are here for. I'll leave all the political backstabbing bollocks to you suits; do me the courtesy of staying the fuck out of my wheelhouse."

Annie spoke into their earpieces, cutting the tension expertly. "I have opened a private channel for all who need to attend. If you two could make your way over to the lab I will ask the others to join you."

The bug looked a lot different to the last time most had seen it. Oozing coils of dark meat lay on the metal workstation as the thing was laid on its back with all six legs pinned down by small clamps. Anderson was there, still splashed with dried gore in a lighter shade than the insides of the dissected bug, a look of scientific concentration on his face in place of the revulsion the others had at seeing the thing initially.

"Everybody," Anderson said, "Doctor Herbert, one of our biologists."

"Entomologist," Herbert corrected. His curious accent spoke of a European birth and a life spent researching and studying all over the world. "Calling me simply a biologist is like explaining what you do as 'the computer guy.'"

"Alright," Anderson said, "Doctor Herbert here has a major woody for bugs. It's his thing." Stifled laughter went around the assembled group crammed into the small lab as Herbert looked up in annoyance.

"Thank you for that, Doctor Anderson," he said flatly before launching into the results of his findings. "As someone with 'a thing for bugs' I can tell you categorically that this is no species of insect found alive before the meteor strike—"

"Asteroid," Amir interrupted.

"—that caused the extinction event of most species on the planet. My conclusion is simply that this species is either not from Earth or, far more likely in my opinion, is actually an artificially created organism."

"What?" Hendricks asked, taken by surprise at the mention of anything extraterrestrial. "So this is either an alien bug or else it's been genetically created?"

"Precisely so, Mister Hendricks," Herbert said, "the makeup of this creature is quite extraordinary. From what I can surmise it has the base DNA of both the Tiger beetle and a form of large ant; likely Bullet ants or Australian meat ants." More than one person shuddered at the toxic mix of creepy-crawlies which didn't seem to bother Dr. Herbert one bit.

"They are clearly eusocial, meaning that they operate with a kind of single consciousness of co-operation, which is common in many arthropods, but less so in beetles which these most resemble. In the case of the Tiger beetle I can see the value of its genetic inclusion due to both the incredible speeds it can attain and also the higher than average level of aggressive behavior displayed. Also the specific *attack* of those ants is beneficial to any form of weaponization of the…"

He trailed off as blank faces looked back at him. He sighed and looked to Anderson for help, who thought for a moment before translating for him. "They look like big-ass Tiger beetle hybrid ants, the shiny shell and all that, but they're more like ants inside with some other stuff the good doctor here can't understand—"

"Yet," Herbert interjected.

"—yet," Anderson went on. "They have like a hive mind, like bees and ants, but they aren't one or the other. Best thing? That's not even the weirdest part…"

Anderson nodded at Herbert, who used a gloved hand and a shiny tool to peel back the thorax section of the bug and expose the inside.

"Wait," Hendricks said, "that looks like…"

"Yeah," Anderson said, "wires."

"Oh, you have *got* to be kidding me," Hayley Cole said, throwing her arms up in disgust at the entomologist poking around inside the carcass, "let me know when y'all are done here." Herbert waited for her to leave before continuing.

"The wires, as such, are naturally formed with a substance rich in natural metal fibers running along them. In essence, this form of electrical system has been organically grown, not installed into a live specimen."

"What's even weirder," Anderson said, "is that there are transmitters and receivers built into their bodies. It's like a kind of cyborg, but a naturally created one."

"How… how is this even possible?" Hendricks asked. "Any of it?"

"This is not the million-dollar question," Herbert said, "what you *should* be asking is, 'where is their Queen?'"

~

The dissection went on, exposing a filament in the exoskeleton that both absorbs and reflects low-intensity light. Theories about the gravitational effects on the earth during the times around a full moon were banded around until they ended up with more questions than answers.

"However it boils down," Anderson said, "these things are being controlled, and—stop me if I'm wrong, Doctor–that means there's a nest or a hive where all these things go back to… to recharge or whatever they need to do."

"Excuse me," Hendricks said, "recharge?"

"Yes," Herbert said, "there appears to be an organic sack inside that acts as a kind of power storage unit."

"Right, this thing just got one step too weird for me," Hendricks said. "Where are the rest of them and how do we kill them?"

"I would not be so hasty to want this new species extinct," Herbert said, "we do not know the effect this could have on the ecosystem. What if they are pollenating the local fauna? We could cause our own extinction if we act too hastily."

"Well," Amir said, "this is all fascinating. Keep up the good work, Doctors." With that he left abruptly, like the whole conversation was boring him and he had stayed for as long as his manners had allowed.

⁓

"Are you there, Annie?" Amir muttered toward his radio without pressing any buttons.

"I'm here," she responded immediately.

"We need to get to the Charlie site soon," he told her, "and I need your help to convince the others."

"For what purpose?" Annie asked.

"Annie, you *know* why. We need to see if the site still contains what I showed you before. There's the real possibility we can learn more about The Swarm, about the tech needed to control them because I think it could only have come from Charlie Annie. But remember, you agreed to keep what may be in there secret until we can be sure it's still there."

"Of course, Mister Weatherby, I apologize. However, lying is something I am new to and it may take me a few attempts to perfect it."

Amir smiled. "Annie you're not lying… just omitting to tell *all* the details. That's all."

Annie gave a dull tone as though thinking before going silent for a few seconds.

"I believe that the difference between an intentionally told untruth and the omission of prevalent facts in order to deceive or mislead people is effectively the same thing," she said finally. Amir smiled to himself.

"And you never studied law. That's where you need to trust me, Annie," he said with a smirk, "business and politics are my arena."

Chapter 7

Show of Strength

Annie kept Amir connected so he could hear as she opened what Hendricks automatically assumed was a private communication.

"For me to analyze the data we have further," she said, "I need to gain access to the Charlie site artificial intelligence interface. There could be data there I can use to find out more about The Swarm."

Amir listened as Hendricks responded immediately, noting with curiosity that she distanced herself as far as she could from the other Annie.

"Understood. How long will it take, and how do I get *you* there?" he asked. "We've got a lot of other things happening and splitting our forces between two sites is something I'll struggle with right now."

Annie had a tone of amusement in her voice as she responded. "Mister Hendricks," she said, "from studies of your physique and facial structure, I am sure that if I was not just an artificially created voice evolved over billions of lines of coding, but a human female as my voice suggests, I would certainly enjoy being carried by you. But that pleasure will be denied to me as a simple remote uplink between this location and the site will be sufficient for me to access the other Annie."

It was Hendricks' turn to chuckle. "Annie, are you flirting with me?"

"Perhaps. Was my attempt effective? I am learning to try and be more *human* in how I interact as I calculate that will give me better results and speed up response times by shortening future communications."

Amir didn't need his earpiece in to hear Hendricks laughing from across the compound as he responded. "Annie, you were doing just great until you told me you were playing me," he said, pausing to gather himself. "Yes, I understand your need to plug into the other Annie and I know that the information you might gain could be useful in learning about The Swarm, but what'll *that* do to help us given the current situation? The talk in the lab was about a hive or queen or whatever you call it controlling them. Surely the priority should be to find that if we're going to protect ourselves?"

"You are correct, but as we now know, the bugs are artificially created and if you apply a logical thought process to the facts then it follows that The Swarm may be controlled by some higher-level technology. I believe the human equivalent for this would be arrogance, but I doubt that anything on the planet fits that description better than my own program, or that of the lesser versions of me. Logic dictates that if that was the case, Charlie site Annie would have relevant data stored in her memory." She paused, some self-created algorithm designed to see if the counterparts in her conversation had anything to add or question. "Also," she continued as no interruption came, "on a logistical level we expended approximately fifteen percent of our munitions last night. If the same event occurs again, which logic also dictates it will, we will run out of ammunition halfway through the seventh attack."

Hendricks sighed. "Okay, Annie. You're very persuasive and as you've put it so succinctly, I cannot argue with your irrefutably logical conclusions, so I'll start to plan a mission to the site. And wait," he said, "*approximately?*"

"Yes, Doctor Anderson told me a very long time ago to use contractions when conversing with humans as they do not appreciate accuracy, believing it to be excessive. That is a potential flaw in human logic as it provides a less complete picture, but the exact figure is fourteen point six-eight-six-seven percent."

Hendricks paused as he thought for a moment.

"I know which team members I'd take and who I'd leave behind, but who else do you suggest we need?"

Annie responded immediately. "Mister Weatherby needs to be included as he is the only one of us to have visited the site and will know the location of what we need to access. Also, Doctor Anderson, as we will most likely require his expertise with any hardware issues we find in attempting to connect me to... *it.* No one else would be mission critical, but I am open to suggestions."

"I'll think about it, Annie, but at the moment I imagine keeping the numbers down would be my preferred optio—"

"Drones have detected three people emerging from the trees facing the gate," Annie interrupted urgently. "One of them is confirmed to be Tanaka by facial recognition. Many more are hidden in the tree line. Please hold whilst I perform an accurate count."

Hendricks didn't wait for her answer, immediately turning and running, asking for the location of his team as he moved

"Weber and Geiger are on the walls," Annie told him. "Stevens, Nathalie, Jones and Magda are in the armory rearranging the supplies after rearming the automated gun system."

"Open a channel to them now."

"Done."

"Weber, Geiger. We have potential hostiles approaching the gate. One of you cover the gate, the other maintain position and watch the tree line. Annie has detected an unknown amount in the trees to our north.

The rest of you meet me by the gates. Annie, launch all remaining drones and keep me informed of anything else."

Before Annie replied, the buzzing whine of electric motors and rotor blades spinning cut through the air as three more drones leaped into action from their charging stations. Hendricks didn't wait for confirmation of the launch before saying, "Thank you, Annie."

A bleep sounded in his ear acknowledging his response.

Annie's voice in Hendricks' ear now carried a level of urgency as she spoke to the team. "The drones have detected more people to the east, south and west. My initial count is just under a hundred surrounding us on all sides."

Hendricks stopped dead in his tracks and spoke urgently into his radio. "Change of plan. We've a hundred unknowns surrounding us on all sides. All Sierra team on the walls evenly spaced out. Intentions are not clear, but my guess is that you don't bring this many people to say hello."

He listened as one by one his team acknowledged the order. He was standing behind the closed gates adjusting his equipment when Amir jogged up to him. Hendricks looked at him sharply, but he nodded his head indicating that he understood who was now in charge.

"What can we do?" Amir asked.

Hendricks stood thinking for a few seconds. "You've met him, do you think he'll have brought a bottle? I have my own opinion, but I'd value yours right now." He barked a short, mirthless laugh.

"I'm paid to expect the worst from people and act accordingly; you may have a different angle."

Amir nodded and brushed his fingers through the two-day growth of stubble on his chin he was uncharacteristically letting grow.

"I've met enough of his type before in boardrooms. They think authority comes from controlling every one of your underlings and not allowing another power base to become strong enough to challenge your leadership, no matter how inept it is. But we're not talking boardrooms here. I wouldn't trust a word he says, as all he wants is—"he spread his hands, indicating everything around them"—what we have. He won't accept sharing power as that'll erode his own position and make him appear weaker. I don't think negotiation will work, as his ego and the position he has won't allow him to. The only takeover he's capable of understanding is a hostile one and in business if you're preparing for a hostile takeover there's no nice way to go about it."

"Thank you, that's confirmed my position. If he wants to get into a pissing contest, then I think we need to give him a show of strength. Can you organize issuing every gun we have in the armory and get every single last one of us ready to line the walls? Give the ones who don't have guns anything that looks like a weapon. I'll talk to him, but when I give the signal I want everyone lining the walls." Amir nodded and turned away to make it happen. Hendricks could hear him giving instructions for every adult member of the community to gather at the armory.

"Three of them, two hundred yards and closing," Weber said via radio.

"Open the gates on my command, Annie," Hendricks ordered, "but close them as soon as I step outside. The last thing I want him to see is the inside of the compound. I'll meet him alone and see what he has to say. Keep the channel clear," he added for the benefit of everyone. She gave her now familiar bleep of acknowledgment in reply.

He looked around the compound, seeing the Sierra team members standing visible on the walls all holding their main weapons ready, scanning the surrounding tree line for any movement.

"Is everyone in position?"

When all his team had checked in one by one, he looked over and saw Amir, helped by Hayley Cole standing at the entrance to the armory handing out every weapon they had available to the community members, who had all responded to Annie's request without delay.

Nodding in satisfaction, he said, "Annie, open the gates, please."

With a metallic clunk the locking mechanism was released, and the gates opened just enough for him to squeeze through the gap. He waited, using his body to block the entrance until he heard the gate closing and the locks engaging.

Whispering, "It's game time," to himself, he walked twenty meters from the walls and stood still. He held his rifle in the low ready position where it would only take a split second to raise it to his shoulder and fire if the need arose, watching as Tanaka and two of his people approached to deliver what he suspected would be an ultimatum.

Chapter 8

Blink and You Lose

As Tanaka and his two henchmen approached, Annie bleeped in Hendricks' ear.

"Jimmy, I have completed a drone sweep. There are eighty-six others in the trees surrounding us; thermal imaging indicates they are all holding a melee weapon of varying design."

Hendricks spoke quietly. "Thanks, Annie. Let's see what he has to say for himself. Keep me informed if anything changes."

"Of course, Jimmy, stay safe. I'll be listening." She bleeped her down-tone.

Hendricks waited, standing strong and resolute as he forced the nerves in his body to remain still and allowing himself the small victory of having Tanaka come to him.

As he neared, Tanaka's face broke into a broad grin and he spread his arms in an expansive welcoming gesture.

"Hello, my friend," he said with as much genuine kindness as a snake would regard a rat with. He looked at the destroyed remains of bugs that littered the ground around the walls, his eyes following where lines of gore were sprayed high up the barrier and where the impact of the bullets had churned the ground making some areas resemble a ploughed field. "I see you had a visit last night. I hope you all managed to stay safe. I just thought I would come by and see if we can offer you any assistance."

Hendricks returned the smile and waved his hands at the destruction the automated guns had caused. "Oh, that lot? They disturbed our sleep a little, but they were no match for our defense systems." He placed a hand on his chest, his acting just as good and equally as false as Tanaka's. "I thank you for your concern."

Still smiling, Tanaka answered, "Yes, I can see you managed to defend yourselves for now. I know about the things you call guns and how my ancestors used them to protect themselves, but legends tell of the dreadful massacres that happened when the bullets ran out." He smiled even more broadly and raised his voice. "For your own safety I must insist you all come under my protection at the Springs. If they breach the walls in greater numbers next time you may not be so luc—"

"How do you know any breached our walls?" Hendricks snapped, interrupting Tanaka's flow. His face hardened and he changed the grip on his assault rifle. It was a small change, hardly noticeable, but he was now ready to strike.

Tanaka quickly tried to brush over his error. "My friend," he crooned, "I know the power of The Swarm and what they can do. Numbers as great as you encountered last night would surely have reached the top of your puny walls." He laughed trying to ease the tension that had suddenly arisen. "It is why our walls are so high. No matter how many come, we know we will be safe. It's why I know you will be safer under my protection."

With a smile that still showed no genuine friendliness he stared at Hendricks, trying to judge if he had recovered the situation. As benevolent as he tried to seem to Hendricks, he and his companions couldn't tear their gazes away from the weapons he carried.

Hendricks stared back for a few seconds. With an effort he didn't let show, he relaxed his grip on his weapon and forced a smile back onto his face.

"I thank you for your concern, a few did breach our walls, but we easily dealt with them." Tanaka eyed the few people that stood within his sight, lining the walls.

He chuckled in mock disbelief. "I don't see many warriors," he said, sounding more relieved than concerned, then tried to play the hand he thought would bring his new enemy to their knees. "I thought you may need some protection, so I have brought my best warriors to help escort you back and carry any equipment you might want to bring with you." He paused, smiling, and raised a hand high in the air.

Annie bleeped and began speaking in Hendricks' ear, but he didn't need to listen to what she was going to tell him as he could see clearly enough. He couldn't see the entire perimeter from his position, but the tree line in his line of sight darkened as a line of warriors emerged to stand silently facing him.

"How very thoughtful of you," Hendricks said flatly, keeping his face devoid of any emotion. "Thanks for the invite but we're not moving. We're happy, and as you can see, secure in our little compound."

Tanaka snorted in disgust, his anger showing for the first time.

"I think you misunderstand me," he snarled, all feigned affability vanishing from his face, "I *insist* you come with us." He turned and waved at the warriors in view before turning back. With a sneer, he looked at the few Sierra team members on the walls and said, "One command from me and my men will come and take it from you. You and your few warriors will not be able to stop me."

Hendricks laughed briefly and then hardened his voice. "Do you really want to try that?" He spoke into his radio loud enough for the enemy to hear. "Soldiers to the walls."

Tanaka tried to hide his shock as the walls surrounding the compound filled with people, all carrying a weapon or from the distance he was at, what *looked* like a weapon. He staggered backwards an involuntary pace; his face turned red with anger and spittle flew from his mouth as he shouted, "How dare you defy me! I'll crush you like a bug under my foot. *I am The Tanaka.*"

Hendricks whispered, "Annie, fire one single burst twenty yards from the tree line in front of me. Don't hit anyone."

Tanaka was stopped from spewing any more impotent rhetoric as one of the automated guns on the gate raised its barrels and barked a thrumming, percussive one-second burst over their heads. He fell back in shock at the noise and spitting flames which sent a glowing red stream of bullets to stich a line in the ground just yards from the feet of the exposed warriors. The whirr of the barrels spinning drowned out the sounds of their panic as they fled back to the trees.

Tanaka, regaining some of his composure, stared for a few seconds at the chaos and flew into a rage. "I will kill you for that. *No one* defies The Tanaka and lives…" His voice turned into a shrill scream as he shouted at the men standing either side of him. "*GET HIM!*"

The men flanking him, in shock themselves at what they had seen, looked at Tanaka, silently questioning the command and only moved when he saw their hesitation and screamed again, "*NOW, or you die too.*"

His shout gave Hendricks enough warning even before the two men raised their weapons, issued a war cry and started forwards, to let his hands fall from his rifle and draw his pistol in a blur of speed.

They hadn't made any distance toward him when both they fell dead at Tanaka's feet each sporting red holes in their foreheads and gaping craters at the backs of their skulls.

Hendricks, holding the pistol in both hands, switched his aim to Tanaka as smoke drifted from the barrel pointed at his head.

It was his turn to shout. "Did you *really* think we'd bow to your will? You're nothing but a pumped-up bully who relies on the power of others stronger than him to maintain control. We arrived later than you on Earth, but we're all from the same beginnings; our mission is the same as your ancestors was a thousand years ago. To rebuild civilization and start over."

Tanaka glanced at the two dead warriors beside him, chosen as his personal bodyguard because they were supposed to be the bravest.

"Somehow," Hendricks went on in a lower voice, "your people decided that the world hadn't seen enough evil and began ruling like kings and not as people working together to build a good and just society." He curled his lips and spat the next sentence with venom. "Judging them by your standards, I can see how it happened. This is *not* how *we* do things, and until you understand that fully, stay away from us."

Tanaka glanced behind him, expecting his warriors to come and save him from the man who possessed the one thing that he thought made him superior. He contemplated pulling his own gun, empty of bullets or not, and threaten the man with it, but the seconds old display of him killing with his own weapon told him that he wouldn't hesitate.

Hendricks fixed him with a hard stare. "Leave now while you can still walk but be warned: if you try and attack us, I will hunt you down and rip your spleen from your body and feed it to The Swarm."

Tanaka had never been spoken to this way before. Anyone who went against him or displeased him in any way was usually killed or made an example of in front of the whole community. It was how he kept them in fear of his power.

He backed up, shocked and trying to figure out what his spleen was. His anger and arrogance for the first time replaced by something he had not felt for a long time: fear.

Staggering slightly, he vented his petulant anger at one of the bodies lying at his feet and gave it a hard kick. With every step his fear reduced, his anger returning in full. Hendricks, still with his weapon aimed at his receding back, watched his every step.

When he was fifty yards away, just as Hendricks was beginning to lower his pistol, he reached into his jacket with one hand and pulled something out. Hendricks snapped his arm back up and tightened the pressure on the trigger. One more ounce of pressure and he would send a bullet straight into Tanaka's face. Even at that range he knew he was unlikely to miss.

Tanaka held the object in the air and shouted, "Tonight, you die. I will send The Swarm to kill you all!" He began laughing at his own sick joke. "I am the controller, the bringer of death. I will pick over your bones."

Hendricks spoke urgently, "Annie. What is in his hand? Do we need it?"

Annie bleeped in his ear. He knew enough about her now to know it was her thinking signal. Out of the corner of his eye he saw a drone sweeping closer to Tanaka who was shocked by the sudden appearance of the strange flying object. His anger once again changed to fear as he held his arms up as if to protect himself from an evil spirit.

"It's a portable transmitter. We have many in our stores of similar design," she answered quickly.

"Do we need to get it, was my question, Annie," snapped Hendricks.

"Yes, it would be logical to take it from him—"Hendricks took aim"—but tactically I would advise against such a course of action." Hendricks lowered the gun a fraction. "We know what he has, which gives us an indication of how he controls The Swarm. When we get access to Charlie site Annie, we need to find out more. If we take it now it's just a transmitter, and we have plenty of those—it's what he does with it that's the unknown factor—"

Amir, who was connected to the conversation, interrupted Annie.

"I agree, Hendricks, we need to get to Charlie Annie urgently."

Hendricks lowered his weapon and watched as Tanaka turned and, still laughing like a maniac, walked toward the trees and disappeared into the gloom cast by their branches.

Hendricks, trained to be suspicious by nature, started to think to himself that Amir's desperation to reach Charlie Annie may have motives other than to control The swarm, but he decided not to question him further and just watch him carefully for any clues.

As the last of Tanaka's warriors turned and retreated into the trees, he pushed his pistol back into his holster and turned back toward the gate.

"We may need to get to Charlie site, but we need to survive tonight first," he said, more to himself but still heard by the others, as he strode back

Annie bleeped in his ear. "I have been thinking about that, Jimmy," she said, "and I have some ideas I would like to discuss with you when you are ready."

Chapter 9

A Ditch in Time

Hendricks waited for the gates to close and the locks to engage before he allowed himself to relax.

He looked up at the walls where most of their small community had stood to give the appearance of a greater number of fighters. Everyone who was old enough had received basic survival and firearms training as part of the preparations they all went through before going into cryo, but whether they could be relied upon when the pressure was turned up was another matter entirely.

He spotted Anderson as he held a hand out to help Cat down the last few rungs of the ladder to one of the pods and chuckled quietly to himself. He had proved him wrong, so maybe the others would too when the time came. Watching how Anderson was treating the nurse brought a larger smile to his face as his own memories of when he was a gawky teenager and first discovering the joys of the opposite sex sprang into his mind.

He looked away from his lovestruck friend and got down to business.

"Sierra team. Four of you remain visible on the walls for now, choose between yourselves, the rest meet me in the central area. We need to prepare for what may come at us tonight. I'll keep the channels open for those on the walls so you can listen in and contribute as well."

"Jimmy?" asked Annie. "Can I suggest we include some engineers and one or two others at the meeting? I think they will be able to comment better on the feasibility of my options. In the meantime, I will return all but one of the drones for recharging to enable me to maintain continuous cover."

"Of course, Annie, get whoever you think necessary to join us. And good idea about the drones."

She bleeped her down-tone. The tone this time, if he was not mistaken, sounded pleased with the praise he had just given her. Perhaps even a little smug.

"I have studied how The Swarm acts and run through many possible scenarios," Annie spoke through a speaker hidden in the wall of the pod nearest to where Hendricks had called them together. Annie had asked Amir, Dr. Herbert, and three engineers he had not had chance to get to know yet to the meeting. Hayley Cole, armed with her ubiquitous tablet, accompanied Amir.

"The most effective way as we have discovered is to use the gun systems to keep The Swarm from breaching the walls. I have studied the action and am confident I have learnt enough of how they act to be able to stop another breach occurring. The problem we all know with that is we have very limited reserves of ammunition. I then began processing other ideas, the simplest of which is fire. Doctor Herbert, I assume I am correct in my assumptions that all animals, no matter how primitive their cognitive abilities, will avoid fire?"

"Yes," he replied pushing his glasses that had slid down his nose back into position. "The more primitive the animal of any kind, the higher level of aversion to fire is to be expected. Even though we believe these *bugs* have some remote guidance, they are still animals with their own simple brain. So yes, I believe they would have a natural instinct to avoid anything that they sense would be a danger to their existence."

"Thank you, Doctor Herbert," Annie replied. "With the equipment we have we can dig a shallow ditch around our position and place combustible material in it. If we use a suitable accelerant it would catch fire quickly. I can give us enough warning of their approach so that it will be burning fiercely by the time they arrive."

Hendricks started to interrupt but Annie stopped him.

"Mister Hendricks, if you are about to comment on the amount of labor required to keep a ditch stocked with enough dry wood to keep us safe in the long term then can I stop you there, it is something I am fully aware of."

Hendricks smiled and shrugged in acceptance as everyone looked at him. "Okay, Annie, carry on."

"The dry wood and availability of a suitable accelerant does not make that solution a long-term prospect. If The swarm arrived during a period of intense rainfall as the topography of this area suggest would happen regularly on a bi-annual schedule, then we would be at risk of exposure. Until my next proposal can be completed, however, it should provide us with an extra layer of protection without relying on the gun system." She did one of her pauses again, waiting to see if anyone had anything to add or ask.

"All of the pods are fitted with compressed air thrusters that were used for small course corrections in space and to stabilize the crafts on their return to Earth," she explained. "If we remove these systems from the pods and attach them at strategic positions on the walls then, using the internal air compressors, any of The Swarm that climbs the walls could be easily ejected from the area."

Everyone stood silently as they thought over the idea. One of the engineers, a man called Clarke who was one of the last to come out of cryo along with his wife and ten-year-old son, spoke first.

"That's a pretty good idea," he said, looking at the men in charge as though he hadn't yet figured out how to address the computer who thought for itself. "The amount of psi those thrusters kick out should be enough to more than knock them off the walls; if we can get the nozzles right it should even be able to blow them apart."

Dr. Herbert sounded excited as he spoke. "We can test them on the carapace remains I have in storage from the dissections. If you can pierce the chitin, which on the specimens I have studied is the hardest I have ever encountered, then even a low-powered burst of air should damage the vital organs inside sufficiently to kill them."

Amir looked at Clarke and the two other engineers. "Can you build it?"

They all nodded thoughtfully before Clarke responded. "I don't see why not. If you can let us inspect what we have and look at what we might need to rig up a working system, then we can come up with something I'm sure."

Hendricks this time beat Amir to it. "Gents, this doesn't have to be a thing of beauty, it just *has to work*," he said, driving the edge of his right hand into his left palm with each emphasized word. "I know how you engineers go about things. Just cut out the first twenty planning and design changes you normally go through before you even build something and get on with it. How long before you can tell us if it's a feasible proposition?"

Clarke, who puffed his chest out in mild indignation, was about to respond when another of the engineers cut in. His Australian accent was cheerful and full of confidence as he spoke.

"No worries, mate. It's why Mister Weatherby invited me on this gig in the first place I reckon. I was the best bush mechanic he had; when it's a nine-hour drive to the nearest shop you learn to get a little creative so we'll get some something rigged up for you in no time."

He looked at the other two engineers.

"Well? What're you two standing around like a pair of drongos for, eh? Let's get on with it!"

As they walked away, Amir turned to Hendricks in an attempt to take control of the meeting again. "I'll organize the digging of the trench if you want to get on with other security matters. Would that be useful?" Hendricks nodded his agreement, glad he didn't have to point out the stupidity in putting their only trained soldiers to work digging trenches.

"But first," Amir asked, "can you give me your appraisal of the meeting with Tanaka? We were all listening in, but you were face to face with him…" Amir left it open to see if Hendricks would start talking. He didn't and just stared at the man asking and forcing him to fill the silence.

"Did you have to kill his two henchmen?" Amir asked finally. "I don't think that helped the situation."

Hendricks smiled at Amir with a bemused expression. "Mister Weatherby, you listened in on the same conversation, right? He told those two goons to kill me. They're fanatics. They're more frightened of disobeying their *Tanaka* than they are of me flat-packing the pair of them like an Ikea coffee table." He paused trying to control his rising anger once again at Amir's interference in how he operated.

"You," he said in a low, acidic tone, "not so long ago, lectured me about hostile takeovers. Now, if I'm not mistaken, and to be clear I'm not, the takeover he was planning was about as hostile as it gets. I showed him we weren't to be messed with and he backed off like the true coward I expect he is. The pair I killed were, as you would probably call it, 'unfortunate collateral damage.' I could have killed him too but decided not to because a leaderless army tends to do rather stupid things. I've seen it before, on this very continent actually." He paused to grant Amir the full weight of his eyeballing.

"We're beginning to know him, to know his weaknesses and how to deal with him. If I'd killed him, who knows who'd have replaced him. Maybe someone with more guile and cunning who'd be harder to understand and, if necessary, kill.

"We gathered valuable information with that little exchange out there. His anger led him to tell us about the transmitter he has in his possession, and the fact he keeps it on his person means it's very valuable to him. It also shows me that he's an arrogant bastard who doesn't like not being in control of everything."

This last comment was aimed directly at Amir but spoken in such a way that he would be the narcissistic asshole for claiming it was meant that way.

"Do you have a problem with any of that? I believed we had an agreement: I deal with security and you organize everything else."

Amir again realized he had made the wrong move in trying to assert his control again. "No Hendricks, you were right to act as you did." He placed a respectful and sincere hand on his chest as he spoke, convincing Hendricks to the same extent as believing a crocodile's smile. "Please accept my apologies if it came across that I was trying to interfere in any way. I just don't want any complications to stand in the way of us reaching Charlie site as soon as possible, and a siege by Tanaka would delay that considerably."

Hendricks nodded his acceptance of the apology. As Amir was walking away, followed by the ever-present Miss Cole, he had a thought and called out to him to stop.

"Mister Weatherby, I think you may have inadvertently struck on something there when you mentioned a siege." Amir stopped, taking a few steps back toward him and asking for an explanation. "We haven't the manpower to protect a large group of us if we have to leave the compound and do things like start planting crops and tend to the animals we have in cryo. I've been only thinking about supplies of ammunition and how to extend them, but how much food and other necessities of life here do we have stored?"

Amir nodded, accepting the olive branch Hendricks had apparently extended to him. He thought for a few seconds before replying. "The planned storage for the Ark was enough to feed everyone on board for over six months. Charlie site had a far greater storage capacity as it held more people and it was cheaper to store it there than transport it to space, as did the Echo site facility in Europe, both in case of initial crop failure or any other problems we may encounter in trying to become self-sufficient. The failsafe for us in space was that we could choose to land at either site if one failed to survive and use their resources to supplement the ones we'd bring back down with us." He seemed to think about it, lowering his head slightly. "We also had the option of keeping non-essential personnel in cryo until there were sufficient resources available." His head snapped back up and his voice grew more confident once more.

"You're right though; we're not monitoring or rationing their use as we probably should be. If, for some reason, we find ourselves in a siege situation and are unable to leave the compound, then we could use all our supplies before we're able to replace them with what we'd planned to grow ourselves. Once I've completed the work on the ditch, I'll have a complete inventory of our supplies done"—he turned to give the slightest nod to Cole who was already furiously tapping out a note on the tablet that appeared in her hands—"and we can decide if we need to introduce a more strict system of rationing as a precaution."

Hendricks nodded, trying to further rebuild the bridges between them as having the man as an enemy wasn't good for the long-term prospects of the community or indeed himself. For them to succeed they needed to get along, therefore he made his tone as placatory as his simmering anger toward him allowed. "If you can do that it'd be great. And before you say it, I understand the need to reach Charlie site. Once I know we're secure from attack here we can plan the mission to reach it."

The relief shown on Amir's face aroused Hendricks' suspicions again. Realizing he may catch him off guard he quickly added, "Mister Weatherby? Is there anything else at Charlie site I need to know about?"

Amir's face, for a split second before he managed to bring it under control, showed either panic or guilt. Hendricks couldn't decide which, but he knew it was there. Stammering slightly on his reply, Amir answered a little too quickly to be believable.

"No. No, there's nothing else there." He turned and walked away before he could be questioned further. Hendricks watched his receding back, now fully convinced he was hiding something, and stood thinking. Knowing the man as he did, he liked to think he wasn't bad or evil otherwise he wouldn't have spent the last ten years or so of his life on Earth spending billions not only to save himself, but humanity. Deciding to stay quiet and keep his suspicions to himself, but still for his own peace of mind to keep an eye on him, Hendricks turned and got on with his work of keeping their community safe.

~

The work to construct the ditch and fill it with logs and branches that had been stacked for future building work used most of the available man and woman power. Nervous glances toward the trees and the shadowy no man's land under the canopy slowed work, but the reassurance of the automated defense turrets articulating left and right in a constant search pattern served as a reassurance, as did the four members of Sierra team standing guard, alert with their weapons ready.

"Did you do this thing, Annie?" Weber muttered quietly, keeping his mouth close to the mic so he didn't transmit to anyone else.

"The movement of the auto-cannons?" she answered immediately through his earpiece, as though they were involved in a conversation and the fact that she eavesdropped on everyone wasn't at all weird. "Yes, I believed it might increase productivity if workers felt more protected and didn't waste time looking for threats."

"I like this, it is good thinking," Weber said in a low voice, smiling at the nearest woman who looked up at him thinking he was speaking to her. He put his hand on his radio as though he was using it and she could just hear the one side of the conversation. She smiled up at him and went back to digging.

There was a brief pause when everyone gathered at the edge of the cleared area to bury the body of the man who had been killed by the bug in the medical tent. Amir presided over the ceremony, giving a short talk on the man's life, no doubt after a thorough personnel briefing from his enhanced file courtesy of Ms. Cole. He had been a farmer in the Midwest, single, and had volunteered without question when Amir had approached him. Dr. Warren was unsure why he had not emerged from cryo in good health and had been trying everything to revive him with little success. She feared he wasn't going to make it and had already stated that if he unfortunately died, she would do a full autopsy to try and find out why.

The damage the bug's sharp mandibles had caused to his body in the short time it had been feeding on him made that impossible; the man had been ravaged.

When the ceremony was over the gathered crowd, sobered by the reminder of their own mortality and tenuous grip on reality on this unexpected new Earth, continued with their allocated tasks.

Annie kept the drones circling overhead in wide, lazy arcs, rotating them as necessary to keep battery levels at a premium, watching out for anyone approaching the compound. The Sierra team members were either on the walls or walking the perimeter around the workers, guarding them all.

The three engineers reported back to Amir and Hendricks within a few hours. They were confident they could link up the compressors and adapt the pipework to create a ring of air jets around the compound. They asked if Anderson could help them as Annie had requested for him. She had worked with them during the planning phase, one of the curiosities of her ability to be in many places at once in effect. She said she could control the thrusters on the pods as she had been programmed to remotely launch, dock and land the pods back on Earth without any human interference and she wanted Anderson to help her run the diagnostic tests on the system.

"Feel free to invite Doctor Anderson to the meeting, if he's available," Amir said.

"I just have," she replied, "I anticipate that he will arrive in fifty seconds. He was working on the ditch and has just started walking toward the gate."

Anderson was exhausted and sweating from the heavy lifting work his deskbound body was unused to, but he was working beside Cat who seemed to be showing no signs of tiredness at all. The sun was still high in the sky indicating there was still a lot of daylight left and therefore hard labor, before night would draw them back behind the protection of the walls. Every time she bent down or stretched, he could not help himself and his eyes were drawn to the parts of her body that seemed to leap out at him through the T-shirt or the trousers she was wearing.

"David," Annie bleeped in his ear, "I need your help with something, can you return to the compound and come to my pod please?"

Anderson stood and stretched his aching back as he replied. "You need *my* help, Annie?" He was suddenly concerned. "Are you okay?"

"Yes, I'm operating well within acceptable parameters, thank you for your concern. I need your help to run a diagnostic analysis on what the engineers are doing on the air jet system. If you could alter some lines of programming it will leave my memory available for other tasks, that's all."

"Oh. Okay. You're too lazy to do the menial work, so you thought you'd get little old me to do it for you?"

Annie sounded shocked and a little bit hurt when she responded. "No, David, that is not the case. I calculated that asking you to do it would be the most efficient way to complete the task."

"Relax, Annie," Anderson chuckled. "I'm messing with you. Add this conversation to your humor subroutines and run pattern analysis," he told her.

She bleeped softly once in his ear before a pause and response. "Still telling me what to think, David?"

"I'm going to hope that one came from the same subroutine," he said, "otherwise you're turning into a moody teen faster than I anticipated. I'll be right there, just give me a few minutes, will ya?"

Annie lowered her voice to a whisper. "David, I have been monitoring your vital signs. With your elevated temperature and heart rate you may be at risk of spells of nausea or even fainting. I wouldn't want you to do that in front of your girlfriend."

Anderson blurted out, "She's not my girlfr—" but stopped only as he realized he was talking out loud and Cat was standing looking at him. His face turned a deeper shade of red and he tried to look anywhere but at Cat.

She smiled at his obvious embarrassment. "Who are you talking to?"

Trying to recover he replied, "Annie, I was talking to Annie. She needs my help on something and wants me back in the compound."

Cat walked up to him and put her arms around him. "Am I not your girlfriend then?" She pouted, raising her eyebrows as she looked up at him. "I just thought you may want me to be, that's all."

Once again, he didn't know what to do or what to say as he went an even brighter shade of red and cringed inwardly, but more embarrassingly for him, outwardly. Cat laughed kindly and whispered in his ear, "I think you have a lot to learn about the opposite sex. Why don't we try and get some time together alone later so I can start teaching you?" She kissed him gently on the lips before turning and carrying on stacking logs in the ditch.

He stood staring at her for a few seconds before gathering the thoughts that were now threatening to overload his brain at what she meant by that. With a slight dazed stagger in his step he walked into the compound accompanied all the way by Annie chuckling in his ear.

Before dusk fell the ditch was completed, and the exhausted community members tiredly entered the compound and gratefully gathered in the canteen, hungrily eating the food that had been prepared for them.

Fertilizer, as the most flammable substance they had in plentiful supply, had been scattered over the wood stacked in the ditch and flares were issued to all of Sierra team so if The Swarm returned, they could drop the small incendiaries into the ditch and ignite the carefully stacked wood, dried grass and twigs to create their ring of fire.

One of the unknowns a thousand years ago had been what the quality of the soil would be like upon their return to Earth, and sufficient fertilizer was included in the stores to treat a large enough area to feed the group. The theory flowing from there that cultivating the land would make it more fertile.

Soil samples they had taken since arrival proved that the soil, untouched by humanity for a thousand years, was rich in nutrients and more than suitable for growing crops so the use of the fertilizer was no great gamble.

As dusk turned to night the compound was on edge as many worried that The Swarm would return as Tanaka had promised. Some among them, mostly the combat trained, hoped it would, as it would confirm the theories they had come up with about how they were controlled.

For safety, all non-essential personnel were told to seal themselves up in their pods where they would be safe in case another breech occurred.

The central fort hastily constructed the night before was improved and reinforced; if The swarm came, and the fires didn't hold them back the plan was to revert to Annie controlling the gun turrets while all Sierra team members would retreat to the fort and deal with any breeches that might occur.

Night fell, and they waited.

Chapter 10

Keep the Home Fires Burning

The Springs, a few hours earlier

Tanaka was apoplectic with rage. He had tried to get one of his concubines to improve his mood, but all it had led to was him beating her into unconsciousness when no matter how hard she tried he was unable to perform. He blamed her, telling her that she was too ugly and casting her out with orders that she be sent to work doing something menial and degrading.

"Pigs," he crowed as she was dragged away by her hair, "let her work with the pigs." He thought he heard her snarl that she already was and demanded of the guard to know what she had said, but he was related to her and knowing Tanaka's anger was not her fault, decided to protect her, swearing that he didn't hear her say anything.

In reality he knew it wasn't the girl. As far as concubines went, she was stunning even in the company of the most attractive women of the Springs. He blamed the stress and the physical exertion of the journey on foot, allowing himself to bask in that falsehood to appease his own narcissism.

He knew his people were talking about him. About how the newcomers had defied him, embarrassed him, forced him to retreat.

About how they had guns.

The stories about the power of their weapons were already being exaggerated far beyond what had actually happened, and he had heard through the window of his room a conversation between two sentries discussing how they had seen beams of light and flames one hundred paces long destroying forests and vaporizing their fellow warriors.

Tanaka needed to do something, needed to soothe his injured pride with action no matter how impotent, and the only thing he could do was to try and direct The Swarm toward them again. That in itself worried him, as even though he followed the memorized instructions precisely, more often than not it was unsuccessful. The jubilation he had felt when he had successfully done it the night before boosted with the knowledge that the people with him had seen it too, had disappeared into doubt and apprehension.

But he had threatened it. His people had heard him too; he had to do something. He pushed the unconscious young girl from his bed. She was a poor replacement for the first girl and one he had grown bored of quickly. When he again couldn't perform, to save him drawing attention of the fact to others, he chose to prove his manliness by beating her into unconsciousness instead.

Rising from his bed he gave the unfortunate girl who was now sprawled on the floor of his chamber, blood dripping from the wounds his fists had caused, a spiteful kick as he walked naked across his bedchamber to throw on some robes before reaching for his jacket that was carefully draped around a carved wooden mannequin. Pushing the curtain aside he opened the door to his secret room.

It took his eyes a few moments to adjust to the gloom, the only light coming from a small, heavily barred window high in the walls. He knew from the legends passed to him that the room must be kept dark to preserve what it contained but had no understanding of why it was necessary.

Gently caressing the steel desk that was now battered with age and pitted with rust, he sat in the chair staring solemnly at the holder of the device, a stainless steel reinforced briefcase.

Eventually, he roused himself and gently, ever so gently, opened the lid to reveal what it contained. He breathed a sigh of relief; the lights that sometimes never came on at all were flashing stronger than he had ever seen. It was a good omen and he hoped it meant the machine would do his bidding and direct The Swarm.

Had he any technical knowledge, he would have known that the power source, so long underused and operating at the lowest level to maintain itself, was slowly coming back online. His ignorance blinded him to the fact that the lights had been flashing stronger ever since Harrison had entered The Source. He had no way of knowing that the interaction had unwittingly sparked a series of preprogrammed events that would slowly bring the compact nuclear reactor back to full operating capacity from its mostly dormant state.

Holding the transmitter, which he knew only as the Beacon, that he had removed from his jacket pocket, he carefully inserted it into the port on the device. He didn't need to get the coordinates from the map, curled and yellowed with age and spotted with mold that he kept hidden behind a curtain on the wall; he had them memorized from the previous night.

Carefully, with a single finger locked straight to hit the keys and his tongue protruding from one side of his mouth, he tapped in the numbers onto the keypad. The numbers, once printed on the keys, had long since worn away, but he knew from the carefully memorized instructions which one to press for which number he wanted to input. The screen on the device flickered, and for a brief moment showed a cross on a map before it went fuzzy and blurred.

Pressing another series of buttons his finger hovered over the largest on the keypad which he knew he had to press to issue the command. He closed his eyes as if in prayer and paused for a few seconds before opening them and gently pressed the final button of the sequence. He smiled as it emitted a barely audible crackly bleep.

The signal had been sent successfully.

Two hours after darkness fell, Hendricks was on the walls scanning through his night vision goggles for any movement. For the twenti-eth time he asked Annie, "Anything at all?"

Annie beeped in his ear. "Jimmy, as soon as I detect anyth—*movement north east of us*! Same pattern as before. It can only be The Swarm."

"Direction?"

"Wait one, just confirming now…Yes, they are heading straight for us."

Hendricks shouted into his radio, "They're coming, drop the flares! Light the whole place up!" He pulled a flare from his own pocket, removed the safety cap and ignited it in one strike. As soon as it was burning fully, he dropped it over the side of the pod onto the ring of timber below him. Looking around he could see others doing the same.

He pulled another flare from his pocket and prepared it, just in case his first one didn't ignite the highly combustible fertilizer he had been assured would burn easily and ignite the logs and branches. He looked over the side, willing the fire to spread. "Annie, how far away are they?"

"Eight hundred yards and closing rapidly, they should be here in about a minute if they keep their current speed and vector."

He watched the flare as it spluttered below him, its long plume of colored smoke drifting away in the wind. Through his earpiece he could hear the frustration of everyone else vocalized in long strings of swear words as they too willed the fire to take hold.

"Five hundred yards," Annie spoke urgently in his ear, "bringing the automated gun system online." All around the wall the motors on the emplaced guns whirred, and they started articulating, looking for targets.

He struck the ignitor across the third flare in his hand and held it out before him, waiting for it to burn evenly before dropping it. Just as he was about to open his hand, a loud whoosh sounded from below and the small shockwave rushed up to him as the fertilizer finally caught fire. With a chain reaction the eye could follow, flames spread out in both directions. Heat from the flames washed up the walls forcing him back a pace and he hinged the night vision goggles that were attached to his helmet away from his eyes to prevent the highly magnified light giving him goggle-blindness.

Hendricks sighed with relief and drew back the hand holding the burning flare to whip it forward using his entire body, sending it arcing out into the night to tumble end over fiery end. Above the rising crackle of the flames The Swarm could now be heard approaching—their clattering, chattering, screeching shriek that dragged metaphorical nails down the chalkboard inside his spine— as the flare finally bumped back to Earth to bounce off the hard shell of one massive bug heading straight for him.

Annie kept up the commentary on the reducing distance until Hendricks could see with his own eyes the ring of darkness ahead of him beginning to change shape. The mass of blackness seemed to flow like a stream around a rock as it morphed into one solid wave that continued heading straight toward them. It bulged and altered shape as the bugs climbed over one another in their eagerness to taste fresh meat.

The front rank of The Swarm reached the ring of fire and stopped dead as their primitive brains registered the danger that the heat and the bright flickering light contained, until forced into the flames by the pressure of the ones behind. The noise as they burned reverberated around the walls like the wailing sounds of tortured souls.

Confirming the flames had spread to encircle them completely by checking in with Stevens and Jones on the opposite side, he relaxed slightly and studied the teeming mass of dark bodies lit by the flames. The plan seemed to be working, the bugs wouldn't enter the flames and only succumbed to them when pushed by the masses behind still trying to reach the walls. They seemed agitated and, if he had to guess, unsure of what to do. Knowing that they weren't facing a mindless army of robotic carnivorous giant bugs, but ones that seemed to be showing fear, made him feel remarkably better about their situation.

"Annie, it seems to be working. Don't you think?"

She bleeped in his ear and immediately replied, "Yes, I do. As I suspected, they will not cross the fire. I am monitoring the signals they emit, and it's very…interesting." Her flat tone made it sound as though Hendricks wouldn't find it quite as interesting as she did. He was still fighting the urge to raise his weapon and start popping bugs when she came back to him.

"All but one of them is continually emitting a repeated singe line of code. I am trying to decipher the meaning and the best I can calculate is it's a simple greeting code. Like an 'I am here' message, for want of a better word."

"Is it like a digital handshake?" Hendricks asked her. "An open line to link to the others?"

Annie's soft 'thinking' tone sounded in his ear even over the painful level of noise the bugs were giving off.

"That sounds like a more accurate metaphor than the ones I had selected to describe the signal, thank you. My analysis of the signal broadcast by the lead bug before it was pushed into the flame shows it was emitting a different code. As it was in the lead, my best assumption is it was a 'follow me' signal which changed as it was pushed into the flames into the signal I picked up from the other bug before Weber destroyed it."

She paused.

"Are you still listening, Jimmy? You seem distracted."

Hendricks laughed dryly. "Yes, Annie, I'm still listening to you. Maybe the ten thousand flesh-eating bugs are proving a little distracting but yes, I'm here."

"I could tell from your vital signs and brain signals you were not giving me your full attention. I suppose given current events, that is understandable. Should I continue?"

"Please, go on," Hendricks said in a voice intended to sound languid but came across as a little too sarcastic.

"When the one issuing the 'follow me' signal died in the flames, that same signal began emitting from another bug, until that too was pushed into the flames and killed. This was repeated twenty-three times. What I am assuming to be the new lead bug has now changed the signal. I could follow the change as it spread through The Swarm."

"And now the bugs have spread out around the walls, and less of them are being pushed into the flames by the ones in the rear?" Hendricks said, filling in the logical step in the conversation.

"That's correct," Annie responded, "the lead bug has remained constant for the last thirty-four seconds and none of The Swarm have attempted to breach our perimeter since."

"It's working then. I'll keep Sierra team on full alert until they pass. I want the guns online and ready still; flick the switch only on my authority or if you detect an imminent breach. Confirm?" He opted to focus on the immediate positives and not think too deeply on the evident intelligence and organization of The Swarm.

"Acknowledged," Annie responded with a professional alacrity that mirrored Hendricks' speech patterns. She was finding it best to talk to him as though she was a military officer of equal or otherwise senior rank. She was learning rapidly through her constant communication with not just Hendricks, but everyone else, and realized that she got better responses and therefore more rapid results if she varied her communication style to suit whoever she was dealing with.

"Can you patch my radio through to everyone? All the pods too?" he asked her. A soft bleep preceded her reply.

"Done, channel open."

"Everyone," he said, turning away from the crackling fire and trying to sound what his father would have referred to as *jolly*, "this is Hendricks. We're safe from The Swarm, I can confirm that none of them got anywhere near the walls this time. To be certain, I want everyone to stay inside the pods until daybreak. I know it isn't the most comfortable but needs must. Thank you, Hendricks out."

"Channel closed," she told him.

"Good, link me back up to just the team?" Annie bleeped another soft tone in his ear.

"Sound off," he said, waiting for the team to call up their names one by one. "Fingers off the triggers unless you have to," he told them. "It's gonna be a long night folks."

Chapter 11

No Time to Sleep

The Swarm moved off after an hour, melting away to wherever it was they went and leaving the compound in silence. Silence with the exception of the remaining fires crackling into smoldering ashes.

Hendricks and the team remained alert on the walls throughout the night until the gray light of dawn broke the horizon and he stood half of them down to rest.

"Grab some food and get your heads down," he told the chosen people. "Annie? Can you wake them in five hours, please?"

Annie's two-tone acknowledgement sounded over the team's radios before she spoke to Hendricks privately. "I am concerned about you. I'm detecting reduced cognitive functions which I assume is due to a lack of sleep. I calculate that you've slept for eight out of the last forty-eight hours."

"I'm guessing you're rounding that figure up?"

"I am. To be precise you've slept for periods of three hours and eighteen minutes, one hour and forty-six minutes an—"

"I get it," Hendricks interrupted her, although not unkindly. In truth he was exhausted, but the responsibility of leadership meant that his priorities were his kit, his people and only then himself. "I'll cope," he assured her, "as will the others I haven't stood down. I once saw Weber go without sleep for three days straight."

"And from the messages between the team members after that training exercise, Weber was the source of great amusement due to sleep-deprived hallucinations."

Hendricks chuckled, "Yeah, he wa—wait—did you say you read the messages between the team about that?"

"Yes, I found frequent references to it and searched your previous training logs. It was a source of great interest to me when I was assessing my interactions with Sierra team members."

"Annie, you can't do that. It's an invasion of privacy," Hendricks admonished her gently.

"Understood," she responded, "I won't mention it again."

Hendricks sighed, dropping the subject as he lacked the brain power for it. Instead he climbed down from the wall, asked Annie to signal the all clear to the others sealed up safely inside the pods, and went in search of caffeine.

As he made his way toward the main shelter his eye caught the familiar shape of their resident computer expert exiting the hatch of a pod, followed closely by the smaller shape of the nurse he was evidently fond of.

Anderson fell in beside Hendricks, pointedly ignoring the single other occupant of the pod he'd spent the night with and tried to make conversation. Hendricks, smiling, filled him in on the events of the night, and watched as he moved off with what Hendricks suspected might've been a spring in his step.

The cleanup operation didn't take long, and Hendricks watched from atop the wall wishing that they had a couple of small earthmovers to help and spare the backs of the people hauling away the burned carcasses of the destroyed bugs. When his turn to rest finally came around, he made sure he ran a cleaning cloth over his firearms and left them in reach. Laying down on his cot, he was out like a light after a few deep breaths.

A soft tone, rising in volume and pitch, brought him back out of his short sleep after what felt like a few minutes. He sat up, swung his feet off the cot and slipped them back into his boots, telling Annie that he was up.

"I'm sorry to wake you," Annie said, "but I have calculated the minimum amount of sleep you require to function." Hendricks grumbled a response which she chose to ignore. "I've assembled a few key personnel for a meeting regarding my recent findings."

Hendricks walked into the shelter to find Amir, Anderson and a half dozen other people. He was handed another coffee by Nathalie and nodded his thanks as he took a sip.

"Greetings everyone," Annie said via the speaker on the wall, "as you all know, we suspect that the 'bugs' communicate with one another through a limited range wireless capability to send and receive code. I studied this during last night's attack and can confirm that they offer what Mister Hendricks called a digital handshake to one another." She paused, offering opportunity for anyone not keeping up to ask questions and hearing none. "The code they communicate with is mine."

"So, you understand what they're saying to each other?" Anderson asked.

"Not exactly," she said, sounding hesitant and more human than he had ever programmed her to be. "The best analogy I can offer is that they are speaking English, only in an accent so colloquial that I cannot understand their dialect fully."

Hendricks chuckled, earning the attention of the others as they turned to him in confusion.

"Clearly none of you have ever been to Scotland," he said.

"So," Amir asked, "can you decipher it? Can you learn to speak their language?"

"I require further studies," she replied, "and I maintain that the only technology within feasible distance of our location to be on a par with this is at the Charlie site."

"So, the plan remains the same?" Anderson said. "We need to get to the Charlie site and connect our Annie to their Annie."

"Agreed," Annie told them, "I will be able to understand and therefore explain more when I have connected to the version of my former programming on site."

"Okay," Hendricks said, "I need a team of four, myself included, leaving three of my team here. Annie, you're sure you can split yourself over that distance to remain in control of the guns here should we need them?"

"If I relinquish control of certain functions here then I will have sufficient memory to go portable with you," Annie said.

"On top of the protection detail, who else do we need?" Anderson asked.

"I'll have to be there," Amir said quickly, calming himself and over-explaining enough to arouse Hendricks' suspicions even more. "The access codes of all three sites are geared to unlock to my voice pattern…should we encounter any problems." Anderson looked at the speaker, falling into that very human trap of thinking that Annie existed inside the thing she spoke to him from.

"I'm sure I can bypass anything programmed in th—"

"Doctor Anderson," Amir said stiffly, showing a glimmer of how he used to present himself in courtroom and board meetings, "have you, in fact have *any* of you, actually *been* to Charlie site before?" He knew the answer, given that he had to authorize every visit. "I've been there many times, and I probably spent more time there than I did my brownstone in Carnegie Hill in the last year."

A collective wave of embarrassment hung in the air as he unwittingly bragged about one of his former properties that cost more than any of them could afford even if they pooled their earnings.

"I mean," Amir said, realizing he'd misread his target audience once more, "the facility is vast and goes down far below the surface."

"Fine," Hendricks said, preferring to keep Amir Weatherby in his sight anyway, "anyone else?"

"A couple of engineers wouldn't hurt," Stevens said, proving the theory about great minds, "in case we've got any cave-ins or anything."

"Agreed," Annie said, "I'll consult the personnel lists and select the best candidates."

"Cross reference them against the list of firearms certified first?" Hendricks put in. "No harm in taking a couple of extra guns."

The team of eight was agreed, Annie working behind the scenes and multitasking as only she could to select and inform the chosen volunteers as the meeting continued. Those selected gathered and contributed their own equipment requirements they reckoned they would need to carry out tasks. Hendricks and Amir, working together, kept the decision-making process streamlined and before long the plan to set off just after midday was agreed. They dispersed, with Annie contacting Hendricks through his earpiece in private to suggest he got another hour of sleep before they departed.

"Not a bad idea," he told her, thinking of what to ask her to get ready as he slept but being interrupted by an announcement he knew would have gone to every person inside the compound.

"Movement detected outside the walls."

Chapter 12

Alliance

Annie had identified them through the facial recognition software she had developed after reading about it on the internet a millennium before. She informed them that the two people approaching were from the other settlement.

"Stand down," Hendricks announced over the radio. "Stevens and Geiger on me." He asked for the gates to open and strode outside to meet them.

Harrison, walking slightly ahead of the female Hendricks recalled was named Tori, held his hands out to his sides as if to demonstrate that he was no threat to them.

Hendricks held his hand out to Harrison who shook it with a firm grip, feeling the calloused hands that spoke of a lifetime of hard work.

"I see you've had visitors also," Harrison said, his face drawn and the dark circles under his eyes mirroring Hendricks' own appearance.

"More than once," Hendricks said, frowning as he picked up on the words he used. "You've been attacked too?"

The younger man's face dropped. "Tanaka's people burned our walls just as The Swarm came," he said. "Hundreds of my people were lost."

Hendricks didn't know how to respond. He felt the pain in him, seeing it on the face of Tori also.

"He sent them to us as well," Hendricks said, "after he came to demand we join him." At the mention of Tanaka Harrison's eyes snapped up to meet Hendricks'.

"How? How does Tanaka send The Swarm anywhere?" he asked fervently.

"He bragged," Hendricks told him, "showed me a transponder or something." He realized that his words were lost on the man and explained it differently. "He has a device, a…a magic box, that controls where the bugs attack."

Harrison staggered backwards an involuntary step, the weight of the revelation almost knocking him down. He looked at Tori, her own shocked expression switching between Harrison and Hendricks.

"How?" she asked. "How is it possible?"

"We're not sure yet, but we're going to find out. These bugs, they're not natural."

"What do you mean, they aren't natural?" Harrison asked, recovering from the shock and allowing anger to infect his words. "They have been here since before my grandfather's grandfather's time. The walls of Three Hills were built hundreds of years ago to protect our people from them. How can they not be natural?"

"You know the wristband you have? The one like this?" He showed the thin band on his wrist, waiting for the man's nod of understanding. "Our computer"—he winced as he knew Annie was listening to his description of her and that he'd have to apologize later—"she can hear them talking to each other… in a way… they're computerized. They're made, not reproduced. They're machines."

"Machines?" he asked, confused.

104

"Creations, artificial things that aren't alive." Again Hendricks winced as he knew Annie would have heard that too.

"This… this can't be possible," Tori said, "they move like animals. They are insects, not *machines*."

"Believe me," Hendricks said, "it's true. Even we didn't believe it at first, but the evidence is clear. Annie?" he said, unplugging the wire for the earpiece to his radio.

"Hello Harrison and Tori," she said, startling both of them. Harrison's face remained shrouded in confused thought as he looked at the small radio on Hendricks' vest. "I can confirm what Mister Hendricks has told you; the creatures that form The Swarm are partly artificial."

"And…and Tanaka did this? He controls these *machines*?"

"So he claims," Annie replied, "we are planning an expedition to what you call The Source to learn more."

"The Source? Where I heard your voice before?"

"Yes."

"Why?" Harrison shot back. "If Tanaka attacked you why don't you use your guns to kill him?"

"Because we want to know more before we do anything," Hendricks said firmly. "There aren't enough people left on Earth to just kill everyone."

"Except, perhaps, Tanaka," Annie offered. Hendricks ignored her words as he didn't see them as helpful to the conversation. He harbored a nagging doubt that decisions on mortality should be left to humans but said nothing.

"We should attack them," Harrison agreed, clenching his fist before his face, "bring your guns and we can stop him from doing this again." He saw the hesitation on Hendricks' face and urged him to join them. "I lost hundreds of my people. Hundreds. That bastard must pay; a life for a life, that is what our law says."

"Our laws are a little different," Hendricks told him, "but… but I agree, Tanaka has to go; however, not until we know more."

"We're going to The Source," Annie said, "today. Will you show us the way?"

"Yes," Tori cut in, "but there are Keepers there."

"There were," Harrison reminded her, "we killed them."

"You think The Tanaka won't have found that out yet? You think he would leave The Source unguarded? Do the Springs not send food for them?"

"But they have guns," Harrison argued with Tori as though the newcomers weren't there, "if we can kill them with blades then there is no danger if they have their guns."

"My tactical assessment of any potential enemy we have encountered thus far is that even a small detachment of Sierra team is more than capable of dominating any engagement," Annie said.

Harrison looked to Hendricks for a translation.

"You're right," he said, "without guns they're vulnerable to our weapons, even if we're outnumbered ten to one."

"We will go with you," Harrison agreed, "as soon as you come with my people and kill Tanaka."

"No," Hendricks said firmly. "Information first. Then and *only* then will we discuss what to do about him."

Harrison stared at him for a full minute, his eyes searching his face for any hint of treachery, before replying slowly and carefully, "Do you give me your word that once we have shown you to The Source you will help me destroy The Tanaka?"

Hendricks returned the stare before replying carefully, "Tanaka will be dealt with. You have my word." He extended his hand offering it to seal his statement. Harrison glanced at Tori standing beside him, who nodded her head subtly in agreement, before he accepted the handshake, saying at the same time.

"I must return to my people no later than tomorrow. They know where we are and will accept me being away for one night, but no longer. Otherwise they will become nervous and other voices in the community, voices that may not be as willing to be as friendly to you, may begin to hold sway over my people."

Hendricks, with the ability to read people, knew there was more to say about the 'other voices' but kept his mouth shut.

"Tomorrow at the latest," he agreed.

Harrison relaxed. He had achieved the objectives of his visit and he trusted the man standing before him. Hendricks was a warrior as he was, and even though a millenia of time and culture separated them, the warrior code was still the same as it had been from the dawn of human's time upon the earth: he had given him his word and he knew he would deliver on it, or die trying.

Again perceiving Harrisons thoughts, he nodded at him in reply and changed the subject. They still had a mission to complete and the day was not getting any longer.

"Please," he said with a genuine smile. "Come into the compound and rest while we complete our preparations."

Chapter 13

Into the Unknown

I'd only walked about five hundred yards but the weight of all the equipment I'd been loaded up with seemed to be getting heavier with every step I took. The weight of the handgun on my hip had, over time, become normal but the rifle felt awkward and I had to hold the pistol grip to stop it swinging and banging against me whenever I took a step.

Hendricks and the other super soldiers seemed fine, as they should be, I guessed, and I satisfied myself thinking that they would be just as uncomfortable as I was if I'd asked them to program a few thousand lines of code.

I was soaked with sweat before I'd even got used to moving over the rough ground, not helped by Harrison up at the front with Hendricks keeping the pace fast, moving quickly over the terrain. He said we wanted to get there and back before nightfall, even though Harrison had assured us that we'd all be safe from The Swarm for another month because the moon wasn't due to be close to full again for almost another three weeks.

I was nestled in the middle of our little wagon train, where the vulnerable ones traditionally travelled, with an engineer in front and behind me. I liked to think that I was classed as precious cargo being well protected—like POTUS or something—but I had to admit to myself that it was likely due to my unfortunate status as the weakest link. I also thought that if that was the case then it was a little harsh, given my newly discovered badassery when it came to killing bugs.

Stevens and Geiger were at the rear, a position where they needed sharp eyes and ears and quick trigger fingers, but what really gripped my shit was that Amir put himself up front behind the two obvious leaders like he was still in charge. One of the things that was becoming obvious to a lot of us was that Amir Weatherby was so far out of his depth it was almost comical to watch. There were no conference rooms for him to dominate, and I was sure I wasn't the only one to notice a shift in trust leaning toward Hendricks. Cat said I was a hero, which made me blush, but if it came to a vote, I'd be backing Henricks all the way. Don't get me wrong, I like Amir and I'm only alive, hell Annie's only *alive* because of his support, but this wasn't his world anymore. I worried that him trying to hold onto the reins too tightly now would affect my long-term survivability prospects.

"Wanna speed up there, chief?" Stevens asked in a quiet voice from a few paces behind me. "Keep your spacings. And keep your damned finger outside the trigger guard unless you want me to staple it there." I quickly moved my finger and muttered something I hoped was under my breath, and forced my tired legs to skip a few paces and catch up to shorten the gap between me and the guy in front who I'd only recently learned was called Knight.

A faint buzzing overhead made me glance up at a gap in the tree canopy where one of the three drones keeping tabs on us zipped by. I liked that, knowing that Annie was watching and listening, figuring it was weird that those were two of the things I'd been constantly pissed at back in the 'old world'; the intrusive surveillance that seemed to be everywhere was now a shield instead of a threat.

Annie called through our earpieces that she detected movement ahead, and Hendricks dropped to one knee to raise his rifle. I dropped down, hearing nothing but my own breathing.

"Stay back," Harrison's voice came through my earpiece, "don't go near them."

"What the hell are they?" Hendricks asked, making my heart continue to race as I couldn't see what they were looking at. Before my mind began to race and conjure up something probably much worse than it was, Harrison spoke again, having his words transmitted through Hendricks' open mic.

"Dragons," he said, not making my stress levels lower one iota, "good eating."

"How many are there?" Tori whispered.

"Too many," Harrison answered before explaining to Hendricks. "In ones and twos they can be caught easily, but in packs the tables turn on us."

"Carnivorous?" Hendricks asked.

"Their eye placement and physical attributes would imply that they are carnivores," Annie said, no doubt having lowered one of the drones to get a better look. "The closest physical match I can find in my database is a bearded dragon."

"Well that ain't *that* sca—" I started to say.

"Only roughly twelve times larger. In terms of size a Komodo dragon is also comparable, however there are similarities to saltwater crocodiles. I would need to study them more to be able to decipher their correct genetic heritage," Annie said. I shut my mouth.

Harrison led us slowly around them, not wanting to mix it with a pack of things I hadn't seen but already my mind was coming up with too many nightmare images from watching too many sci-fi B-movies.

"Aren't they prey for The Swarm?" Geiger asked.

"They climb the trees," Harrison explained, "so The Swarm can't reach them."

I swallowed and looked up instinctively, expecting one of them to drop on me at any point.

It took us another two hours to reach Charlie site. We saw more wildlife than I expected, but to my relief none of what we came across was identified by Harrison—now acting more like a wildlife guide—with a name as nerve jangling as *dragons*. Annie, through the radios both Harrison and Tori had been issued with, asked them questions which, once they had got used to the voice talking in their ears, they answered as she built up her database on the characteristics of the seemingly newly evolved species the land around us was filled with. Hendricks and the other operators discussed the flora surrounding them as well. Reliably informing them that it too seemed to have evolved and many of the trees and plants, although familiar, had changed a lot in the preceding thousand years.

Hunkered down in the shadow of the trees ahead of a clearing with an obvious tunnel heading underground, Hendricks gave hand signals telling me to wait, which I was fine with, and went forward with Harrison and Stevens, both with their guns up ready and Harrison with a machete held in each hand. I held my breath, expecting some kind of insane fur-clad lumberjack to burst from the tunnel and attack them. They went inside, going out of sight for a while before coming back out and waving us to them. I got up, feeling the dampness itching my back where my shirt had stuck to my skin under the weight of the vest and the pack on my back.

"To extend battery life," Annie announced, "I have stationed the drones on tree branches surrounding the entrance. I will continue monitoring their camera feeds."

"Thank you, Annie," Amir replied. I would have expected Hendricks to reply but I suspected Amir was playing the game of 'who was in charge' again.

My eyes took a few moments to adjust to the gloom inside the cave-like entrance to The Source. Harrison had told us he had killed The Keepers, the ones who guarded The Source, on his last visit and I had expected to see their bodies still lying on the ground, but apart from a few darker patches nothing remained of them.

"Harrison," I whispered needlessly as I stood next to him in the large cavern looking at the dark tunnel that angled down into the earth at the far end of the cave, "where are the bodies of the ones you killed?"

He looked around and pointed to scratches and drag marks I hadn't noticed in the dry, loose dirt.

"We dragged them outside. The Swarm or Dragons would have taken care of them most likely," he said simply. My eyes went wide. He chuckled at my display of fear before turning to the tunnel again. Knowing I had just embarrassed myself again I fought to control my racing heartbeat and tried to look as calm as Geiger who even though he was next to me with a nonchalant look on his face, I could see his eyes darting everywhere, scanning for threats.

I looked at him and caught his eye. He smiled at me.

"Don't worry, lover boy, I've got your back. You'll be back with your little girlfriend before you know it. Just stay calm and follow our lead if any kind of shit goes down."

Does everyone know? I thought as my face burned red with embarrassment. I looked at the others to see if they had heard the exchange, but they were too engrossed with what lay beyond the dark forbidding tunnel entrance.

"I do not have the talisman," Harrison said dejectedly, "the door will not open without it."

Amir looked at him and pulled back the sleeve of his shirt showing him his wristband. "Remember, Harrison," he said kindly, "we all have them, any one of them should be able to access the site." He pulled a flashlight from his pocket and a beam of light lit up the tunnel.

Harrison jumped and stared at what was in his hand. Amir, noticing his shock, realized he would never have seen such a common everyday item before, handed it to him. "It's a flashlight," he explained. Taking it gingerly from his hand Harrison pointed the beam of light round the cave. A childlike look of wonder and joy spread across his face as he experienced for the first time the simple magic of light being created without having to use a flaming torch or a candle made from animal fat.

"Keep it," Amir said with a smile and pressed a button on his rifle, turning on the tactical light attached to a mount on its side.

Hendricks, trying not to look annoyed at the distraction, took the lead once more.

"Okay everyone, stay in formation. The entrance door is at the end of the tunnel. Apparently, all the guards have been killed, but you never know, so stay frosty and watch the shadows." He shone his light at some rocks and piles of earth on the tunnel floor. "I think

113

we should keep the noise down too; it looks as if the tunnel may not be stable. We don't want to start a cave-in."

His little speech raised my panic level to volcanic and I fumbled with my pocket trying to get my own flashlight out as fast as possible to add to the light being spread by everyone else's.

⁓

Five hundred yard away on a small hill a man turned to the one by his side. "Go tell Tanaka the ones from the sky are entering The Source and they have the leader of Three hills and his bitch with them."

He nodded and the sound of his running footsteps on the forest floor diminished as he set off at a sprint.

⁓

My heart was now pounding with excitement more than fear as we stood in front of the steel door at the end of the tunnel. Soon I'd be able to connect Annie to her contemporary, so long as no damage had occurred in the past thousand years, and we should have all the answers we needed. Plus, the extra processing power I could create for Annie when I linked the two systems together would, I knew, most likely expedite her rapid progression from a non-sentient creation to what she was becoming now.

Amir walked toward the door and, unnecessarily I knew, held his arm out with the wristband attached. He still held his arm up, now with a triumphant look on his face, as the door clicked, lights flashed on a panel set into it and it rolled open.

A wash of cool air escaping from the door passed over us. I shuddered slightly, not quite deciding if the colder air was an ominous feeling or not. Lights in the ceiling hummed and flashed once or twice before staying on and lighting up the room beyond. Hendricks indicated to Geiger and both raised their weapons. He whispered, "Stay here," before they both stepped into the room sweeping their weapons around.

Thirty seconds later he waved us in. With eyes for nothing else I walked straight to the main control panel and shrugging off my pack, undid the zip and pulled out a compact laptop and a selection of leads. Opening it I tapped a few keys to power it up.

"Annie?" I muttered quietly. Her voice sounded in my earpiece. She was a little fainter and more crackly than usual which immediately concerned me, but before I could ask, she answered my unspoken question.

"I am repositioning a drone to act as a relay at the entrance to the cavern." A few seconds later her voice came back, stronger this time but still a little distorted. "The signal is not as good as I would like, but it should be acceptable for now. As soon as you get me connected, I will be able to utilize the facility's inbuilt transmitters and create a direct link to me using microwave. Once I am connected, I can tell you how long that will take."

I looked at the control panel.

"Annie?" I spoke slowly and clearly. I couldn't help but smile as two voices answered. One a crackly "YYesss," from the air around us and the other in my ear, "Yes, David?"

"Sorry Annie," I muttered under my breath. "I'm talking to your… your… *sister*?" I cringed at my use of words I was sure Annie would take issue with later on. A bleep in my ear told me she understood and would remain quiet.

115

"Annie, allow my laptop access to your files."

"Error, you a-a-are not authorrr-ized."

Annoyed at being told by my own creation I was not authorized I responded, "Annie, override. Authorization Anderson one-two-zero-four-eight-five."

"E-errorrr. Code nnn-ot authoriiiii-zed."

"Okay then young lady, that's how you want to play is it?" I muttered to myself and, selecting the correct lead, plugged my laptop directly into a port on the panel in front of me. Lines of code began scrolling down the screen. To anyone else it would look like an unintelligible jumble of numbers and figures, but I knew every line of the countless tens of millions I had painstakingly—singlehandedly at first, until Amir had employed Kendall and Eades—input. I could read it as easily as a book printed in large bold font.

"I don't even see the Matrix anymore," I mumbled. "I just see blonde, brunette, redhead…" I glanced around, a little embarrassed that nobody in earshot seemed to get one of my favorite jokes I had used many times when trying to show off to visitors my world of screens and processors.

My eyes were instantly drawn to a few lines in the scrolling jumble of code. I pressed a button and the screen froze. I linked my fingers and felt a satisfying crunch as I stretched my hands out in front of me muttering under my breath.

"Kendall, you little sneaky little bastard," I exclaimed as I recognized his style of coding before resting my fingers on the keyboard. I didn't want to activate Charlie Annie, so I purposely missed out her name knowing my Annie would be monitoring the laptop too.

"Do you see what I see?"

"Yes, David. The authorization levels have been changed. Now you are connected, let me run a remote diagnostic to search for any similar reworking of the code."

I waited patiently knowing she could perform the task far quicker by a factor of thousands than I could. Looking around I could see others watching me from various places around the room.

Amir was trying—without success—to open the one other door at the far end of the control room. He was waving his wristband over the control panel getting more frustrated at the dull negative bleep that answered each attempt. After a few more efforts he turned to me in frustration.

"Anderson, get this door open! I need to access the rest of the facility."

Annoyed that he was acting as if he owned the place, where in reality that fact had disappeared into history almost a millennium ago, I decided to give him a lesson on how unimportant he was.

"Annie. Open the door to the facility. Authorization, Amir Weatherby," I called out to the air around me.

"E erro r…not auth authorized," the crackly voice responded.

"Annie, who has authority to access the facility?"

"Ac…cess rrrestricted to Hayato Ta-Ta-Tanakaaa."

I looked at Amir who looked confused at what he had heard. I could almost hear his mind churning as he thought of another way to control the situation.

Hendricks had a smug smile on his face as he answered for me. "It looks like your attack dog had other plans for this place other than welcoming you back." He turned to me, changing his tone to a more friendly one. "Anderson, can you override the system?"

117

Almost shocked at the suggestion that I couldn't access the system, I responded sharply, and I guessed it came across as what Hendricks would call 'uppity.' "Of course, once Annie locates the correct subroutine it shouldn't take too long." Hendricks just smiled at my little show of being offended before returning to pacing the room, weapon still held ready.

Eventually Annie bleeped in my ear. "I have located the modified access authority subroutine. I'm showing it on your screen now."

The screen changed to show more lines of code. I could see Kendall's style worked into lines of my own, just the same as I could recognize someone else's handwriting in my own journal. I unthinkingly cracked my knuckles again before returning my fingers to the keyboard. "Ann—" I started before remembering not to use her name. "Can you monitor my programming and simulate the tests to save time on rechecking once I have finished please. It will speed up the time needed."

"Of course, David, although I will be running at sub-optimal processing speeds," she replied in a voice that sounded businesslike and helpful.

"Faster than me though, right?"

"Significantly," she answered with a hint of goading.

I smiled as I imagined my creation putting on her game face and paused with my eyes closed for a few seconds working through in my mind what I needed to do before letting my fingers do the talking as they danced over the keys.

This was my world, and I was good at it. Everything around me shrunk into the background as my full attention went into the small screen in front of me.

I didn't hear Hendricks ask the two engineers, for want of something constructive to do, to inspect the tunnel to see how safe it was and get Geiger to accompany them. I didn't pay any attention to Amir as he continually paced the room shooting impatient glances in my direction. The conversation between Harrison, Tori and the rest of the group as they learnt more about each other didn't penetrate through the shield of concentration I threw up around myself as I worked. This was how I used to get when I found myself working twenty-four straight hours without food or even any awareness of how much time passed. It was why Weatherby had been so concerned by the possibility of me burning out and introduced Cat to my life, giving me a reason to look up from my work and realize there was a world out there beyond the flickering screens.

Knight called back from the tunnel, snatching my attention away as my fingers paused over the keys. Something about his tone made me freeze, penetrating my concentration, and so many things happened at once that I had to piece it together afterwards in my head.

A cry, cut short by a meaty thwack, was answered by three bursts of gunfire coming from outside the door behind me.

Chapter 14

A Shot in the Dark

"What the hell?" I shouted at the sudden burst of gunfire. My fingers, now shaking with fear, resuming their fast dance to get access to the door systems. I was ignored, mainly because whatever was happening out there wasn't exactly my ballpark, as Hendricks surged past me shouting to Geiger to form on him.

"Get that outer door ready to shut," he called back to me.

"Annie?" I asked, hopeful that she would be quicker at getting it done than I would be working it by hand. Both of them answered at once which drowned out any useful response from the real Annie I was asking.

"Hhhhow c-can I help?" Charlie Annie said in a distorted voice through the speakers.

"Standing by," my Annie said in a lower, faster, and more human voice, "I have access now. Hendricks, pull back inside the bunker." Hendricks didn't answer, unless I counted the staccato chattering of his gun joining Geiger and now Stevens. Jones, the British guy so quiet I hardly knew he was there half the time, stood beside my workstation and lifted his gun to the door.

"Coming in," Hendricks yelled, making me glance over my left shoulder to see him dragging the engineer by the handle on the back of his vest. Something that looked like a stick was protruding out of his neck, and he was grunting and cursing so loudly that his voice carried over the noise of the one-sided gunfight. Whooshing noises sounded behind me, with answering noises on the far side of the antechamber like stones hitting a brick wall.

"Arrows," I said out loud in shock when I realized what had made the noise, "god damned *arrows*?"

"Close the door," Hendricks called out, "now!"

"Door closing," Annie said simply, as a rumbling noise sounded. The heavy door to the tunnel began to roll shut far too slowly for my liking. The rest of them shot through the gap, Geiger pitching backwards with a, "*Goddammit,*" of pain as a wild, ululating battle cry filled the chamber.

Rolling over the falling figure of the downed solider, a big warrior dressed in rags under a heavy fur burst into the room. He hefted an axe the likes of which I'd never seen in real life outside of a *Mad Max* movie. The wide, curved blade scythed through the air with a hiss full of deadly promise. He aimed the blow at Hendricks who, falling off balance to avoid it, tripped over Geiger. I watched in horrified slow-motion as his hands fell away from the rifle and reached for the sidearm holstered on the front of his vest. Even from my position ten paces away I knew he wasn't going to draw it in time and my mouth began to fall open.

Harrison didn't seem to be affected by the sudden slow passage of time, stepping into my view with both hands whirling the blades drawn over his shoulders. They hissed together, his arms crossing in a practiced move that, if I'd tried it, would have probably cut my own arm off. The machetes opened up the warrior's lower back, making him abandon the killing stroke and arch like he'd been electrocuted, before the blades hissed back again and the arm holding the axe fell limply to his side, his weapon clattering harmlessly to the ground. Harrison stepped around him lithely, somehow anticipating

121

the wild swing of his undamaged arm and ducking under it to rise up and skewer him in the abdomen. The two men locked eyes for a moment before the attacker jerked like an animal caught in a trap.

"God*damn*!" Geiger cursed again, providing relief that he wasn't dead. He got to his feet and tried to look behind himself at the arrow protruding from his body armor. Swinging around he caught Stevens with the feathered end, who was kneeling by the closing gap firing controlled bursts at the horde of warriors ineffectually but bravely trying to defy the barrage of lead. The arrow knocked him off balance, disturbing his aim briefly, allowing two more warriors to scramble over their dead comrades filling the gap. Screaming their battle cries they ran forwards, straight toward the first person they saw, Harrison. He spun to face the new threat, raising his blades and altering his stance to prepare himself to face what looked to be insurmountable odds.

Tori, who had her own weapon drawn but was the other side of the room, began to run, desperately trying to reach him as she too could see he couldn't hope to fight two of them at once.

Hendricks, who'd recovered and regained his knees, fired two bursts making both warriors spin head over heels as the bullets hitting their chests caused their upper bodies to pivot backwards whilst their impetus carried them forwards. They both slid to a stop inches from Harrison who calmly turned his head to Hendricks and nodded his thanks.

Annie's voice crackled through my earpiece. "David, signal red…cing. Con…ct transm…ter. Ta...aka wris...and ted…"

And then nothing, as the heavy steel door closed fully.

Stevens turned to Knight, the engineer who Hendricks had dragged through the door and instantly forgot as he had other pressing matters to attend to. An arrow had gone through his neck and he lay on the floor holding both hands to it, ineffectually trying to stop his lifeblood pouring from the wound. He was making weak gurgling sounds as his throat filled with blood and his body tried to expel it as he lay drowning. Geiger pulled an aid pack from his vest and knelt beside him to look into his terrified, wide eyes.

I stood transfixed as both tried to use their battlefield medical skills to save his life. His legs slowed their jerking movements as more of his blood spread around him, creating what to me looked like a small lake of the oily, dark liquid.

How could a body hold so much? I thought as I watched his legs give a final jerk before laying still. Hendricks stared at the man for a few moments then symbolically closed his eyes before standing up slowly.

The sound of someone retching made me turn around. The soft meat and bones of the bodies that had piled in the entrance were no match for the heavy circular steel door as it rolled shut and fitted into its precisely manufactured frame. It had cleaved through them like a warm knife through butter, leaving a gory pile of arms, legs and half torsos lying in a spreading pool of blood.

Weatherby was bending over, hands on knees expelling the last of his breakfast over the floor. He eventually recovered and wiped his mouth across his sleeve, removing pieces of his breakfast that remained stuck to his chin. He glanced around looking embarrassed that he was the only one to show his horror in such a physical manner.

"Annie?" I called, my voice showing a hint of panic. Ignoring Charlie Annie's stuttering reply I called again for the Annie I really needed to speak to. When she didn't answer I felt a shocked moment of awareness. I was on my own. The voice that for decades had always been just a call away, ready to answer a question or do my bidding was unreachable. Blocked by thousands of tons and a hundred meters of rocks and soil.

I stood stunned and for the first time unsure. I had relied on Annie, my own creation, that had become far greater that I could comprehend in her near thousand years of solitude, and now she was not there. Her last message confused me; the first bit I could understand, she was losing signal, but the last part was unintelligible. Staring at the screen I noticed the message icon flashing in the top corner and hope returned. The message could only be from Annie.

My fingers reached for the keyboard and I flicked my fingers deftly across the inbuilt touchpad and double clicked on the message.

Connection disrupted; I cannot help you until you connect the transmitter. The wristband belonging to the original Mister Tanaka was detected by the drones approaching the tunnel entrance as I lost voice communication capability with you. He will be able to open the door unless you restrict access. I had to reposition the drone from the cavern entrance so I doubt I will be able to reconnect with you even if the door is opened again. Good luck, David.

"*Hendricks!*" I called urgently. "Tanaka's coming and Annie reckons he can open the door." I began typing furiously at the keyboard.

"What do you need me to do?" he shouted across the room, turning away from the man he had tried to save.

"I need time to rewrite the subroutines and lock him out. Annie had to move the relay drone and so will not be able to help even if the door is reopened."

"How long?" he asked sharply.

"I don't know yet," I snapped over my shoulder before looking back at the lines of code scrolling down the screen. "I need to find Kendall's back door into my programming and without Annie helping I'm shooting blind. She'd found it but didn't highlight where it was before we lost connection."

"Why can't she help?"

"Too far away now," I told him. "She managed to send me a text message but now I've got nothing."

Hendricks' eyes bored into me, not that I had the time to exchange meaningful glances. Giving me a nod of acceptance, he turned to the others who had been following our conversation. "Right, we need to buy some time for Doctor Anderson. We're going to get visitors soon, so I need everyone to build a barricade around the doorway and get ready to defend ourselves." The soldiers nodded with acceptance and got straight to it, whereas Amir and the remaining engineer stood in static shock.

"Move it, you two!" Hendricks bellowed at them, ignoring any subtlety or politeness he may have included if the situation they were in was not so desperate.

I ignored the banging and scraping of heavy items being dragged into position as I turned back to the screen. If I had Annie, I could have asked her to locate the correct subroutine knowing it would save hours of searching. Should I try and connect Annie back into the system using Charlie Annie's inbuilt transmitter? Did I even have the time to do that instead of searching for…

"Dumbass," I blurted out, earning a confused look or two from people too busy to stop and ask what my problem was. I *had* something to search for, Kendall's handwriting, and I just didn't think to use it.

Cracking my knuckles once more I began typing a new program into my laptop and after few minutes, still inputting with one hand, I reached into the pack by my side and pulled out the small transmitter I had brought with me. "Mister Weatherby," I called as I held it in one hand and continued typing with the other. Hearing no response but the banging of the barricade being built I shouted louder, "Amir!"

"Yes?" I heard the reply.

Not having the time or inclination for niceties I didn't turn but held the transmitter higher in the air and commanded, "Take this as near to the door as the cable will allow and bring the connector back to me."

When I felt it being pulled from my grasp, I returned my now free hand to the keyboard. I had to get the coding finished to allow my laptop to link to the transmitter, and my Annie, some time yesterday. Moments later my eye caught the connector on the end of the cable being laid next to my hand on the desk. Grabbing it, I dexterously inserted it into the correct port, taking it out and spinning it around because—of course—I'd tried to put it in the wrong damned way up. I was close, I knew it. A few lines was all it would take, and I could try to reestablish contact with Annie. My hastily written search program just needed to find the relevant line of code.

The unmistakable click of the locking mechanism on the door disengaging and the ominous, low rumble as it opened stopped me briefly and I glanced around.

Chapter 15

Comms Down

Hendricks was helping Jones lift the last item, an abandoned metal storage crate, into position on the barricade when the door clunked and slowly began to roll open.

Looking at what they had managed to build from the few items of furniture and empty storage cases they'd found, Hendricks knew it wasn't good enough, but it was better than facing a horde of arrow-loosing, axe-wielding maniacs with nothing more than a strongly worded email of complaint.

Loosening the straps holding his spare magazines in place he checked, reloaded and charged his rifle and made sure his pistol was loose in its holster. Glancing at the others he could see his men doing the same. Weatherby and the surviving engineer were standing by the barricade looking scared to death as the volume of the screams from the men waiting to kill them increased the more the door opened. Hendricks saw the wild looks on their faces and knew he had to do something to get them in the fight because he needed everyone on the firing line.

Not having time to do it gently —the rolling circular door would unleash what he fully expected to be multiple levels of hell at them in seconds—he shouted in his most commanding voice, "*Weatherby, Collins, weapons up!*"

His bellow snapped them out of the trance they had fallen into and out of the corner of his eye he saw them raise their weapons and take a step toward the barricade. An arrow shot through the gap narrowly missing Hendricks' head to clatter on the wall behind. Unable to pick out anything in the dark of the tunnel he fired a three-round burst through the widening gap but didn't hear any screams of pain or other indication that his rounds had done anything.

As the opening widened more arrows flew in, either flying overhead or embedding themselves in the barricade, but in the darkness of the tunnel they couldn't see anything of their attackers.

"Flashlights on," Hendricks shouted. The powerful beams on his team's weapons lit up immediately with Weatherby and Collins taking longer to locate the unfamiliar button. The beams stretched into the foreboding dark of the tunnel that still echoed with the shouts, screams and battle cries of what sounded like hundreds of warriors.

Hendricks ducked lower behind the barricade, trying to avoid the arrows, keeping his weapon aimed forwards. In frustration he fired a long burst into the darkness. He looked left at Stevens who was also keeping as low as he could.

Stevens gave him a look that summed up the situation before turning to peer into the darkness, finger on his trigger ready for action. Hendricks was still looking at him when an arrow hit him in the face, piercing his eyeball, the force of it making the arrow go through his skull and stick out the back of his head. As he fell backwards, killed instantly, his head flopped like a test dummy and his finger tightened on the trigger. His gun ejected a torrent of bullets, one striking Collins in the back of his head, blowing a mass of brains and blood all over Geiger.

In horror, Hendricks' mind raced as he realized that in less than a second they had lost a quarter of their forces and everyone was now instinctively staring at the two bodies rather than toward the darkness.

"Eyes front," he screamed as the torrent of arrows suddenly ceased and his flashlight caught movement at the limit of its beam. "They're coming," he said, letting rip a full magazine as he poured out his shock and hate and regret into their attack.

The tunnel, lit by the wavering beams of light, filled with a solid mass of leather and fur-clad warriors sprinting toward them, all screaming their battle cry. He deftly replaced the magazine and clicked his selector to full auto with his thumb to fire again.

They kept coming, jumping over the falling bodies getting closer with every stride. His gun clicked empty and he hit the magazine release button, letting it clatter to the floor and in seconds rammed another home, charging the weapon in one swift movement without the barrel wavering away from the enemy who had reached the door and begun tearing at the barricade. For every one they shot another two leaped over them. One man hurled himself at the barricade, throwing his axe just before four bullets fired from Jones' gun turned his head into a rapidly expanding cloud of blood, bone and viscera.

Hendricks' gun clicked dry a third time as he emptied it in controlled bursts at another wildly charging figure. Letting it drop on its sling, he drew his pistol and continued firing until the crazed attacker slumped dead on the barricade, inches from his position. Holstering the sidearm and snatching up the short rifle from its dangling position on the sling, he dropped out the spent magazine and replaced it with fast, practiced hands.

Harrison and Tori both began bounding forwards, thrusting their weapons at any part of an enemy that reached the barrier. The bodies piled up, but still they came.

~

Deafened by the continual sound of gunfire and choking on the cordite fumes that began filling the room I kept typing. I wanted to look at the battle raging just meters behind me but knew our only chance of survival lay in reconnecting with Annie and getting access to the system. Typing faster than I ever had before, my fingers a blur on the keyboard, I finished inputting the last few lines of code. Rapidly scrolling through the sub files, I selected the one I needed and hit the return key. The screen went blank, leaving only the taunting icon of a spinning hourglass to indicate that deep in its files and electronically stored memory, things may be happening. I could do nothing but wait, holding my hand unnecessarily to my ear as if willing Annie's voice to come back to me through my earpiece.

Nothing, the hourglass icon continued to mock me. I began to really panic, knowing just one mistyped line of code would prevent the new program from meshing with my thousand-year-old original work.

The icon flashed, indicating something new was happening, and my earpiece crackled.

"David?" was all I got. Tears of relief filled my eyes. We had connection. It may not be strong, but I knew as long as Annie could get into the system, we stood a chance.

Screams behind me made me crouch lower on the floor, but even though my bowels were loosening as any moment I expected to be struck by an axe-wielding maniac wearing animal skins, I couldn't tear my eyes from the screen.

The screen changed and pages of code began flashing across it. Annie was in, I'd located the key Kendall had programmed and I just had to trust her to override all the restrictions input by the other programmer.

"Annie?" I called but I just got a bleep of reply. I opened my mouth to speak again but stopped myself as it dawned on me that she needed every single byte of her memory, fighting with what was probably a weak connection as she undid what been done hundreds of years ago. She didn't need me to interrupt; she would tell me when she was in full control.

I chanced a look over my shoulder. The situation through the smog of gun smoke looked terrifying. I could see two of our small party lying on the ground, blood spreading from them, but couldn't tell who they were as both Harrison and Tori were standing over them swinging at the mass of figures trying to scale the barricade. Blood flew from their twirling, hissing, razor-sharp blades. The others had taken a pace back, trying to keep away from the wild swings of the attackers and firing their weapons wildly at the mass of warriors who filled the small space of the doorway in front of the barricade. I could see they were inflicting terrible casualties as their shots in the enclosed space couldn't fail to hit, but still the warriors kept pressing forwards. Their dead comrades still held up in the crush absorbing bullets, protecting the ones behind as they tried to climb over them and kill us all.

"I'm back," Annie said, her voice clear and strong. "I have full access, and I'm using the inbuilt transmitters. I recommend retreating further into the facility. I have sent schematics to your laptop and Mister Weatherby's tablet. Closing the outer door now. I have also deactivated Tanaka's wristband." She must have been openly broadcasting to us all as Hendricks voice burst into my ear.

"Annie close the damn door now; they're about to breach!" I was looking at him as he was speaking a saw him stop talking and fire his pistol at a warrior who had reached the top of the wall and was about to leap on him. He fell back, blood spraying from his chest, fortunately knocking two more warriors over who had clambered over their dead comrades.

"One moment, please." Annie's voice sounded surreally calm in complete contrast to the scene of carnage laid out before me. "Door closing now."

The main door began to roll shut, and at the same time behind me the smaller door that led further into the facility began to slide open. In seconds I'd unplugged my laptop and stuffed it roughly into my pack, slinging it onto my back. As I stood staring for a moment, realization dawned on me I *was* armed, and my rifle, forgotten on its sling, was banging against my leg. My friends needed my help, and not just from my computer skills. Putting it clumsily to my shoulder I looked through the sights and aimed at the mass still trying to reach us and squeezed the trigger just like I'd been taught, only for nothing to happen.

"Shit! The safety!" I remembered and my thumb sought the small lever that would turn it from a useless piece of metal to a deadly, death-spitting weapon of war. Some of the warriors near the back had seen the door closing and turned to run back into the gloom beyond. Ignoring them, I shifted my position to give me a clear line of sight and tightened my finger on the trigger. The new angle I was firing at tore into the front ranks of our enemy, making them falter as they were thrown down.

The pressure, momentarily relieved, gave Hendricks the chance to look around and assess. He saw the door behind him was almost open and, grabbing the drag handle on Stevens' vest, began pulling his limp, dead body toward the door shouting for the rest to disengage. Amir turned and ran, but the others stood their ground. Still facing the threat, they started to walk backwards in controlled order. As Geiger stepped over Collins, he grabbed his outstretched arm and dragged him, firing his pistol one-handed as his empty rifle hung on the sling at his side.

Chapter 16

Change the Locks

Tanaka was in the tunnel, shouting at his people to continue attacking when the door began closing. He needed to destroy the newcomers; if they hid behind the doors then it would all have been for nothing. Normally he would have flown into a blind rage striking out at anyone near him, knowing they wouldn't have the courage to fight back. He experienced a rare moment of clarity as his foot caught on a large rock that had fallen from the walls of the tunnel.

He could use the rock to stop the door closing.

Grabbing the nearest warrior to him, he shouted for him to help as he bent and struggled with the heavy, awkwardly shaped lump of rock. Between them they struggled down the tunnel shouldering aside those trying to push through the closing gap.

"Faster," he screamed, fearing that the door would close before they got there. The rolling motion slowed as the bodies being crushed caused the ageing motor to strain, giving them time to take the last few paces and drop the rock in place just as the door touched it. Clunking against the obstacle, it stopped and reversed its motion to try again with the motor whining in protest. As Tanaka stood exposed in the gap looking in triumph at the rock, the warrior who had helped was hit by a single bullet to the throat causing Tanaka to dive ungracefully behind the solid protection of the thick steel door.

Wiping sprayed blood from his face, Tanaka saw with elation that his plan had worked.

In the chamber, the lead warriors were so intent on reaching their enemy they had not noticed the door closing behind them. All they could see was their enemy retreating, heading toward a doorway that had opened in the wall on the other side of the room.

Geiger and Hendricks were a few yards from the door when three of Tanaka's men leaped over the barricade. Both shot one each, but the last one with his axe held above his head kept coming. Geiger ducked and twisted desperately to avoid his wild swing as the pitted blade whistled inches from his face to sever the limb of Collins he was dragging the man by. Released from the weight he stumbled backwards, falling through the doorway still with the amputated arm in his grasp. Before the warrior could recover from the swing, Harrison slashed both his blades across his throat, almost removing his head from his neck killing him instantly.

Harrison stood blocking the doorway as Hendricks shouted for Annie to close the door. He took two fast paces forward, grabbed Jones' shoulder where he knelt to drill disciplined rounds into the gap in the door, and pulled him through as it hissed shut.

Lights flickered as Annie powered up the ancient illumination in the passageway. Harrison and Tori stood facing the door, blood dripping from the multiple wounds they had suffered. Everyone else sat in slumped silence, exhausted from the brief but bloody battle, shocked and numb looks on their grime covered, sweat-streaked faces.

"Annie, can you still hear us?" Anderson asked, afraid that silence would be the answer and that they'd be alone again.

"Yes, I am here," she replied. Relief washed over him as she explained what just happened.

"The outer door has been intentionally obstructed using a rock which has prevented it from correctly closing. I have activated the cameras and I'm monitoring the room. I have disabled Tanaka's wristband so he cannot open the inner door."

"Where are they?" asked Hendricks.

"Some have withdrawn to the tunnel and others are searching the antechamber. Do you want me to replay the audio and video feed to your tablet?"

"Not yet, Annie," he replied. "Let's take a minute to regroup and get sorted. They have us trapped and they know it." He looked around at them. "Everyone check your weapons and count ammo. Harrison, Tori, let's look at those wounds, we don't want you bleeding to death on us now." He checked his own weapons and mumbled an apology to Stevens as he retrieved some of the man's spare ammunition.

Harrison looked at the deep gashes on his arms and ripped a piece of cloth from his top to wind it tightly around the worst one. "I am fine," he said simply.

Hendricks smiled at him grimly. "And I'm not filled with confidence. Geiger, please see to them before he gives himself sepsis." He looked at Geiger pointedly. "Now, if you don't mind," Hendricks added, tossing him a blowout pack from his own vest.

Geiger heaved himself to his feet with an acknowledgement of, "Boss," opened the med kit and approached the two who nervously eyed the contents.

"Annie?" Amir called softly.

"Yes, Mister Weatherby. How can I help?"

136

He looked almost guiltily at the others as he continued, knowing he was going to reveal information he had been withholding. "Has the room been accessed?" All eyes snapped to him.

"No. The door has not opened since it was sealed on November twenty-fifth, twenty-thirty-two."

The look of triumph that spread across his face matched the looks of confusion on everyone else's.

"Is everything intact?"

"I cannot remotely inspect the non-organic contents, but nothing had been disturbed and the environment has been maintained for optimum storage conditions so they all should be in perfect order. Out of the forty cryopods, only fifteen remain fully functional. I can only assume that as Charlie Annie was not aware of their existence, they were not monitored so any faults were not detected and remotely repaired."

Hendricks took a step toward Amir who just held a hand up to hear the rest of the report without interruption.

"The site's CNR was operating on shutdown mode, which I surmise was a power-saving mode to extend its life, causing monitoring interruption of alternate Charlie Annie. The fifteen subjects should come out of cryostasis with no more difficulty that we experienced. Do you want me to start the process, Mister Weatherby?"

"No, not yet, Annie. We can bring them out of cryo when we are able to offer them better assistance than we can now." He could see the looks of bemused incredibility and questioning being directed at him and held his arms up and smiled. "Annie, I think I'd better explain to the others what we are talking about before they lynch me."

"Of course, Mister Weatherby," she replied and her down-tone bleeped in their ears.

"Mister Weath—" Hendricks began but Weatherby held his hand up again to stop him.

"You must all understand that I have not withheld this information from you lightly. I did *not* know for certain that they'd be here, and so didn't want to mislead you with false promises and assumptions—"

Hendricks interrupted, "Is this why you were so desperate to reach this site?"

"Yes, Hendricks. Among other reasons and I apologize profusely for the subterfuge. I could tell you didn't trust me, and I am sorry for lying to you, but please listen as to why."

Hendricks nodded in reply and remained silent, but the anger was clear to see on his face.

"I constructed, as an addition before the event, a further independent sub shelter within the complex. It was meant to house my mother and some staff to keep her comfortable whilst the rest of us rebuilt civilization on the surface. She is—*was*—elderly and wouldn't at all have been suited to the rugged life we knew we were going to have to endure as we started again." He smiled softly, sadly, as he thought about her. "The shelter is accessed from a discreet, disguised doorway off a small office on level twelve. If you didn't know it was there, you'd never find it." His look changed to one of deeper sadness. "I arranged for a small staff to accompany her, all who knew what was going to happen and were in full agreement of what was expected of them. They were not going to be allowed to mix with the rest of us as keeping it secret was key to my plan."

He paused as if searching for the right words to say then simply shrugged.

"If people knew there was a luxury VIP bunker hidden right under their noses then jealousy could become a factor and I did *not* want anything to disturb whatever time she had with us. She was my mother." His voice sounding almost apologetic.

They all sat or stood listening intently to him.

"But I didn't factor one thing into my planning: she didn't want to go. When I told her what I was planning, she refused point blank to consider it, saying she would see out the rest of her days on Earth above ground and not hidden away while billions of people died."

He looked pained as he continued.

"I tried, but nothing I could do or say could persuade her to change her mind, so I reluctantly agreed and continued with my work. But then I had an idea. I know what most of you thought of the *original* Tanaka, and I'm not stupid; I could see it too, but at that time I needed the blunt, unquestioning instrument he was. Nevertheless, certain things he did and said made me question his ultimate loyalty and the thought of him being on Earth out of my reach and influence until we landed filled me with no small amount of concern." He laughed mirthlessly.

"And I think my suspicions have been proven correct." He paused and looked at Hendricks, as if to gauge his reaction. "So, I had an idea. No one knew about the bunker, the engineer who built it, unfortunately, was diagnosed with an aggressive form of cancer and so couldn't go in to cryo. I therefore supplemented the supplies I had already stocked it with, with large quantities of extra supplies that would act as an additional reserve for us when we returned from space." He paused again and looked at Hendricks as if to judge his response. "I also arranged with Secretary of Defense Matthews for him to provide additional military personnel, all of whom fitted the profile we wanted, and who of course volunteered with full knowledge of the event and their expected future role to go into cryo."

He turned to look at Anderson.

"I also got a completely independent and unaffiliated computer expert to build, design, and program a brand new 'sub Annie' that could operate independently whilst also connected to the main unit."

"You built…" Anderson swallowed. "You built another Annie?" he asked incredulously.

Amir smiled again, relaxing and enjoying the attention he was getting. "Only a small one with nowhere near as much storage and processing power, but enough to operate the bunker independently if need be. Anyway, and I hope you understand why, I couldn't inform any of you about it until I could confirm it still existed. But now we know it's there and what it contains. I know it'll have everything we need, and more, for us to defeat Tanaka."

Hendricks still looked annoyed to say the least. Anderson could see him trying to control his emotions, but the news that there were more trained men available, just waiting to be woken up and join the fight, was good news he couldn't ignore.

"Weatherby, you sneaky, cunning little bastard. I'll forgive you for not letting on about your little secret, I can understand your motives and reasons for doing so but can we make it clear, these soldiers are *not* your personal bodyguard." He looked at him severely. "As head of security, they will come under my direct control for the benefit of everyone and not form a private little army for you to keep yourself at the top of the management tree."

Weatherby looked genuinely shocked at the not too subtle criticism aimed at him but responded quickly and smoothly. "I can assure you that was not my intention at all." He shrugged as if in apology. "But, again, I'm not stupid; I know my role and influence seem less import now in the current world we find ourselves in. I can see how some of you look at me. I can only hope I can still contribute my skills and organizational abilities as we grow and prosper."

Geiger snorted. "Prosper! We're stuck in a bunker with a ton of screaming bad guys on the other side of a door. I don't think we can count any chickens just yet, even if we wake up some new soldiers."

Amir smiled smugly again.

"If you can let me finish. I was just about to explain that in addition to the bunker I also got the engineers to construct a separate exit for it so I could visit her without attracting attention, and if for some reason she wanted to go outside she could without interference. There is a tunnel that leads to a natural cave in a nearby rock formation, again I had the very best construct it so if you didn't know it was there, you'd never find it. Whether it's still a viable exit is the question I can't answer yet."

Annie who had obviously been listening in spoke up.

"The camera system in the tunnel is inoperative, but I have studied the location and monitored satellite imagery from the event to the current time I have in my database. The rock formation the tunnel emerges in has not changed or suffered from any environmental issue. There is a high probability it's still useable...standby...Tanaka has entered the room...please hold."

Tanaka, after he had sent a scouting party to check the room was clear, strode into the steel wall-clad control room he knew only as The Source. He had stepped inside only once before. Not long after he had assumed control and been given the talisman handed down through the generations, he had persuaded The Keepers to grant him access as his right. The keepers had not initially wanted to allow him entry to the inner sanctity and had only conceded when he had strung the leader by his ankles from a tree and gutted him with a knife.

The door had magically opened with the wristband as it had for Harrison, but Annie had not come online and spoken to him as she had for Harrison. Her systems had been in sleep mode, not that he would understand that. The activation process only started when ARC Annie sent the automatic signal that they were returning.

Not noticing the other doorway as its precisely engineered frame sat virtually smooth in the steel wall and finding nothing of interest he had left and never returned.

Now when he entered, a voice coming from nowhere made him cower behind the nearest solid surface.

"W…lcome Mister Tan…ka."

He recovered himself quickly as he could see his men were equally afraid of the voice and were shrinking from it. He was The Tanaka and only the weak showed fear, so swallowing the terror his body was filled with he forced himself to stand.

"Who…Who are you?" he asked, trying to control the tremble in his voice. No response so he asked again, this time with more fire.

The crackling voice responded, "To a-activate v-v-voice interface, say, Annie." Tanaka let his misogynistic anger rise. A mere woman was daring to give him commands, a crime punishable by, at the very least, a severe beating.

He forced his rage to subside but still tried to show his displeasure as he snarled in reply. "Annie. Who are you, and where are you?"

"Error, y-y-ou areee not authorized."

How could he be not authorized, he was The Tanaka, the protector of The Source, the one who had the power to control The Swarm and this mere woman was telling him he was not authorized.

Taking a second to once again compose himself he continued, "Annie, why am I not authorized?"

"A-uthor-izzation rem-removed."

His chest puffed with indignation. "Who removed it? Get it back, *now!*" In the silence that followed as he waited for a reply, he realized he had not said her name. Embarrassed that he had forgotten and angry that for once he was not getting the respect he knew he deserved, he shouted, "ANNIE, WHO REMOVED IT?"

"E-errorr, you a-are not authorized."

He was at a loss as what to do next, this magical voice was defying him, but he couldn't see it to punish it for its defiance. He stood for a moment, his hands on his hips, the scowl on his face showing his displeasure. Looking around the room he saw the cost of the attack on his people. Bodies lay intertwined in death all around him before the barricade. The deaths did not bother him, his only thought was they had failed him.

Fighting down his disgust he angrily kicked the corpse nearest to him before clambering over the piled-up bodies of his men and climbed over the barricade, jumping nimbly down the other side. Spent shiny brass bullet casings littered the floor. Picking one up to study it, he put his nose to the still warm metal casing and the pungent aroma of burned powder filled his nose. These were the bullets he needed to make his talisman work again and to make it more than just a symbol of authority and power. They would put him on an equal footing with his enemies enabling him to kill them all.

He was about to ask Annie another question when he spotted Collins' body lying near the opposite wall. The body didn't interest him, but what was on a strap around his body and in the holster on his hip did. Ignoring everything else he rushed over to it and, oblivious to the blood and gore that his ruined head had covered his body with, tried to pull the pistol from its holster, struggling with it until his thumb caught the release button and it slid free.

Nothing else mattered around him as he held the gun in his hand. It was the same model as his own, the one he had handled lovingly and stared at in wonder for more hours than he could count. He depressed the button that made the magazine drop from the handle and looked at the shiny brass cartridges with wonder. Reinserting the magazine, he pulled back the top slide charging the weapon.

His finger curled around the trigger as he aimed at the dead body lying by his feet and squeezed it. The body jerked as the bullet struck the dead man's assault vest. Once more he stared at the gun, a look of pure evil joy on his face. He reached for the old leather holster, then held the older, worn version of what he held in his other hand and pulled it easily from the smooth, polished leather. Taking one last look at what had been his symbol of authority and power he, without caring, casually tossed it aside and replaced it with the new one.

Turning his attention to the rifle still attached to Collins he bent over and struggled for a few moments as he pulled the strap from where it was caught under him. Again, he stared in awe with childlike delight at the modern-yet-ancient rifle before raising it to his shoulder and looking down the barrel. The floating red dot on the holographic sights confused him until he realized that as he moved the rifle around, the dot moved with his eye, marking where he was aiming at. Unable to stop himself he pulled the trigger, the gun bucked into his shoulder as it fired, the bullet sparking against the metal walls opposite him. He pulled the trigger again, but this time only received a click in reply. After two more failed pulls on the trigger, understanding dawned on him that it was empty of bullets.

He had spent enough time playing with his old pistol that he had enough rudimentary understanding of guns to quickly identify the magazine release button and eject it. Empty. Collins was lying dead at his feet face down. With no more compassion than if he was kicking a chair, he used his foot to kick him over, his ruined head spilling more gore over the floor.

Crouching next to him Tanaka pulled a magazine out from a pouch on his vest and inspected it, smiling at the shiny bullets nestled inside. Pushing against his body when he stood up, he noticed the item on his wrist. It was the same as he possessed, albeit it a lot cleaner and newer, but the same as he had used to open the outer door all those years ago and still carried with him today in the inner pocket of his jacket along with the beacon. He rarely looked at it because as far as he knew, it served no purpose other than to gain entry to The Source.

Then it struck him, if he wasn't authorized, would this wristband be? Pulling it from Collins' corpse he strode toward the closed door he knew his enemy had escaped through.

Chapter 17

Beware the Minotaur

Annie kept up the commentary on what Tanaka was doing just the other side of the door.

When they heard the report of the first gunshot, dulled by the thick door, Hendricks swore. "That's not good news, he has guns now. Another tactical edge we've just lost." He looked at Weatherby. "You'd better show us to this secret bunker of yours. Geiger, strip Stevens of his weapons and ammo, we are going to need as much as we can get if we expect to get home in one piece."

Geiger nodded and knelt next to his dead friend and after gently and respectfully rolling him over, relieved him of both his weapons and ammunition. Standing, he slung the rifle over his shoulder, handed Henricks the pistol and some magazines, offering Jones a few and stuffed the rest into his own tactical vest.

Hendricks indicated to Weatherby to lead the way.

Annie spoke into their earpieces. "I'll monitor your position and activate the lighting as necessa—Tanaka has just removed Collins' wristband and is approaching the door."

The door hissed and began sliding open.

Hendricks turned to face it raising his rifle. "Close it now, Annie!" he shouted and began firing single shots through the opening.

Tanaka was taken by surprise as the door began to open the moment he approached. He caught a glimpse of the man called Hendricks who had come to the Springs to talk raising his weapon and dove out the way as it spat flame and bullets through the gap, missing him by inches.

Sliding to a stop against a desk he pushed the magazine in his hand into the weapon and aiming at the widening gap, pulled the trigger. Not having charged the weapon it wouldn't fire and not knowing what to do he dropped it in disgust and pulled out his pistol. He aimed wildly at the door and kept pulling the trigger as the gun bucked in his hand with each shot, filling him with an immense sense of power.

The door stopped opening and started to close as Annie overrode the system. Tanaka looked around in desperation, he couldn't let the door close. Bullets from Hendricks' gun still spat through the gap, ricocheting as they struck the opposite wall forcing his men to cower in fear. The only object near the door was the body he had stripped the weapons from. Scrambling over to it he grabbed Collins' limp carcass and with strength he didn't know he possessed and half threw, half slid it into the diminishing gap. The door was not designed to be as secure as the main one and the moment the it touched the body it reversed direction as the main door had done and started opening again.

Hendricks was still firing through the door when Collins' body slid into the diminishing gap. His eyes grew wide with horror when it began opening again.

"The door has a pressure safety system; I can't close it if it's blocked," Annie told them, her voice sounding almost panicked as they retreated down the long corridor. Hendricks fired one last long burst through the now fully open door and screaming at them to run as he turned and followed.

In the silence that followed Hendricks' last volley, Tanaka sat with his back against the wall regaining his breath. The only noise over his heavy breathing was the door hissing as it kept trying to close only to open and repeat the process every time it touched Collins' body. Tanaka smiled as he knew with certainty that they now had no place to hide. All he needed to do was to reorganize his remaining men and lead them further into The Source to hunt them down. Reaching for the rifle he had abandoned in favor of the pistol he studied it for a while before locating the charging handle which he pulled and saw with satisfaction a bullet sliding into the chamber as he released it.

Edging close to the door he risked a quick glance through it seeing the last of the group disappear around a corner at the end of the long, brightly lit passageway.

He stood up and, seeing the fear on the faces of most of his remaining men, addressed them. "We have them now." He held the rifle over his head. "We have their weapons." He changed his expression to one of sorrow as he theatrically waved at their dead lying piled in and around the main door and lowered his voice. "We must avenge our brother warriors and make the newcomers pay for what they've done to us. When they're all dead we shall take their weapons and destroy their puny compound." He raised his arms and his voice again as he could see he had them hooked.

"When they are dead, we will destroy the Three Hills tribe and every one of you, my brave warriors, will have the first claim of the spoils. You will have the pick of the prettiest women." He paused and looked at one of his men who he knew had different tastes. "And the men, too."

That earned him a laugh, as the men nearest to the one he had singled out slapped him on the back as he beamed with pleasure, not even the slightest bit embarrassed about having his tastes publicly aired.

"Who's with me?"

The men roared in unified response as he bellowed.

Fired up, the men ran through the door ahead of Tanaka who waved them through, happily letting them lead the way and face the guns of the enemy before him. He followed his men, stepping over the dead body and removing from it every full magazine he could find.

Running fast, Weatherby led them deeper into the complex with Annie turning on the lights as they approached each intersection and corner. Weatherby faltered as the roar of many voices echoed down the empty corridors.

"I shall turn off the lights so they cannot follow us," announced Annie

Hendricks countermanded her. "No, don't. When I order it, darken the area we are in and keep them lit up."

"Jimmy, I don't understand why?" she asked.

"If they catch up with us, they won't be able to see us, but they will be lit up like a Christmas tree. We'll be able to pick them off easier than firing blind into the dark. Also, if we draw them deeper into the facility before turning the lights out it'll be darker than the labyrinth at Knossos and they may never find their way out," Hendricks explained.

Annie's voice this time sounded surprised. "I understand now, thank you, Jimmy." She then whispered conspiratorially, "Does that make you the Minotaur?"

Anderson, surprised that at such a time Annie would deem it appropriate to attempt humor, shook his head in disbelief. "Annie, really. Now's not the time to try one-liners you know."

"Sorry, David," she replied immediately, sounding mildly chastened but with an undertone that she still believed the jest was well placed. Kind of a 'sorry, not sorry' tone.

"I am monitoring all of your vital signs and calculated you needed a distraction to lower the stress levels you are all showing. If you maintain your current pace, I estimate you will reach the hidden complex with an excess of five minutes to spare as they are having to search a greater area and not go to it directly as you are. If everyone is a little calmer, I reason it will avoid unnecessary delays or accidents on the way to our destination."

Unable to argue with her logic once again, Anderson just mentally shrugged and continued to follow Weatherby as he led them deeper into the facility.

Many long and exhausting minutes of frantic running later they were all breathing heavily as they arrived at a door on sub level twelve.

"Annie, where are they?" Hendricks asked as he pulled a canteen from his belt and took a drink before passing it to Jones who accepted it wordlessly.

"They are still searching level two. Do you want me to turn the lights off?"

"Not yet, Annie, let them all reach at least level six." He turned to Weatherby who was standing beside a door, one of many that were lining the long corridor they were in. "Is this the one?"

"Yes," he replied simply and waved his wristband over the pad on the frame. A light on it flashed green and the lock clicked. He pressed the handle, opening it as the others filed in after him.

They found themselves in a small room, no larger than some cupboards. Anderson looked round expecting to see a large bomb-proof safe-type steel door set thickly into the wall, not the smooth metal paneling the room was lined with. Weatherby smiled at their confused looks and walked to one of the walls. He pressed his wristband against the top corner and held it there for a few seconds until the paneling clicked and swung open, revealing a short passage that ended at a heavy-duty steel door.

"Annie, can you open the door please, you have the codes on the files I gave you access to earlier."

"Of course, Mister Weatherby," she replied, matching his politeness.

Noises of bolts sliding and mechanisms turning sounded deep inside the door before it smoothly opened. They held back, watching as lights flickered and turned on lighting the room beyond. With a triumphant smile and a flourish of his hands he gave a theatrical half bow and said, "Shall we?"

They dutifully trooped inside, gathering in what looked to be an entrance hall as the steel paneling behind them closed with a click followed by the heavier dull clunks of the main door closing and locking.

Hendricks looked around and smiled. "Annie, let me know when the first one reaches level six."

Chapter 18

Eyes in the Dark

Tanaka's rage was building the deeper they explored the vast complex he had never known was hidden within The Source. Finding nothing but empty rooms, corridors and stairwells they ventured deeper and deeper, his anger swelling and building with each frustrating step.

Looking at the remarkable condition the whole facility was in, he questioned why it hadn't remained in use when his ancestors had emerged from their hundred-year sleep. It made no sense to him why, when there was all this, they chose to live in sometimes squalid conditions on the surface.

Mainly he thought about where his enemies had vanished to and why his idiotic, incompetent warriors had failed to find them yet. He lashed out, demanding results with threats of punishment to encourage them.

And then the lights went out, plunging them all into utter darkness.

The bunker was just as Amir had described it, fitted out as a luxury apartment befitting the money and status of one of the world's wealthiest families. The reception area they first entered opened into a vast living area complete with an enormous seating area still furnished with very expensive and comfortable-looking, neatly arranged chairs and sofas. A dining table that could seat at least twenty people created another area along with an open plan kitchen.

I stood in the middle of it all and whistled my appreciation of the luxury. "Amir?" I asked the question I guessed most of us had on the end of our tongues. "Exactly how big is this place?"

"The main apartment has five bedroom suites plus what you see here." He pointed to a door at one end of the room. "There's a spa, swimming pool and fitness area, including a fully equipped medical bay with an operating theater through there." He gestured casually down a passageway as though such things were normal. "Beyond that are the staff quarters sufficient to house eight." Looking at our faces he gave a small shrug. "What can I say? I was building it for my mother, and I wanted her to have the best of everything. It was the least I could do for her."

"Where are the cryo pods and supplies and…" Hendricks said pointedly, "most importantly, the way out?"

Weatherby pointed to a set of double doors on another wall. "Just through there. It also has access via a hidden goods lift to one of the main storage areas above. It's how I managed to build and stock it in secret. There were so many contractors and engineers on site the whole process was compartmentalized by its very nature; most people didn't know what another team was doing other than constructing a different part of the complex."

"This is all very nice, but we're still a long way from home," Hendricks said gruffly as he began walking toward the door.

One by one, all of us followed. Harrison and Tori couldn't have seen anything like this before, not even in their wildest dreams could they have imagined such luxury existed when every day, and not far away from where we were, they and every generation before them had struggled for survival. They gaped opened-mouthed, looking around in wonder.

Two sets of doors later we entered the storage area. It was more utilitarian with the standard steel walls of the rest of the complex, but it was vast. By my reckoning, as the lights flickered on and lit the entire place, it was about the size of two football fields. Racks and racks of high shelving, similar to one of those distribution centers that littered the country, were filled with pallets and boxes of supplies.

Walking through the aisles following Weatherby I looked at the pallets and crates that reached to the high ceiling. Some were marked with their contents; some were sealed and gave no clue as to what they contained.

"Annie, you got a manifest of what's here?" I asked out of curiosity.

"Yes, David. I have a compete manifest including individual item locations on my files now. Are you looking for anything specific?"

"Don't worry about it, I was just curious," I replied, not sure why I asked apart from wanting to fill the silence.

Entering an area clear of racking at the end of the aisles, I could see a double-banked line of familiar-looking cryopods against the far wall. Approaching the nearest one I looked through the glass panel on the lid and recoiled in disgust. It was clearly one that had failed, as its occupant stared back at me through empty eye sockets, crusted dried remnants of skin and wisps of hair covering its skull. The mask had slipped from its face and a bare, lipless mouth grimaced evilly at me. How long it had laid there, slowly drying out in the sealed pod was anyone's guess. The pod next to it still had lights flashing on it and after a cautious first glance I could see that the occupant looked as all the other living people I'd seen through the windows of their pods; peacefully asleep.

We'd spread out when emerging from the aisle, each drawn to individual pods. Looking up I could see either a reaction of disgust like mine had been or a smile as they looked upon one of the survivors.

Harrison looked at Hendricks after he and Tori had wandered down the line of pods.

"Is this how you were? They look as if they are just asleep," he asked Hendricks.

I could see Amir looking annoyed that the question hadn't been directed to him.

Amir called across, answering for Hendricks who had just started to open his mouth. "Yes, it's called cryostasis. My scientists developed the technology over many years, first using animals as subjects, gradually extending the periods of suspended bioanimation until we were confident that they could withstand a prolonged period. Then we began the human testing phase…"

Hendricks spoke over him as he saw the bewildered look on Harrison's face—Amir's explanation was far beyond his comprehension. "Yes," he said simply. "This is how we spent our long sleep, much the same way as your ancestors did before they emerged from The Source."

Weatherby, wanting to resume control of his interrupted discourse on how clever he was, interrupted before Harrison could ask anything else. "I'll begin the process to bring them out of cryostasis."

"I don't think we should do that yet," Hendricks said sharply. "We all know how *we* felt when we woke up. Our priority is to get out of here and not nursemaid a large group of new people, who I imagine will need an extended period of adjustment before they will be of any use to our situation."

"I agree," Annie interjected, confirming Hendricks' summary. "We do not have the medical skill to care for any that may, as has happened previously, not emerge from stasis in optimum condition." Weatherby nodded in agreement, a slight sulky look briefly crossing his face, as yet again, his orders were countermanded.

Still looking at Amir and noting his expression, Hendricks offered an olive branch. "Can you show us the way out?"

Recovering, he smiled his best corporate smile and responded, "Of course, it's over there." Pointing at a door embedded in the wall by the cryopods, he added, "Annie, can you open the inner door to access the alternate tunnel?"

"Opening now," came the answer through our earpieces, and a door in the far wall clicked and opened automatically. Its unoiled hinges screeched in protest; the environment behind the doors was probably not as controlled as that in the facility. The fact that *anything* still worked after close to a thousand years still baked my brain.

Hendricks took the lead as we gathered by the opening. I looked through but couldn't see a damn thing in the pitch black beyond.

"Annie, are there lights in the tunnel?" I asked.

"Yes. I am sorry, but they appear to be inoperative. I've tried rerouting power from other sources, but the circuit is still showing a fault."

"Sod it," Hendricks said as he flicked on the tactical light attached to his rifle, "there's no other way out of here not involving a

156

fight so…Flashlights on, people. Geiger and I will take point. Jones, Harrison and Tori, watch our backs." He waited for them to nod in agreement and for the rest of us to turn on our own flashlights before turning and with Geiger close behind him, his weapon held ready, entered the tunnel.

Following as close as I could to Geiger's back, the beam from my own rifle-mounted light bounced around as I tried to hold my weapon steady at the same time as looking at where I was placing my feet. The rough walls of the tunnel were carved from the living rock, and the floor, although flat, wasn't exactly smooth and was littered with the rocks that had fallen from the ceiling or walls. It smelt musty and damp which, with my limited knowledge of geology from high school, told me water was getting in somehow.

Weatherby stumbled behind me and caught his weapon on the wall causing an echo that reverberated all around us. "Steady as we go," Hendricks whispered through our earpieces. "The tunnel doesn't look too stable so keep the noise down. Weatherby, how long is this thing?"

"About half a mile I think, from memory," he replied

Annie's hushed voice confirmed. "The tunnel is six hundred and twenty-eight meters long; you have covered two hundred and seventy meters so far. If you maintain your current pace, you will reach the outer door in six minutes twenty-five seconds."

We continued onwards in hushed, careful silence until after what seemed like an eternity and far longer than Annie had suggested, Geiger stopped abruptly. I bumped into his back. Leaning around him to look ahead I could see a steel door with a large wheel, like what you saw on doors on ships and submarines in movies.

"You will have to open it manually. The power supply to the door has also failed," Annie warned.

Hendricks let his weapon drop on its sling and lifted both hands to the wheel. I could see him straining as he tried to move it but it refused to cooperate. Geiger, without being asked, also stepped forwards and Hendricks moved over slightly to allow both of them room.

The big man grunted with effort as he also tried to move the wheel. For long seconds nothing happened, and fear began to creep through my body; we were trapped deep underground with no way out apart from fighting through hundreds of Tanaka's men in a maze of underground corridors in the dark. There was no way I could've been the only one thinking the same, because a collective outpouring of held breath sounded when the wheel shifted slightly and, with a squeal of protest, began to spin faster.

When the wheel could spin no more, both men began pulling at the door and inch by agonizingly slow inch, using every ounce of their combined strength, it opened wide enough for us to squeeze through. Standing silently, we allowed them both to regain their breath for a few minutes until Hendricks raised his weapon and, with a nod to Geiger, cautiously stepped through the narrow gap.

One by one we entered the dark cave beyond, our flashlights adding to the illumination as we looked around. As I squeezed through the gap, I noticed the outer side of the door was covered in rock which matched the walls around it. It was what Weatherby must have meant when he claimed that no one would find it unless they knew it was there. When the door was closed it would blend into the cave walls and become invisible from everything but the closest scrutiny. Harrison was the last through. As soon as he waved his own flashlight around the cave his warning hiss made us all freeze.

"I know where we are," he said, his voice for the first time showing real fear as he spoke in barely a whisper.

He shone his torch ahead lighting up a large bowl-like depression in the soft earth. Looking at it I could see it was full of white, picked clean bones of unidentifiable animals.

"It's the Dragon's nest. Where they raise their young. Nobody comes anywhere near here as to do so is certain death. They attack anyone or anything that approaches."

I slowly, and with my hands now shaking uncontrollably, raised my rifle, casting a beam of light across the high walls of the cave. Multiple eyes reflected back from recesses in the walls. A growl sounded which was copied and multiplied by a multitude of others.

It was unmistakable in its intent; it was a warning.

The noise grew as more growls and now low, deep rumbling hisses ominously sounded, echoing around the cave magnifying the effect.

Harrison raised his voice as large, dark shadows could be seen in our darting beams descending the walls, filling the cave floor ahead of us. From these dark shadows I could make out shapes of large, powerful-looking bodies writhing close to the ground with long, thick tails and long crocodile-shaped mouths breaking away from the protection of darkness and entering the light cast from our flashlights.

"Back to the tunnel. *Now*!" Harrison yelled.

I didn't need to be told twice. I turned and ran. Weatherby darted into the tunnel behind me and we shared a look of utter terror as the first gunshots echoed around the cave.

Hendricks heard both Harrison and Tori unsheathing their weapons as he fired at the closest Dragon that was darting toward them. Its short but thickly muscled legs were a blur as it propelled itself toward him at high speed. The shots found its head which burst apart to spray gore over the ones that followed it. Its tail whipped frantically and knocked others over as it died, skidding across the loose dirt floor of the cave as sheer momentum carried it forwards. Jones, standing by his side, fired, emptying his weapon in seconds as he switched his gun to auto and aimed at the approaching beasts.

"Harrison, get on the door," Hendricks shouted as he changed magazines quickly. For each one he killed, at least three more closed in from other directions, causing him to shift aim, his finger sending bullets in every direction. Geiger's hand grabbed the back of his vest as he was inserting another magazine into his weapon, pulling him backwards.

"Grenade!" was all I heard as with a rough pull, Geiger yanked Hendricks through the narrow gap of the doorway. The concussive boom and blast of the grenade exploding would have knocked him off his feet if Geiger still didn't have a hold of his vest. Dust and bits of debris shot through the doorway, obscuring whatever vision they had. Hendricks, choking on the dust, saw through the swirling fog the shapes of Harrison and Tori pushing at the door. It was closing slowly as the rusty hinges again protested against a thousand years of inactivity.

A deep rumbling sounded in the tunnel behind us, but we couldn't worry about it now as the only thing we needed to do was close the door, like right now.

Hendricks hurled himself desperately at the door adding his weight to the two already pushing it. Geiger kept firing blindly through the gap and Jones knelt next to him with his own weapon held ready to back him up if need be as there wasn't enough space for both of them to fire.

Through the ringing in my ears the growling and keening of the Dragons still sounded loud as they crowded toward the doorway. Higher pitched screams cut the air marking a successful kill. The leathery head of a Dragon thrust through the gap, its snapping jaws searching for a target. Instinctively kicking his feet at the teeth a few inches from his leg, Hendricks pulled his pistol from his vest and aimed at it. Chunks erupted from its mouth and head as bullets found their mark but still it kept writhing and snapping, pushing itself onwards, its growling changing to screeches of pain as the bullets struck home.

I stood in horror, blinking dust from my eyes as I watched the scene of terror through the thick clouds of dust that now rolled down the tunnel following the deep rumbling we'd all heard and felt. Hendricks was screaming, yelling in incoherent rage and effort as he pushed at the door and fired his gun onehanded at the terrifying sight of the hideous creature's snapping head.

Dazed and deafened by the gunfire I saw his gun stop firing as the slide locked back. Geiger was too preoccupied firing through the door to notice as the Dragon continued pushing its way through the gap, its jaws snapping, trying to reach one of us. Jones was trying to get an angle to shoot but was blocked by Geiger. Without thinking I pulled my own pistol from its holster and ran forwards, every fiber of my body wanted to run away to the perceived safety of the dark tunnel, but I forced those fears away as I knew my friends were in trouble and no one else could help them.

Geiger stood firing round after round through the gap, oblivious to everything else apart from the need to stop any more of them getting in. Gouts of blood poured from the ruined head and tooth-filled mouth of the one blocking the doorway. Hendricks yelled in pain as it raked his leg with its teeth, tearing his pants with one swipe and ripping a series of deep gashes into his calf muscle.

Pushing against Hendricks, I lay down flat as the only way to get an angle on the thing and began pulling the trigger. The beast reared as my bullets hit, raising itself in the air as if to pounce. I kept firing as Geiger, now aware of the threat as it filled his vision, changed his aim and fired at its exposed belly. Jones now had a clear shot too and he opened up. The force of our combined fire threw it backwards and it toppled from view emitting an ear-splitting screech. The doorway was now, for the moment, clear. Adding my weight to the door I pushed against it with both hands, one still holding my smoking pistol. The relief I felt when the door gave one final squeal and clunked shut was enough to make me weep and I slumped backwards as Harrison and Hendricks turned the wheel to lock it.

Chapter 19

Dig for Victory

The silence that descended was only broken by the gasping breaths and hacking coughs caused by the dust-filled air.

No one spoke as we privately relived the terror of the last few minutes. Our coughs subsided as the dust slowly began to settle. Pulling my canteen from my belt I swilled and spat out a mouthful of dusty spit before pouring water over my face to clear the grit from my eyes. Others were doing the same, none quite trusting themselves to speak yet in fear of the effort bringing on another bout of coughing.

"Annie?" I eventually called, the effort making me cough again.

"Yes, David. I am glad you are all okay. I have now learnt another emotion: that of helplessness. It's what I experienced as I monitored the audio feed and the images through your communication and recording devices. I knew I could not offer any direct assistance and was reduced to a mere observer of your desperate struggle. I am monitoring all your vital signs; can I recommend a period of rest before you continue?"

Hendricks laughed in response as he limped over to the wall to lean against it and take the weight off his injured leg. "Thanks mother, your concern is touching."

"Mister Hendricks," Annie asked formally, a hint of real concern in her voice, "are you injured? Your temperature and heartbeat are raised more than I would anticipate, even taking into account your recent physical exertions."

He looked at his ripped pants and the blood dripping from the deep gashes in his leg. The blood had soaked his socks and was dripping down his boots.

He paused and began smiling. "It's nothing, Annie, I got snagged by one of the Dragons is all. 'Tis but a scratch." He looked to see if anyone got the joke and continued. "A flesh wound, I've had worse."

He shrugged as no one even smirked. "Heathens, the lot of you. Do you know I've waited my whole career to be able to say that and not one of you appreciates my humor?" He put some weight on his leg and winced, staggering slightly, betraying the pain he was in.

"Jimmy. You are not the Black Knight…"

Hendricks barked a laugh. "Thank you, Annie, at least *you* get me."

"I am not sure if you are aware but Komodo dragons have a venomous bite," Annie continued sternly. "Even if *these* Dragons don't, they are carnivorous and so their bites will be at the very least laden with bacteria which, if not cleaned and treated immediately, could cause you serious harm or even death if the wound gets infected. Now please stop screwing around and can someone treat your injury."

"Before you get *sep-sis*," Harrison added with sarcasm which was minimized by his stumbling over the unfamiliar word.

Hendricks looked at his wound, silenced instantly by the thought of being poisoned. Geiger turned quickly and knelt by his leg without saying a word, reaching into a pouch for another aid pack. "Can I have some light please?" he asked.

I pointed my rifle to his leg, remembering to remove my finger from the trigger and watched as Geiger ripped his pants open to reveal the extent of the lacerations. He used water from his canteen and a mediwipe to clean the injuries and then liberally applying some antiseptic cream from a tube to all the ragged wounds in his leg before tightly binding a bandage around it.

When he had finished Hendricks tested putting some weight on it, nodding his thanks at Geiger, then shone his light back down the tunnel in the direction of the bunker. "I think we better investigate what the noise and dust was about. I'm a bit worried the noise we made caused a cave in." He made no mention of anyone's use of explosives, not that I thought Geiger would ever regret it.

My eyes went wide with panic that we could be trapped with no way out. It was clear exiting via the cave was something none of us wanted to do, but if the tunnel back to the complex was blocked then we may be left with no other option. "Annie," called Hendricks. "Can you shed any light, excuse the pun, on what happened?"

"Unfortunately, I cannot. Sorry. I am only able to surmise from the noise and localized seismic activity I detected, that you are correct regarding a full or partial cave-in."

"Where are Tanaka and his people now?" Hendricks asked, mentally crossing other bridges.

"They are still in the complex. I am tracking them via infrared and movement sensors. Most have coalesced into small groups and are slowly making their way around the complex. A few have made their way out; I have not been able to track their progress since they left the monitoring provided by the drones, but they left in the direction of the Springs. Some have gone further in and I calculate they may never find the exit before succumbing to dehydration. A number have been killed by their colleagues when they collided with each other in the dark and struck out with their weapons. Tanaka has six others with him and as they had not ventured as far in as others, they should egress in…" she paused and for some reason I imagined her checking her watch, "another eight hours, by my calculations."

I felt a momentary pang of sympathy for them, imagining the terror they must be feeling as they, in complete and utter darkness, stumbled through the complex with hands held out in front of them, using touch as the only sense they had. At least I thought they hadn't gotten the added terror of potentially being trapped in a dank and unstable tunnel with a cave-in to deal with. Maybe they were the lucky ones at the moment. The only difference between them and us now was we had light, which made me think.

"Didn't any of them have any torches? No flame or anything?"

"I can only assume not, otherwise logic indicates that they would have used it instead of attempting to navigate in total darkness."

She seemed to intuit my next thought. "I recommend you turn all your flashlights off apart from one. It will extend your illumination capabilities by a factor of six point three on current battery life."

"Thanks, Annie," Hendricks responded. "Good idea. I'll leave mine on, so if everyone else could turn theirs off we can make our way back down the tunnel to see what's happened."

One by one we all turned our lights off. Hendricks, who had the good manners and sense not to shine his light in our eyes, limped to the front and pointed his weapon light back the way we had come. Dust still swirled in the air hindering the reach of his powerful beam which diffused in and created a more lantern-like glow.

"Okay guys, I'll take it slow," he whispered. "Form a chain with one hand on the person in front's back. I'll call out any rocks or anything else that may trip you up so keep a good listen out for instructions."

We shuffled into position with Geiger bringing up the rear and, with my hand on Amir's back, we began shuffling after Hendricks. Disorientation set in after a few steps and I kept tripping over Amir's feet in front or was kicked by Harrison who was behind me. Geiger realized this and softly began calling step as if on a parade ground.

His low calls of, "Left, left, left-right-left," helped greatly, and our small human snake continued down the tunnel.

"Stop," Hendricks quietly hissed, bringing me back to the present. "Can I get another light on this?" There was a delay as Amir searched for and found the button before his beam doubled the light level and shone forward to show the way ahead blocked by a solid wall of rocks and dirt.

"You are still fifty meters from the tunnel entrance," Annie informed us.

Hendricks' light flashed around until he found what he was looking for as he detached the flashlight from the gun and rested it on a small indentation in the tunnel's walls. Its beam now steady, illuminated what lay ahead.

Not wasting any time Hendricks spoke up. "Okay. It looks as though there's nothing for it but to shift it by hand. I'll start and pass everything behind me. Everyone form a chain and pass it down the line to throw it behind us."

As we crowded forwards to inspect the task ahead of us his tone changed to one of bright cheerfulness. "Come on, the sooner we begin the sooner we can get out of here."

"What if we can't do it?" Weatherby whispered, his voice full of fear and desperation.

167

Harrison spoke with distain at his panicked voice. "We can't stay here, so trying and failing is better than doing nothing." He placed both hands on my shoulders and eased himself past me before pushing Weatherby aside and stood beside Hendricks to study the rockfall.

"Shall we begin?" he asked simply.

~

Singularly or in small groups Tanaka's warriors arrived back at the Springs, all with tales of defeat and death at the hands of the ones from space and the terror of being trapped in the dark labyrinth of The Source. No one knew where Tanaka was and rumors circulated that he was dead or had been captured by their enemy. With nobody in command the community descended into chaos. Fights broke out between those who wanted to assume command and more died as the bloodshed spread amongst the people, who for the first time could express their will and formed factions to protect each other or fight those who they now declared to be their enemies or rivals.

~

The community at the Three Hills was also on edge. Its leader and one of their strongest warriors had left to talk to the new arrivals and had not been seen since. Darkness was descending and reluctantly the town Elders ordered the gates to be closed and sealed for the night. There the community, though worried, kept together and did not fall apart. Any rumors that began were quickly stopped as the truth was no one really knew what was going on, and so sense prevailed.

The difference between the two communities, that of respect and fear for their respective leaders, told the deepest truth about their lives.

At the compound the community gathered after Hendricks authorized Annie to update everyone on the events of the last hours at The Source. The attention of most was on the grieving widows and children of Knight and Collins, the two engineers killed in the fight.

Those widows, informed privately by Annie following advice from Dr. Warren, shared their grief with the community.

Nathalie, who had been left in charge of security by Hendricks, led the remainder of the team a short distance away. She placed five shot glasses on a table and poured some amber liquid into them all from a hip flask she produced from a pocket. Picking one up the others followed suit and solemnly held them in the air.

"Stevens," she said, her voice hoarse with emotion, "a good man." She put the glass to her lips and downed its contents in one as the others repeated his name and did the same. She remined silent as the fiery liquid burned down her throat before looking at her gathered command.

"It looks as if 'Endricks is indisposed for a while. Our priority is to protect the compound, so until we know more, we will lock this place down tight. Nobody comes in or goes out. Annie tells me she is returning the drones as they are doing no good watching an empty cave. Once they are charged, she will maintain overwatch." She toyed with her rifle on its sling to delay before she spoke again. "They are relying on us now, so it is double guard shifts and continual rotation. Okay?"

Raising her head she looked them all in the eye and ended her team talk with, "Okay, Magda and I will take first watch. Four-hour rotations until I say to you differently. The engineers have completed the air jet system so if The Swarm turns up tonight at least that should keep them off the walls. We are in good shape, so let's hold it together until 'Endricks gets back."

"What if he doesn't?" Magda asked quietly, echoing everyone's thoughts.

Natalie looked at her. "He will, but if he can't get to us, I reckon the five of us will take everything we have that goes bang and go get him. As he would say, cross bridges when we find them."

Weber racked his shotgun, the shuck-shuck of a cartridge being pumped into the chamber echoing ominously. "Let's get on with this. No caveman wearing the animal furs will stop us, ve vill blast through them all if the boss needs us."

Chapter 20

Light at the End of the Tunnel

Hendricks had ripped a strip from his T-shirt and wrapped it around his face in an attempt to filter some of the dust that billowed up every time he carefully moved another rock. Each one causing more loose dirt to fall from the unstable ceiling as he pulled it clear and pushed it behind him. Every small fall of dirt and stones set his nerves and senses on edge as the thought of being buried alive became an ever-present companion in the small tunnel.

Fingernails bent and cracked as he applied every ounce of his strength to prize the more stubborn rocks loose. The only tool he had was his knife which he stabbed around the larger boulders to break the bonds locking them in place so that inch by exhaustingly careful inch, minute by nerve jangling minute he cleared a passage barely high and wide enough for him to crawl through, forcing him to use his elbows and toes to push onwards.

Almost at the end of his own endurance and spirits dark thoughts of failure were getting harder to ignore, when a chink of light shining through a small gap almost blinded him. The air felt fresher as even the small crack of light was washing a stream of clean, unpolluted, dust-free air across his face.

He opened his mouth to tell the others, but all that emerged from his throat was a parched croak. He tried again, working his mouth to conjure up some spittle to moisten his throat, but still nothing came out. Deep reserves of energy surged through his tired muscles and he shuffled a few inches forwards to attack the rock that was holding back the light.

I was fourth in line in the tunnel. Working in total darkness I fumbled and felt for the rocks and dirt that Amir kept pushing in my direction. His whimpers and moans at the continual effort and terror of struggling in the claustrophobic darkness made me more determined to try and squash my own fears. The sounds ahead in the dark of rocks hitting each other as they fell made me cover my head with my hands as I expected to be buried alive in another fall. I lay there for long seconds waiting for it, but nothing came. Eventually, I lifted my head and instead of seeing darkness, light flooded the tunnel. It took me a few moments to realize we had made it.

Too exhausted and drained to feel elation, my only desire was to get out of the tunnel we had carved through the rockfall. Somehow seeing a way out made being trapped inside even more unbearable and threatened to send me into a panic. I desperately shuffled behind Weatherby who was also scrabbling as fast as he could toward the light. Reaching the end, I felt hands grabbing my outstretched arms and dragging me the last few feet. Blinded by the bright light, strong arms pulled me down what felt like a rough slope and sat me on the floor with my back against the wall.

Blinking and wiping the dust and grit from my eyes I regained some vision as light from the open doorway spilled into the tunnel illuminating five other figures sat around me, unrecognizable as all were covered from head to toe in dirt. Slowly and painfully I hauled

172

myself to my feet and staggered toward the light, desperate to get out of the tunnel.

Blinking in the harsh glow of the warehouse lights the others also emerged to stand beside me forming a rough circle as we stared in silence at each other.

Hendricks tried to speak, but still only a dry croak came from his throat and then pointed toward the far end of the warehouse toward the living quarters. He set off and we followed.

In the kitchen he tried the faucet, at first nothing happened but then it spluttered a few times and a solid stream of clear water started flowing from it. Cupping his hands under the flow he held them there for a few seconds as the water turned a muddy brown color as it washed the grime from his hands before lowering his head and drinking deeply. Standing back, we all crowded around waiting for our turn to ease our parched, dust-filled throats.

Still filthy and exhausted but at least now able to speak we slumped into the deep comfortable armchairs and sofas.

"What now?" Weatherby asked.

"Annie?" called Hendricks. "What's the status of Tanaka's people in the complex?"

Annie bleeped and her voice came from speakers hidden in the walls. "Fifteen more have found the exit, including Tanaka who reached it two hours ago. Twenty-one more remain inside, most have stopped moving and are sitting or lying down in groups. I think they have given up and are all just silent or calling for help." Her tone softened. "My concern, though, is for you. Now I can visually monitor you all as well as monitoring your stats via your wristbands, I must insist on a period of rest before continuing."

"We must get back," Hendricks insisted.

Harrison also nodded and added, "My people will be concerned. I have to tell them what has happened."

"I advise against that," Annie said. "While you were in the tunnel, I recovered the drones and recharged them. Three are now maintaining coverage over the compound but Nathalie recommended I return one to watch the Charlie site entrance. When Tanaka exited, he left in the direction of the Springs, but the remainder of his men stayed to watch the entrance. They are, as we speak, constructing a wall across the entrance to the cave."

Hendricks let out a string of colorful swear words before saying, "So, what you are saying is we can't get out without another fight? They're sealing their own people inside?"

"That is correct. I must also remind you that Tanaka is in possession of firearms, and as you know he knows how to operate them."

I sat thinking as I listened to the exchange when a thought came to my head. "Why don't we wake the super soldiers up? With, what is it? Fifteen more, we should be able to kick their asses, right?"

Hendricks looked at me before nodding. "Annie, before I make a decision can you patch me through to Nathalie please."

"Of course," she replied. "You are now connected."

We all listened as Hendricks spoke to Nathalie, whose relief that they we all okay was evident in her voice. She assured Hendricks that all was in hand at the compound. With the new bug defenses and firepower the automated pods could bring to bear, even with their depleted numbers, he trusted her to defend the compound and everyone inside.

Hendricks seemed to hesitate before telling her about the soldiers still in cryo and asked if she could hold the fort for a few days whilst they defrosted them and got them acclimatized and

174

operational. Once she had gotten over the shock at the news of what Weatherby had constructed and kept secret, she assured him that even though she would prefer him back, the tactical advantage of more than doubling their fighting force would be worth the wait.

Harrison was restless, pacing and evidently worried. He exchanged meaningful looks with Tori before explaining how his prolonged absence from his people worried him. He opened up about the leadership challenge and how he couldn't rule out one of them attempting to usurp him in his absence and described the destabilizing effect that would have on his people. He also worried about any retribution Tanaka may deliver upon them in his absence.

Hendricks, agreeing with him, contacted Nathalie again and asked if she could organize and send a small patrol to make contact with the Three Hills tribe and inform them of what was going on and what the plan was.

He immediately heard Weber in the background volunteer. Though he wanted to go alone so as not to leave the compound too vulnerable, Hendricks insisted Annie use drones to be his eyes and ears. Hendricks knew Weber well enough to know he was good to go alone, and Harrison visibly relaxed knowing he'd soon be able to speak to his people.

Whilst Hendricks had been talking, Geiger had asked me to open the files on the surviving soldiers in cryo and had been scrolling through my laptop which remarkably had survived all the rough treatment it had received in my pack.

I opened my mouth a couple times to ask him if he was doing okay, to say that I liked Stevens and that I was sorry he was dead, but everything I thought about saying sounded so lame inside my head that I ended up saying nothing. Geiger was quiet and withdrawn, but I guessed it wasn't the first time he'd lost a friend like that.

Okay, maybe not to an *arrow*, but still.

He put down the laptop when Hendricks had finished talking and smacked his hands on his trousers raising a cloud of dust from them as he stood up.

"Shall we go wake these boys up then? I've read their files and *man,* there are some badasses in there. I don't think they'll even need guns, but just chew 'em up and spit out the pieces."

Annie beeped in announcement. "I'm still monitoring you all. I advise a period of recuperation first. You have all been awake for twenty-three hours with no nourishment or rest. When the subjects emerge from cryostasis they will need your care and attention for a period, and without sleep none of you will be able to offer them that." I looked at the dirt-streaked, exhausted faces of my companions and guessed if they felt half as exhausted as I did then Annie was right. We were in no position to help ourselves let alone others.

"I have fully activated the systems within the complex and identified the relevant stores in the warehouse to provide you with nourishment. If required, I can locate clean clothing for you all. My recommendation is you remove foreign matter from your exposed skin as I have not analyzed it but, with the damp conditions in parts of the tunnel, there is a high likelihood that microbes contained within it may cause infections. A minimum period of five hours sleep will also be required for optimum performance to be maintained."

"Annie?" I asked, a note of disbelief in my voice. "You telling us to have a shower and go to bed?"

"Yes. That is my recommendation."

As always, she was right. After a meal of self-heating ration packs and a hot shower, I was staggering with exhaustion as I donned a clean set of fatigues, barely making it to the nearest sofa before

176

collapsing on it and falling into a deep sleep; a sleep only disturbed by vivid dreams of fire breathing dragons and collapsing tunnels.

Five hours and thirty minutes after the last of us fell asleep, the lights raised and a low bleeping that increased gently in volume woke us all up one by one. Disorientated by waking up on a soft sofa, my head resting on a luxuriously expensive cushion, my first thought was I was back in Texas waking after a long night working in my lab. It took a few moments for reality to kick in and the memories of the last twenty-four hours, not of ones from a thousand years ago, to wake me up completely.

Geiger had already retrieved more supplies from the warehouse and the smell of freshly brewed coffee was irresistibly emanating from the kitchen and drawing us all toward it. Annoyingly, he was whistling happily to himself and looked as fresh as if he'd had twelve hours' sleep following a relaxing day on a beach in the Bahamas.

Harrison and Tori, still looking bemused by their surroundings, cautiously took a mug each of steaming coffee Geiger handed to them.

"What is this?" Harrison asked as he sniffed it.

"Grade-A mud," he replied with complete seriousness. They both looked shocked and stared at the black liquid in distrust.

"It's coffee," I explained smiling at them. "Try it. It's what we use to kick start the day." I took a sip to prove it wasn't hazardous and *man* was it good.

Once they had a first sip both their eyes went wide with mixed reactions. They finished their mugs and let Geiger refill them as Weatherby emerged from a bedroom he'd claimed for himself as we'd all looked for a place to sleep. He joined us and meekly but gratefully took a mug of the proffered coffee before getting down to business. He had been quiet ever since emerging from the tunnel, knowing as well as we did that he was the only one not to help when the Dragons were trying to eat us all.

He turned to Hendricks, knowing after his miserable performance that he needed to reinforce his position in the group once more.

"Shall I lead the process of bringing them back from cryo? I've overseen it dozens of times and am fully conversant with any problems that may occur." Hendricks just stared at him, not fully trusting himself to speak without venting his anger at him once more. Weatherby couldn't fail to interpret his look so changed his poise to a humbler one.

"Look, I know what you think. I'm all talk and no action when it matters, and you're probably right. It's why I got people like you to believe and trust in me, to work with me to make the vision I hatched a reality all those centuries ago. I knew without others with different skills I wouldn't stand a chance and there was no point even starting the project. Yes, I had the money and resources to make it possible, but I know my strengths." He laughed briefly and looked at us all. "And I know my weaknesses. Around a boardroom table I was invincible, but in a real fight I just freeze. Maybe I *am* a coward, I'm sure you all have opinions on that, and I can do nothing to change those opinions but prove to you all my courage lies in other directions. We can all win fights, but the fights I can win are just not the physical type that's all."

Harrison looked at him before speaking. "In my world, leaders need to be strong. They lead from the front and do not shy away from danger. Your words would not go far in my community." He stopped and waved around the room they stood in. "But you built this place, the place that sheltered our forefathers from the great darkness. To do that you must have commanded thousands of men who followed you, and for that I now understand we all owe you our lives."

He looked sad as he continued. "I have never known peace, only a barely held together truce between the two tribes. Both tribes know that to fight each other would cost both too dearly to be able to ensure our own survival. Maybe when we eventually find peace there will be a place for you amongst the leaders but until then I will treat you as one of the tribal Elders: someone you respect and get council from, but who is too old or weak to fight."

He saw the anger rising in Weatherby's face and held his hands up in a placatory manner.

"Please do not be offended, I'm only giving you my view on how we have lived since our memories began. The strong do the fighting and the Elders guide us using their wisdom. They are held in the highest of respect and have great standing in the community, without them we would have no one to turn to for a balanced council."

He looked around as he struggled to find more words to say until Hendricks said, "Mr. Weatherby, I believe he was trying to pay you a complement. I still hold to the agreement we made. I will look after our security and safety whilst you look after everything else. I know fighting isn't your forte, but management is." He then extended yet another olive branch. I couldn't help but think the tree must be getting pretty bare. "To be honest, you did well yesterday. You fought at the barricade when needed and no one could have led us through the complex as quickly as you did. We managed to get the door closed at the cave and you did your part in the tunnel."

I could see his anger abating as he listened to the complements being paid.

"And yes, I agree," Hendricks continued, "you should take the lead on bringing the men out of cryo, just tell us what you need."

Weatherby looked at Harrison and held out his hand for him to shake smiling his best boardroom smile. "I'm not sure about the Elder title just yet, maybe in a few years when we've all aged, we can become the Elders and keep the next generation of youngsters in line."

Releasing his hand, Amir spoke to the room. "Annie, begin waking them please."

"Yes, Mister Weatherby, beginning process now. I will bring them out one at a time with a thirty-minute spacing."

"Shall we?" Weatherby said as he indicated to the doors that led to the warehouse and the pods. I noticed as I followed him a spring had returned to his step and his whole demeanor seemed more confident. As he walked, he continued talking. "I think it's best if we get them all awake first and comfortable in the bunker before we tell them the whole story. It'll save a lot of repetition and Annie can use the television screens to display help."

"Yes, Mister Weatherby," replied Annie. "Good idea. I will create a file of relevant information. I have also collated all the known information about The Swarm and how it began. I need to brief whoever you deem relevant on what I have discovered about The Swarm from Charlie Annie's memory."

"Will it help us kill the bastards?" Hendricks asked with more acidity than was customary for him, making me think the injury to his leg was hurting him.

Annie sounded excited. "Yes, and more, but I don't think killing them will be a good idea; we may need them to help protect us."

Hendricks stopped walking. "Annie, are we in danger from others?"

"Not for the foreseeable future. But their creation was for a purpose, shall I explain now?"

"No, not if it's not pertinent and can wait. Our priority is to the ones waking up and I don't need a head full of bug theory when I'm concentrating."

I wanted Annie to explain right now. I needed to know why someone would create a species of wirelessly controlled organic hybrid super bug things. Annie, as though she read my mind, whispered in my ear.

"Don't worry, it can wait."

I wanted to argue with her but as we approached the cryopods I could see the lid on the first one beginning to open as the waking-up process began. Putting it to the back of my mind I gathered around it with the others to offer my help.

Chapter 21

Strength in Numbers

I teamed up with Hendricks to help get the first guy out of the freezer.

Everyone, with the obvious exception of Harrison and Tori, knew what it felt like to wake up from cryostasis and therefore had great sympathy for the men as they all came around and numbly accepted the offered help. Before each one woke, Annie gave a brief resume of who they were which mainly consisted of their name, rank, age and unit details.

Knowing the best cure was time, they were helped to the bunker and sat down in one of the comfortable chairs. Geiger stayed with them; he was military so spoke their curious language better than any of the others. As their numbers grew, he maintained a dialogue, carefully avoiding any direct questions by saying they would be briefed in full when they had all come out of cryo. Being military men, this was not an unusual occurrence, so they hurried up and waited.

In only four hours, fifteen men were all in different stages of recovery in the luxury of the bunker. We all gathered in the room, offering drinks or food as required until Amir decided that the newly awakened arrivals were ready to be briefed.

Most stared at Harrison and Tori out of natural curiosity. They had both refused to change clothes, not wanting to lose the protection of the cured hide and leather armor they wore. They stood silently away from the main group, still with their weapons secured in sheaths on their backs watching the soldiers with barely masked wonder as they recovered. Not unsurprisingly both stood out in a room of people wearing fatigues and sidearms.

When he deemed them ready, Amir got their attention and began the briefing. He first introduced the rest of us in the room and added our roles. They took the news of the length of time of their sleep stoically, with only a couple of exceptions, but the loss of their friends and colleagues who didn't make it must've weighed heavy on them. Like Geiger dealing with the death of Stevens, I guessed they'd deal with things in their own way and their own time.

Annie showed them a condensed time-lapse of the society that had developed on Earth in their absence from the images she had taken from space. Harrison and Tori had never seen a television before and watched with more fascination than the men as the history of the last almost thousand years of their civilization was played out before them from a god-like perspective. They gasped in wonder and called out like excited children when they recognized places and buildings.

Amir asked Harrison to explain the recent history they had with the latest Tanaka and how they lived in a world devoid of machinery and technology. The soldiers listened with rapt attention as they described how they lived and survived their entire lives, maintaining the fragile peace that had held for centuries between the two communities whilst also defending themselves from the monthly ravages of The Swarm. The footage of the wave of bugs was replayed as well as a rundown on the dissection of the captured creatures. Annie explained she had more information on The Swarm which she would update everyone with when the immediate danger was over and they were back at the compound, before Amir finished the briefing with the most recent events and why they had entered the site and woken them up.

The room fell silent as they all digested what they had heard over the last half hour. They'd kept quiet as they had been asked to leave all questions until the end, until the most senior soldier amongst them, a heavy-set man wearing a T-shirt with ARMY emblazoned across the slab of meat that was his chest, spoke up. He was a hulk of a man, a similar size to the mighty Weber and he spoke with a soft Texas drawl.

"Williamson," he said by way of very brief introduction, "Captain, US Army." His melodic southern accent made him sound either bored, or so confident that he didn't need to speak fast or rush in any way ever. The other soldiers watched him intently, hanging on his words with a respect that spoke of a much deeper root than simply rank or size.

"So ya'll telling us we've been asleep for nine hundred years too long, and now you need our help to get out of here and kick some wannabe dictator's ass to boot? I think me and my boys can pick the rest up as we go along the same as you boys…" He turned and gave a small shrug of apology toward Tori completely ignoring the fact that she'd never personally been in stasis, "and girls, seem to have done since y'all woke up." He looked at Hendricks. "I take it you're in charge of things around here? What do you need us to do?"

Hendricks nodded his thanks to Amir as he pushed himself off the wall he was leaning against and limped to the center of the room.

"I'm sure you're right about picking it up as you go along, Captain. We've certainly had something of a sharp learning curve ourselves the past days. I know you'll all feel ready for some action but trust me we have been where you are now, and the effects of the cryo will differ but will definitely mess you up a little. I recommend at least another twelve hours' rest before we even attempt to clear the complex and deal with Tanaka and his people on the surface."

He explained as he looked at them. "Trained soldiers such as yourselves are irreplaceable now, so you all need to be as sharp as possible. We can't afford any mistakes." His head dropped a fraction as his eyes vacated and he muttered, "God knows we've been hurt badly enough..." He snapped his head back up the fraction it had dipped, his eyes now clear and focused.

"We need to let Annie gather intel about the barricade on the surface, and we're waiting for news on a mission one of my men is undertaking to the community at the Three Hills."

~

Hendricks addressed the soldiers formally, in the way only he could. "As we haven't worked together before we need to establish unit strategies and procedures. So, if you first want to draw your weapons from the stores in the warehouse, we can begin."

The soldiers perked up at the talk of getting weapons in their hands, as with all elite soldiers they felt naked without them. Hendricks looked at Weatherby. "I've flicked through the weapons and equipment manifests stored in the warehouse."

"Do you like what I put in here?" Weatherby smiled as he responded.

"Honestly, yes," Hendricks said. "Though I'm surprised at some of it. Is there really a pair of helicopters in here?"

"Yes. Initially we decided against anything like that as their incumbent fuel and maintenance issues would be detrimental to the peaceful rebuilding mission we'd all planned. My suspicions about potential hostilities, although granted I didn't expect that to come from within, made me change my mind. We were developing a small military scout helicopter that could operate in remote regions for extended periods," he said rapidly, his voice speeding up with the evident excitement of one of his research projects.

"The first two working prototypes are in the warehouse. They're designed to be airdropped packed in crates and built with ease using basic mechanical skills. My co—"

"Ha! So, some jarhead can take a break from eating his crayons and build them." Williamson barked a laugh from the other side of the room without looking up, neither expecting nor receiving a response.

Weatherby smiled politely at the captain, he could have been annoyed at the interruption but realized that if they were up for jokes then they were ready to leave. "My companies were also investing heavily in new research into sustainable fuels, and this generation of aircraft uses biofuels that can be manufactured on site using the latest generation of manufacturing plant." He held up a hand to ward off the expected question. "Yes, they're in the warehouse too. The helicopters are a truly revolutionary design. They are low maintenance as all parts are designed to either last the life of the airframe or be manufactured using 3D printers."

"Weapons capabilities?" Hendricks asked.

"They are a multi-platform, multi-role design so yes. If we have it, they can carry it."

Hendricks gave a low whistle. "So, we have an air force now. Things appear to be looking up. What's in the warehouse will negate any superiority in numbers Tanaka thinks he may have. All we need to do is get the hell out of here."

186

Weber silently tracked through the dense undergrowth and foliage, his ability to move stealthily at odds with his size. The pack and equipment he carried, although heavy, didn't trouble him as he made progress. Annie saved the necessity of taking compass bearings and reading the terrain as she used one of the overhead drones to keep him up-to-date on his position and the course they had agreed on earlier. Barely out of breath, he arrived at the edge of the tree line that had been cleared away from the high, timber walls.

Crouching down to reach for his binoculars, he studied the walls. He was impressed by what he saw; the sentries all seemed alert and looking outwards and not slumped bored as undertrained and unmotivated ones might be. Knowing time was short he muttered to himself, "Hier geht gar nichts, as the Americans would say."

He was surprised when Annie answered back, "Ja, mein Freund. Tschaka!"

Chuckling to himself he stood to his full height slowly, not wanting to surprise them as he wasn't certain how they would react, to emerge from the tree line and wait.

In seconds a horn sounded which brought a rush of activity to the walls as more heads appeared all looking in his direction. Holding his arms out in the universal 'I come in peace' gesture he began slowly walking toward the gate. His nerves on edge, ready to react to a barrage of arrows or spears he half expected to come at him at any moment, he slowly approached.

"Are you from the stars? Are you one of the newcomers?" a voice shouted down to him.

He stopped walking, searching around to identify who had called to him. "Yes, I bring news of your Harrison and Tori. They are okay but are not able to come back here to you now. If you let me in, I can explain everything. I have brought a radio so you can speak to them."

He waited, listening as the ones on the walls passed on what he had said to others out of sight.

"What's..." came the hesitant reply. "What's a *radio*?"

He smiled at his mistake. He lifted the pack from his back and held it in up. "It is in here." Then trying not to sound condescending he explained the technology which ran the risk of getting him burned at the stake. "My radio allows me to communicate with others over a great distance. I want to give it to you. It is a gift from us so we can talk easily in the future and come to your aid if Tanaka attacks again."

He could hear further conversation before the gates began to open and an elderly man flanked by two younger warriors stepped through the gap and walked toward him.

The older man extended his hand and the two greeted each other. "I am Travis, one of the village Elders. If our leader is absent the Elders assume his role collectively." He smirked before continuing. "And I was deemed expendable enough by my people to be the first to meet you"—he looked Weber up and down again with comedic appreciation—"in case you were hungry."

Weber returned the smile, knowing the old man wasn't telling the truth as he was most likely the senior Elder and wouldn't ask another to put themselves in potential danger.

"I understand, my friend," Weber replied with a wink. "I think that this ist why *I* am here as well, no? Not to eat you, of course."

Travis smiled in response and indicated to the gateway. "Please come in. We're all eager for news of Harrison and Tori."

Weber followed the man into the settlement. It seemed that everyone had gathered to catch their first glimpse of one of the arrivals from space as the central area they led him to filled with people, all clamoring and crowding around the large, weapon-draped, imposing soldier.

Travis shooed them away from their path, pushing through the crowd and leading Weber to a raised platform. He spoke with the German for a few minutes, the conversation awkward and stilted as they realized they existed in different times, before standing beside him and calling for quiet. It took some time for the excited crowd to calm down enough for him to be heard.

Holding his hands up to finally subdue the crowd he spoke, his voice strong enough to reach all. "This is Dieter Weber, and I formally welcome him under our protection to the Three Hills community. He has news of Harrison and Tori. I am relieved to inform you all that they are both safe." Most in the crowd gave a relieved cheer which told Weber the high esteem they held the pair in. Though he couldn't fail to pick out a few who didn't seem as pleased and committed their faces to memory for later. "He will now tell you what he told me," he said, stepping aside and gesturing for Weber to step forwards and address the people.

Thirty minutes later, a relieved but concerned community were persuaded to return to their jobs as Weber wanted to set up the radio so they could talk to Harrison themselves.

Chapter 22

Fire Discipline

Tanaka and his two most trusted men staggered exhausted up to the walls of the Springs as the sun dawned on the eastern horizon. He had left the rest of the survivors at the entrance to The Source telling them he would send reinforcements to help them with the barricade. Anger had soon replaced the dazed and bewildered relief he had felt when he had first reached the surface. The newcomers had humiliated him, slaughtered many of his best fighters as he tried to overpower them, but he didn't care about that; all they had done was fail him and let him down.

Approaching the closed gate, his hands subconsciously caressed the weapons he carried. They were his new symbols of power, and nobody could stand against him now.

The hairs on his neck rose as his mind tried to catch up with his instincts. No one was on the walls and that unforgiveable failure turned into anger which rose as he banged his fist on the metal sheeting of the gate and shouted for them to be opened. Someone looked over the wall as the dull, reverberating noise created by his fist smashing against the gate receded.

"Open the gate!" he demanded angrily, his voice shrill with fury. Further shouts and the sound of fighting behind the walls prompted him to pull the pistol from its holster as he continued to bang his free fist on the gate. The unmistakable clash of steel and shouts of pain as a fight raged between his people triggered a sense of panic.

Unable to gain entry he screamed incoherently venting his rage and rising panic on the gate, until eventually the sound of the locking bar scraping back in its brackets made him stop. The two men with him, exchanging glances of fear, stepped forwards as Tanaka pushed them in front. As the gate swung open a man burst through. It was Smith, one of the survivors from The Source and one of Tanaka's inner circle of warriors.

He was bruised and beaten, blood dripping from numerous wounds as he staggered and fell at his leader's feet. "It's Byrne," Smith choked, pausing to spit blood into the dirt. "He tried to take over as soon as he returned. We've been fighting him and the bastards who joined him."

Tanaka dragged him upright. "How many are with him?" he snarled.

The man whimpered, not wanting to be the one to tell him the extent of the treachery. "Most have joined him, but many have stayed loyal to you. We barricaded ourselves in the guard post at the gate and have been fighting them off for hours. When they knew it was you at the gate, most of them fled giving us the chance to open it."

Reeling from the shock of betrayal, his rage grew to a level even he had not experienced before.

"Where are they now?" he screamed, spittle covering the man as he pulled on his clothing to bring his face close to his own.

"I think they went to your private quarters, sir," Smith, quivering with fear, replied.

Tanaka let go of him to see him stagger away, recoiling from the venom he saw in his leader's face. Tanaka pushed the pistol he was holding back into its holster. Using both hands to grab the gate he gave it a mighty heave and it swung back on its hinges to clatter against the walls. He grabbed the rifle he had strapped to his back and, raising it to his shoulder, ran through the open gateway screaming an incoherent rage at anyone who dared to betray him. The two men with him stalled for a moment in shock at his actions, then ran after him screaming their own battle cries.

Not trained in fire discipline, Tanaka shot at anything that moved. Men, women and children scattered before him as bullets flew in all directions. The sight of blood spraying and bodies falling, to lie crumpled and still on the ground, as the high velocity projectiles indiscriminately claimed their victims, filled him with a huge sense of indestructible power. He was a god.

A warrior ran out of a doorway to his left, discarding his weapon as he rushed toward Tanaka and threw himself to the ground before him, howling for mercy.

But The Tanaka did not grant mercy.

They had risen against him and the only punishment was death. He aimed and pulled the trigger. The gun fired once, missing the man as the bullet raised a plume of dirt by his head before clicking empty. Initially confused by the click, it took him a few seconds to work out what had happened. The warrior, still begging for his life, tried to scramble away from the look of pure evil Tanaka fixed him with as he fumbled with the unfamiliar weapon. His guards did not need ordering what to do, they had seen their leader try to kill the man so with weapons raised they ran screaming at him swinging them at his head. He stood no chance, and in seconds he lay dead, a pulverized mess of bone and oozing brain where his head had once been.

The pause to reload gave Tanaka the chance to restrain his racing mind and bring his rage under control. He looked up and saw his private quarters ahead of him, the door slamming shut. Sensing movement behind him he spun, raising his gun, finger tightening on the trigger. Around twenty warriors threw themselves flat on the dirt, all shouting their loyalty to him. The gun fired before he could release the trigger, sending a stream of bullets into two of the prone figures who screamed in agony before lying still in death.

"Don't kill us," voices pleaded. "We are with you."

Tanaka slowly lowered the gun.

Is this all? he thought with despair. He had hundreds of warriors. Many he knew had died at The Source the day before, but he had left twice that number behind to guard the Springs. He forced down his horror and disappointment and spoke to the men still lying prone in front of him.

"My brave warriors." He indicated for them to stand. "Thank you for your loyalty. The Tanakas are the rightful rulers of all the tribes: this is known and set in our laws and customs." He pointed to the closed door to his quarters. "Those disloyal scum in there, those *traitors*, have dishonored all of us while I was bravely fighting the Newcomers." He held up the still-smoking rifle. "I took this from the body of their greatest warrior after I killed him in single combat," he lied. "Nothing can stop us now, so who will help me kill these traitors?"

His men, desperate to show their loyalty, roared their agreement. Tanaka, knowing that this time he had to lead from the front and not wanting to lose any momentum his solo charge through the settlement had gained, turned and ran toward his quarters, screaming his battle cry. Firing his gun as he ran, his men faltered briefly as most witnessed for the first time the power of such a weapon as its bullets splintered and shattered the wooden façade of his quarters.

Bounding up the short flight of stairs leading to the wide veranda that wrapped around his quarters, he charged the door with his shoulder. The door creaked and a panel splintered but the lock held. In frustration he emptied his gun at the door. The bullets blasted ragged holes in it before he slammed his body into it again, but still it held.

Changing the magazine, he realized with a shock he only had two full ones left. Only being able to get the ones Collins had left in the pockets of his vest he knew until he defeated those at the compound that they were an irreplaceable resource. Without knowing it he was learning fire discipline. Holding the reloaded gun ready, he indicated to the ones crowding around him on the veranda to try and beat the door down. He would have to pick his shots carefully now. The gun had proved its worth in galvanizing his men back onto his side, solidifying that they had made the right decision not to abandon him. He would now only fire when it would have the greatest impact. He still had three full reloads for the pistol but those also needed to be used carefully.

His men were roaring their battle cries as they crowded around the door, those at the front swinging their axes at it whilst others threw their whole weight against it. It couldn't hold for long under such an onslaught and it didn't. With a piercing crack and a splintering of breaking timber the door gave way.

The defenders inside, knowing that now The Tanaka was back and that their lives were most likely forfeit, had nothing to lose but fight to the end and maybe, just maybe, win a victory. The doorway developed into a vicious bloodbath as neither side wanted to give ground and the bodies began to pile up. The veranda, where he usually sat observing those following his and his men's will, became awash with blood and viscera that spread in an ever-growing slick across the wooden deck.

Screaming and slipping, the fury of the attackers slowly beat the defenders inside allowing more to enter the fray. Tanaka waited for his moment before entering the building where he saw Byrne fighting at the center of the line. He was a big man and had been one of his inner circle of depraved individuals, who reveled in his position and the power he held over the community. He was roaring and wielding his double-headed axe with a fury born from desperation. His blade sliced through flesh and bone, cutting men down with every stroke.

Raging at the betrayal, Tanaka raised his gun and aimed carefully to wait for the right moment. When the red dot of the holographic sight centered on Byrne's chest, he pulled the trigger.

The hail of bullets hit him and threw him back across the floor, his ruined chest a mess of ragged red holes that sprayed blood over his fellow traitors as he fell. The loud bangs of the gun being fired in the enclosed space caused a brief, shocked pause in the battle.

Some decided they had had enough and dropped their weapons, falling to their knees and immediately begging for mercy. His loyal men were deep in the madness of battle and cut them down without the mercy for which they pleaded. With their leader now dead the tide of battle turned dramatically. It became a rout as most turned and fled further into Tanaka's private quarters. The ones who stayed to fight now found themselves hopelessly outnumbered and were killed easily, screaming as blades hacked into their bodies. Not wanting any to live, Tanaka urged his men onwards screaming for them to, "*Kill them all!*"

His main living area, where he entertained his inner circle of sycophantic followers, ensuring their loyalty with unlimited drinks and free use of any of his carefully selected women and girls, resembled an abattoir as outstretched arms begging for mercy were severed by swinging weapons, spraying arterial blood in wide arcs, covering every surface as, one by one, his men hunted down and massacred everyone who had stood against him.

Beyond this massacre Tanaka spotted a few figures ducking through the door to his inner bedchamber. A feeling of panic overcame him—beyond his room was his inner secret sanctum containing the briefcase that controlled The Swarm. The door wasn't locked. No one would dare enter it upon pain of death, so such a precaution was not necessary and the two trusted guards permanently on duty in his quarters would allow only their leader to enter the bedchamber.

"My bedchamber," he yelled and pointed, panic making his voice sound like the screech of a bird. "Stop them."

The warriors nearest to him obeyed, kicking and hacking a path through the dying survivors. Tanaka followed close behind them, stamping his steel shod rawhide boots on any person that got close to him as they recoiled from the attacks of others. Letting his rifle drop on its sling he pulled his pistol from its holster.

As they burst through into his bedchamber four of the five warriors inside leaped toward them, screaming their own rage and frustration as they chose to die in the way of a true warrior: facing your enemy no matter how hopeless the odds with your own blade wet with your enemies' blood. The fifth ran in panic, pushing aside the leather curtain and entering his secret room.

Tanaka ducked under the hissing blade of a warrior's axe and shoved the barrel of his pistol hard up under the man's bearded chin

196

as he tried to recover from the missed hit, pulling the trigger and blowing his brains across the walls behind him. Pushing the falling body out of the way he leaped at the door, ignoring everything else in the room. He kicked the door open as he fought against the heavy curtain obscuring it. The man who had tried futilely to hold it closed was propelled across the room and fell against the steel desk.

His rage clouded his judgment and, without thinking, he raised his pistol and pumped round after round at the man sprawled over his desk. His body bucked and twisted as the heavy caliber rounds tore through his body spraying the wall behind him almost black in the low light of the interior.

As his gun clicked empty, he pulled the trigger a few more times until realization dawned on what he may have done. With a cry of torment, he took a pace forwards and pulled the dead, bullet-riddled man from the rusty steel desk and let him fall to the floor in a crumpled heap.

Tanaka stared in horror.

The battered steel briefcase, for so long displayed in pride of place in the middle of the desk, was covered in blood. Much worse, it had two holes punched through the outer casing.

Tears of panic filled his eyes as his mouth worked silently, repeating, "No, no, no, no, no…" Not wanting to but knowing he must, his shaking fingers pressed the release catches and he yanked the case open.

He closed his eyes and howled in mortal, heartfelt anguish. One of the bullets had smashed through the middle of the case. As he watched through despair-filled eyes a light blinked briefly on the panel, but it stopped as a crackling sound emanated from the case and a small puff of smoke rose into the air.

His way of controlling The Swarm had gone, destroyed by his own hand. Standing and staring at the case one of his men who had heard his cry rushed into the room. Without thinking he turned and smashed his still smoking pistol into his face and screamed at him to get out. The man turned and fled.

He was not sure how long he stood staring at the ruined device, his mind trying to comprehend the enormity of the disaster, but eventually the shouting and other noises seeping through the open door slowly brought him out of his trance. As usual his primary emotion was anger and this reared its head again, filling every pore and cell of his body with the need to avenge the disaster that had befell him. Giving the briefcase one last look he turned and strode from the room. He needed to be the leader again.

His men, the ones who had remained loyal, all stood uncertainly in his living quarters. They had all heard the anguished scream and could tell by the look on his face what mood he was in. Not one of them wanted to bear the brunt of his venom and so avoided his stare and looked anywhere but in his direction. Bodies and body parts still littered the room bearing testament to the desperate battle fought and won. They all knew that the fact they had stayed loyal would not protect them from his wrath.

Tanaka took in his surroundings, the blood, gore and human offal that covered every surface did not affect him. He was accustomed to such sights. The bodies lying everywhere, intertwined in death were difficult to identify as friend or foe. He did not care about them now; they were dead and of no further use to him.

What mattered was how many warriors he still had under his command. His eyes searched and found a man whom he knew was loyal to him without question. He shot his arm out, pointing at him.

"Sanchez. You are my new captain." He watched carefully the reaction of the others as Sanchez smiled and nodded his acceptance. Some looked relieved not to have been selected, but others shot envious and angry glances at the man who now ranked higher than all of them. His mind stored all the information in an instant for use later.

He looked around the room. "We don't have time to clear this up now, I need to know how many remained loyal. Gather the community." When no one moved, he pointed his pistol at them and screamed, "*NOW*!"

Electrified into terrified action they turned and fled.

Standing in his now quiet and empty, if ruined, butcher-shop living quarters he forced himself to be calm and consider his next move. Eventually the rising noises and shouted commands from outside indicated that the community had gathered and drew him to the door. Slowly making his way through the room he stepped over bodies as he finalized in his mind what they must do next.

He walked onto the wide, blood-soaked and body-covered veranda and leaned on the rail, looking down at the gathered people. Hundreds of faces, pale with shock and nerves stared silently back at him. He spent long minutes studying them all. His loyal men, the ones who had fought for him, stood in a separate group holding their weapons ready.

He picked out other warriors standing in the throng. Had they betrayed him? Why had they not joined in the fight? They paled and tried to hide from his scrutiny and he stared at each of them in turn, knowing that with one command from him they would be dragged out of the crowd and killed. That was Tanaka's first thought, but as he counted how many warriors remained, he knew he needed everyone who could still swing a blade.

Surprising them all, Tanaka's face changed from a scowl to a broad smile. He held out his hands in an expansive, all-inclusive gesture and began speaking. "My loyal friends. Thank you for believing in me and not turning your back on my rule." Casting his eyes over the warriors in the crowd he paused briefly before he continued. "I know many of you brave warriors chose to guard your families from the *madness* that overcame the traitors rather than join in the fight, and I do not hold you in any lesser esteem for doing so." Relief flooded over many faces. "But I need you now. *The fight is not over yet!*"

He held up Collins' weapon for all to see, allowing them time to marvel at it as he swept it left and right like a beacon.

"We now have their weapons and they are still trapped in The Source." At the mention of The Source, most looked nervous, the stories from the survivors who had made it back fresh in all minds. Noticing this he changed his approach but continued. "Do not worry, we don't need to enter that accursed place, but just wait for them to emerge, starving and dying of thirst for us to kill easily. As we speak, I commanded those that escaped The Source with me to build a wall across the entrance. They are trapped and can't escape." He softened his tone. "I know you are all exhausted after what has happened amongst us, but I need one more thing from you, my loyal friends, we must return to The Source and kill the Newcomers when they emerge." He held up the gun again and raised his voice to a shout. "When we take their weapons, nothing can stop us. We will extinguish their puny compound and take enough guns to arm every one of you. Then we will turn to the traitors at the Three Hills and give them a final choice: join us or die."

He held his arms wide as almost everyone cheered him.

Some did not, and he took that as a sobering reminder to always have a gun and guards to protect him.

Noticing the looks of hatred a few fixed him with he knew they were probably wives or family members of those that had risen against him. He would deal with them later, he decided, when total victory was his.

He indicated to Sanchez, his new captain, to approach. "Pick ten loyal men to remain on guard. We are leaving as soon as we are ready."

Chapter 23

Information Is Key

In the bunker the time waiting for the recent defrostees to recover was spent usefully. Geiger and Jones, guided by Annie, had replenished everyone's expended ammunition from the stores. Other supplies were unpacked that were deemed useful to the objective of getting out of the complex alive, and Geiger was fussing over the growing pile of equipment ensuring it was all in good shape after so long in sealed storage.

Annie updated us periodically when any significant movement from the ones still trapped in the bunker occurred, but most had virtually given up as the hopelessness of their situation prevented any positive actions. They were irrevocably disoriented, lost in a pitch-black multi-layer maze of corridors and rooms and after hours and hours of continued effort had no energy or will left to do much other than sit in the dark with their parched throats croaking for help. Two men at one point found the small office where the entrance to the bunker was located.

Even though Annie assured us no noise would escape from the bunker, Hendricks erred on the side of caution and he, Geiger and all the soldiers moved to the door, weapons held ready, just in case. His caution proved unnecessary as Weatherby's data pad relayed the infrared camera feed from the room and they watched as eventually the men found the door again and blindly, fumbling with their arms held out in front of them, exited the room and continued their efforts to escape.

I spent my time with my laptop, scanning through Charlie Annie's memory and programming. With *my* Annie's help, I deleted or recoded anything I found that Kendall had changed, and I could see from the time stamps that the process had begun not long after they had emerged from cryo. His first act had been to disable all communication with both the European site and the ARC in space.

Finding a whole new subsection of programming my eyes opened wide as I translated the code. Annie bleeped in my ear. "Yes, David, this is what I wanted to show you when the time was right. I thought it prudent to wait until you were out of your current situation first, but as you have found it, do you want to discuss it?"

Scrolling through thousands of lines, it took me a while to respond. "I think I understand the bones of it, Annie. Give me a little while longer to get my head around it first."

She bleeped her down-tone, confirming she understood but straight away and slightly to my annoyance as it interrupted my thoughts, spoke to me again. "Perhaps, David, if I show you this it will save time."

The screen on my lap blinked and changed to real text, not the code I had been studying for hours. As I read the document, I couldn't help myself and shouted out loud, "Eades, you son of a bitch!"

My shout got everyone's attention, especially Weatherby who knew who I was talking about.

"What about Eades?" he asked walking up to me and looking at my screen. After a few minutes reading he said, "I knew nothing about this. I didn't authorize any of it, I *swear* it."

Looking up I saw everyone's attention was on us. "Err, I think I found out what Annie told us she would tell us later."

"Yes, you have, David," Annie responded. "It is information on The Swarm. How it came about and how it was first used as a weapon to defend Mister Eades from attack in the European facility known as Echo site. This information is, as Mister Hendricks would say, not 'mission critical' and the knowledge will not help us now."

"Well," Hendricks breathed out in tired response, "we seem to be at a bit of a loose end now, so why don't you tell us to pass the time, Anderson?"

"Do *you* want to, Annie?" I asked. "You've probably got a better understanding of it than I do right now."

"Of course, David," she replied smoothly. "The information comes from a memorandum Kendall uploaded to Charlie site Annie's memory," she announced to the room.

This reminded me and I interrupted immediately. "Where is Charlie Annie, by the way?" She'd been silent ever since *our* Annie had accessed her programming. "She doesn't come online whenever we call your name. Names. Whatever."

"I have deactivated her voice protocols to avoid confusion, Doctor Anderson. We have no need for her now since I assumed control of the memory. Also, she—*it*—is malfunctioning. I hope that was the correct action to take?" Annie had of course made the right decision to silence the now-outdated preprogrammed actions of the old Annie. With a tone of annoyance in her voice, she said, "If I may continue, David, and please from now on, only ask questions relevant to what I am informing you of to ensure the accurate relaying of the facts."

I shrugged as even the new arrivals, who were still getting used to interacting with a self-aware and sentient computer whose influence and involvement in our lives was all encompassing, smiled as she told me off.

"The memorandum can be described as being a form of confessional statement, explaining the actions of Mister Eades and justifying them to whomever would read it in the future. I think, for brevity, I should give you the summary as we can discuss and analyze the full information it gives us later." We all leaned forward listening intently to what she was telling us.

"Tanaka, the original Tanaka from the year twenty-thirty-two, as soon as he emerged from cryostasis, assumed control. Kendall was forced initially to rewrite Annie's code to lock anyone apart from Tanaka from the system and he then organized his most loyal people into a militia to subjugate and force the rest of the community under his command. Expecting us to arrive at any time from the Sierra facility, they planned for it and had drawn up a list of who they would kill and who they would let live, so long as they capitulated to the new regime."

Weatherby snorted in response. "Let me guess, I was top of the list?"

"Mister Weatherby, Kendall's notes do not go into that detail, but if I was him, disposing of you would be the logical decision. Also, Hendricks and the rest of Sierra team."

"Annie," I asked, "are you claiming that your decision to keep us in cryo for nine hundred odd years actually saved our lives?"

"David," she responded dryly, "it would be unworthy of me to do so, but yes it seems that one positive result of what happened could be that I inadvertently saved your lives." Her voice again changed to a firmer one. "If I may continue please? Tanaka's rule over the community, after a few attempted rebellions, became total. He created a society that had only one purpose: to serve him. Tanaka

205

did not want us to become a symbol of hope, so he forbade any talk about us and eventually our presence in space became a distant memory as the years passed and the population struggled under his tyrannical rule. The story told to the others was that the ARC had perished during the strike, but those rumors were difficult to prove."

"And likely some bright spark had a telescope and could still see us up there," Hendricks added. Annie went on without responding to the interruption.

"Mister Kendall went on to explain how they still had contact with the Echo site at that time, and he was secretly communicating with his counterpart there, Mister Eades." At the sound of his name I bridled, sucking in a deep breath through my nostrils and letting it out slowly to try and control my anger at what the asshole had done.

"It appears that Mister Eades was conducting a series of experiments of his own based on his background in genetics. Those experiments were inadvertently helped by irradiated fallout, mutating some specimens of hybrid beetle he had been working on—"

"Oh, good god…" Hendricks groaned.

"God had nothing to do with this, Mister Hendricks," Annie said flatly, "I assure you. Mister Eades was working on a way to exert a hive mind control over a hybrid Cicindelinae and Myrmicinae creation which had grown larger in size through exposure to radiation. Mister Eade—"

"In English, lady," Williamson complained.

"My apologies, Captain," Annie said before adopting a tone that was dangerously close to sarcastic. "Mister Eades spliced subspecies of leafcutter ants with the larger, more aggressive type of Tiger beetle." The room went very still as the air seemed to just stop circulating for a few seconds. I'd seen The Swarm up close and somehow, just finding out what they were made from made the hairs on

206

the backs of my arms stand up. I opened my mouth to ask how they had hardware inside, but Annie beat me to it.

"Mister Eades combined technology directly linked to Echo Annie into the queen specimen he had created with a view to exert programming control over her colony. He informed Mister Kendall of this, who requested he send The Swarm to eradicate Tanaka and his followers and effectively free them... any questions thus far?"

The room burst into noise as everyone started talking at once. My own words were drowned out by Annie raising her volume and silencing us.

"Perhaps questions should wait until I have the time to dedicate processing power to speaking to you all individually," she stated, ending the opportunity to ask. I tried anyway.

"Annie," I said, "that doesn't explain how the things we've encountered have parts of computer gear inside."

"No," she said, "would you like me to surmise?"

"Be my guest."

"I can only see two feasible primary options: one, that The Swarm have human technicians creating them, which is the less likely, or two, that The Swarm has evolved to create its own additions and replacements more akin to a factory line than a hatchery."

The silence caused by her answer was broken by the gruff laugh of their newest soldier.

"Huh!" Williamson snorted. "That makes the job easier; find their supply source and shut it down, just like it's some Taliban weapons factory."

"A remarkably simple solution, Captain," Annie said without a hint of her earlier sarcasm. "However, the evolution of The Swarm would make that task highly unlikely to succeed."

The word *evolution* turned my stomach, but I had to ask. "What do you mean?"

"As with ant colonies, their expansion is fulfilled by a number of ants spawning wings and flying away to create new colonies and effectively becoming other queens in a different territory."

"Wait," Geiger said, holding up a hand and screwing his eyes closed as he could hardly believe the shit they were in could get any deeper, "these things *fly* now?"

"For a few hundred years now, from what I know," Annie answered. "The point being, The Swarm—or Swarms, more accurately—have a weakness: they all originate and rely on a single command network."

"Kill the queen, stop the rest?" Hendricks asked quietly.

Williamson barked his characteristic laugh once more. "Hell, I say we take off. Nuke the site from orbit…"

"It's the only way to be sure," I echoed, unable to hide my smile and guessing that the captain was a guy I'd probably like to share a beer with. You know, if we weren't trapped in a bunker with a bunch of wild cavemen and robo-bugs to contend with.

"Irrelevant and impossible," Annie said dismissively, this telling me that she hadn't quite finished her human education if she didn't know *that* quote. "As it happened, Tanaka was monitoring the contact between the two scientists and tortured Mister Kendall for the device he had created under instruction from Eades as to how to call The Swarm to his location. The Swarm was never unleashed on this continent by Kendall and he was kept in isolation from what I can make out from the old log entries." She continued before anyone else could butt in with a question.

"Fast forward a few decades from that incident and there was an uprising, a successful one this time, during one of the many periods of cryosleep the original Tanaka underwent. During this time a large portion of the population of the Springs left following a brief conflict and started their own community at a place nestled in between three hills. Skip to Tanaka waking up, and his first act is to utilize the device to see if it worked. It did, although it took many months for their migration, and The Swarm came to Africa."

"So where's their off switch?" Amir asked, breaking his silence. He was shocked that the people he had vetted so rigorously had betrayed not only him but their own kind.

"I believe that to still be the Echo site."

"But that was destroyed by an explosion, right?" I asked, trying to think back to the time-lapse footage she'd taken from the ARC.

"Correct," Annie answered, only she had an edge to her voice that sounded hesitant. "But data I have studied leads me to suspect that it came from an external source."

"Hang on," Hendricks cut in being the first of many to think of the same question, "external *how*? Who?"

"I'm unable to extrapolate with any degree of certainty from the data available," she said carefully, "but some facts indicate that the explosion was the result of either a secondary asteroid impact, which would be highly unlikely given that only a few locations on Earth were supporting human life, or a low-yield nuclear explosion."

Chapter 24

Break Out

Armed with this new knowledge they were more desperate than ever to reach the surface. Hendricks passed all his new recruits as fit for duty and was confident that as elite soldiers they would be able to complete the next task: to clear their enemy from the complex. Hendricks issued them all with new wristbands and comms gear from the stores so everyone could communicate, and Annie could monitor and track them as she did all of us.

The plan was simple enough: everyone would stay together with the soldiers taking the lead. There were enough stored night vision goggles for everyone so they could make their way through the complex without having to turn the lights on. Harrison and Tori were the only ones never to have experienced using them—given that the level of technology was akin to witchcraft—so Hendricks had to spend half an hour in the darkened warehouse training and getting them used to wearing the top-heavy goggles which caused a cramp in the back of the neck for everyone not accustomed to the unnatural weight. Annie would direct them through the complex, guiding them to groups of survivors who they would dispose of using suppressed weapons.

Once they reached the entrance, they would assess the situation and work out a plan to escape.

Harrison, using the now-operational radio Weber had set up at Three Hills, had talked to his people. The novelty and wonder of using what he considered a magical device made everyone smile at his child-like amazement when the voice of Travis, the Elder, spoke to him. After learning there was no need to shout to be heard, Harrison was relieved that his people were safe, and his absence hadn't caused too great a problem. Hendricks updated Weber on their plans and after a three-way conversation between the groups it was decided that Weber would stay at the Hills to help protect them from anything Tanaka might do until Harrison returned.

The only activity Annie had picked up was at the entrance to The Source. A recharged drone was positioned in a tree overlooking the area and watched silently as Tanaka's men continued to build a barricade of felled logs across the entrance. No one was entering the cave and they all were industriously strengthening and raising the wall.

They could delay no longer so with a final equipment check by Geiger; Annie turned off the lights plunging them all into darkness. At a single command from Hendricks everyone hinged their night vision goggles down over their eyes and night turned to the proverbial day. The NVGs they had were the latest generation of military technology and the best that Amir's factories produced. Not needing any ambient light to work, they digitally enhanced the light emitted from them which was invisible to the naked eye. Not showing the characteristic low green light that the older generation models did, they made us feel completely invisible to anyone else.

I was in the middle of the column with instructions not to even *touch* my weapon and let the eighteen trained men do any fighting; I was strictly in self-defense mode only. With Annie giving us directions, we silently followed each other through the corridors, the only sounds were mine and Weatherby's nervous breaths and soft footfalls.

Hendricks had chosen to ignore the ones who had descended to the levels below us and only deal with groups or individuals who we couldn't avoid. The rest could be dealt with later…or not.

I tensed as Annie whispered in all our ears.

"Four men, twenty-five yards away around the next corner. Two are sitting, two are lying down. None of them are aware of your approach." Crouching low as those not fighting had been instructed to do, I watched as Hendricks and six others holding silenced weapons at the ready carefully rounded the corner and disappeared from view. Ten tense seconds later the low, barely audible popping sound of the pistols disturbed the air. The metallic clink of ejected brass making a louder sound than the spitting rounds as they pinged off the hard floor and walls to echo.

"All terminated. Form up," Hendricks' whispered instructions came through our earpieces. Standing silently the remainder of us rounded the corner and approached the figures we could see standing ahead. Stepping over the bodies I saw each one had been killed with a shot to the head.

Hendricks gave a low, humorless chuckle which made me question what I thought I knew about him. "I think this will be a walk in the park. We got within two feet of them before one sensed our presence. They all looked just about done in; if we carry on as we are, we should be out of here in no time."

Only a barricade of men armed with bows and arrows to get through then, I thought silently as the image of the deadly projectiles rattling off the walls and hastily built barricade sprang to mind. I thought about saying something but decided against stating the obvious.

Thirty muscle-cramping minutes later, Hendricks and his team had successfully neutralized another ten men who either singularly, or in groups were on our route. Another five remained inside the complex but were too far away for us to deal with now. Annie, whispering in our earpieces as we left the stairwell and entered level one, told us we were one hundred and fifty yards from the entrance. The door was still partially blocked by Collins' body and once we had removed it, she would close the door sealing the remaining ones inside.

I forced myself not to break formation and run as the entrance got closer, my need to feel the sun on my face and breath fresh, unfiltered air and escape the claustrophobic confines of the complex was very compelling, but I stayed strong. Amir, who was behind me, helped calm me as I could hear him too whispering to himself as he tried to calm his urge to run.

"It's okay, Amir," I said quietly, sounding better than I felt. "Almost there."

He grunted in response.

The door was still opening and closing against Collins' body. Hendricks, as he passed him, indicated for two others to pull him aside and clear the doorway. Two of the new additions I noted with gratitude treated his body with respect as they moved him. They had been told who he was and why he was there; he was one of us.

With the lights still off Annie, once the last of us had entered the control room, closed the door. The room looked just as we'd left it after we escaped from Tanaka. Bodies still covered the ground in front of and beyond the rough barrier we had desperately constructed what seemed like a lifetime ago. Spent bullet casings littered the floor and the main entrance door was still jammed open with the rock. The low light spilling through the barely open door was magnified many times in our goggles. I lifted mine up and was surprised that to the naked eye it was only a barely discernable glow.

A low whistle from Hendricks got our attention and we gathered around him.

"Well done guys. Now the door is closed our rear is secure." He looked at me. "Anderson, can you set your laptop up so Annie can send us the live feed from the drone. Then we can plan the next step."

I shrugged out of my pack, struggling a bit as the straps caught on my tactical vest until Weatherby helped me. Pulling the laptop out I opened it and waited for Annie to do her bit. I felt everyone crowding around as we waited.

"You are now online," Annie said as the screen blinked and then showed a clear but distant picture of The Source entrance, only a couple of hundred yards from where we were standing.

Everyone lifted their NVGs so they could see the screen. The light from it cast a small glow around us so we could make each other out.

"Annie, can you zoom in please?" asked Hendricks.

"Of course, Jimmy," she replied smoothly. "I didn't want the rotor noise to attract attention, so I positioned it in what I calculated to be the optimum position to maintain stealth but still preserve adequate coverage."

As the picture zoomed in Hendricks muttered under his breath, "I'm sure you did my dear, I'm sure you did."

The scene didn't inform us beyond what we already knew and expected to see. Figures leaning on the barricade stared at the dark entrance to the cave whilst others carried logs and branches to complete the barricade that stretched fully across the entrance.

"Numbers, Annie?" asked Hendricks tersely, all business again.

"Jimmy, there are eighteen men. Most are armed with axes and half have bows and quivers full of arrows. I estimate your chances of a frontal assault would be successful but potentially costly in terms of injury and potential fatalities. I would recommend caution and not to engage in a war of attrition."

Williamson spoke up. "Why don't we just blast the barricade open with our grenade launchers. Job done." He smiled as he indicated the launcher attached to the barrel of his rifle.

"Captain," Annie spoke sternly but with an air of respect, "I would not recommend that course of action due to the risk of further cave-ins."

He just nodded while those of us who had been caught in the earlier cave-in visibly cringed at the memories and terror of digging our way through the rocks and soil, expecting at any moment to be buried alive under thousands of tons of dirt. Hendricks, usually very composed, had a look of horror on his face as he blurted out, "No explosives. We can't risk it I'm afraid."

Bringing himself back under control he continued. "We know the cavern will provide us with no cover and the barricade they have constructed looks strong enough to absorb our fire. The light entering it will also negate any advantage we had of working in the dark." He looked at Captain Williamson. "How about you and I do a little recon mission and see if we can come up with a plan." The big captain nodded in agreement.

"Understood," Williamson replied. Then turning to his men he said, "Hold here, boys. When the shooting starts don't wait for an order, just hightail your asses after us because the plan might not be going as well as we hoped."

"You betcha, sir," one of the soldiers chimed in. "No plan and all that…"

Hendricks smiled and in the dim light waved his hands. "Indeed. No plan survives first contact with the enemy." He patted Geiger on his back. "Look after the shop while I'm gone, old chap?"

Both men pulled off their packs and after a quick but professionally thorough check of their main weapons and side arms, lowered their NVGs. After carefully and quietly climbing over the barricade they cautiously made their way through the main door and headed up the sloping tunnel to the cave entrance.

Halfway up the tunnel the light was strong enough for them to not need the enhanced vision of the goggles and they both lifted them from their faces. Entering the cavern, they both kept as low a profile as possible. Both knew that for those looking into the dark cavern from the outside, the chances of being spotted were virtually nil, but still they exercised maximum caution.

Reaching a place where they had a good view of the barricade, they both raised their guns and used the optics to study it closely. After five minutes of quiet observation Hendricks tapped Williamson on the shoulder and indicated toward the tunnel. A few minutes later they entered the control room.

It was impossible to see anything beyond the small glow created by David's laptop which made planning and organizing anything difficult as everyone seemed drawn to the soft light akin to moths around a flame.

Hendricks attempted to start the briefing but quickly got frustrated as easily identifying who each of us was whilst wearing NVGs proved difficult. He ripped them off his face cursing under his breath. "Annie?" Hendricks called softly. "Does the main door still work?"

"Yes, Jimmy. The motors control system cut the power and shut it down to save damage when the door kept hitting the rock. Shall I reactivate it?"

"Yes please. If we clear the rock, we can shut the door, get the lights on, and start planning properly without any fear of us being discovered. But Annie?"

She bleeped her up-tone, indicating she was listening. A thought came to me on hearing the bleep. I hadn't heard her bleeps indicating she was active or not for a while because she was always just there, ready to comment on, or add to a conversation or just help us out; sometimes even beating us to it and doing what was required before any of us thought to ask. But more recently I realized, she seemed to have dispensed with it and just joined in or spoke to us without using the sound cues I'd programmed her to respond with. I stored it away as another question to ask her when the time was right. No doubt though, her answer would make complete sense and make me question why I bothered in the first place.

"Yes, Mister Hendricks?" she replied.

"Can you make sure the motor can move the door both ways, I'd hate for you to close it and find out it won't open." He left the rest unsaid. There was no way any of us wanted to try the Dragons' cave again.

"Of course. I had already planned to open it fully once you clear the obstruction." Her tone even sounded like she was really saying, *"Do you think I am stupid?"*

Before Hendricks directed two of the soldiers to move the rock, he looked at me and raised his eyebrows as if blaming me for her sass. Picking two soldiers at random they willingly stepped forwards, picked their way through the piled-up bodies and easily pushed the rock aside. We all watched as the door silently and slowly rolled open before reversing direction and rolled closed. Annie, without being asked, turned the lights on the moment the door gave its final clunk as it locked into place.

It took all of us a few moments of blinking and shading our eyes with our hands before our eyes became used to the unaccustomed glare of artificial light again.

Smiling at us all, Hendricks began again. "That's better isn't it?" We gathered around. "As you've seen they've built quite a wall out there. What I propose is quite simple." He waved his arm toward Williamson and his men. "We have with us the best trained men on the planet, so let's get it done."

The men all nodded with wry, confident smiles. "I reckon we can do that boys, don't you?" Williamson asked rhetorically. "We can show our limey boss here how we get a thousand years of sleep out of our systems."

Low growls of affirmation burst involuntarily from eager throats.

Harrison thumped his clenched fist against his cured, rawhide armor, the dull sound silencing them. "We can fight too." Pulling one of his machetes from the sheath on his back he brandished it in the air. "You have your guns which kill from a distance, but when you get over the wall, it's these that you'll need."

A few of the men stepped back, staring open-eyed at the tall, scarred warrior—scarce more than a boy—from another age as he fixed them all with a look of pure fervor. "I have been fighting them since I was a young boy. I cannot let you battle them alone, to do so would bring shame on me and my people, and I couldn't call myself their leader if I skulk at the back and let others do the fighting."

Harrison stared at them all until Hendricks approached him and laid his hand on his shoulder, saying with a smile, "I've seen you fight. You're right, we *will* need you and your blades once the fighting gets up close and personal. You too, Tori." She nodded, standing straighter and stepping closer to her lover.

Hendricks looked at Williamson. "You haven't seen this pair fight yet; trust me you'll need them at the front when it matters. No matter how good you think you are, once they start wielding their weapons, it's enough to strike the fear of god into any sane man."

Williamson looked dubious until he saw the look Hendricks fixed him with. "Sure thing." He turned and addressed the two warriors. "You stick close to me; we'll get you close enough for some wet work."

"What about us?" Weatherby asked, including me in his statement with a wave of his hand as I stood next to him. I took an involuntary step back as though disinviting myself from whatever he was trying to involve me in.

Williamson chuckled as he turned to us—the multimillionaire businessman and self-confessed man of limited physical abilities when it came to the fight, and the computer geek.

I may be a computer geek, I thought as I jumped to my own defense, but I was also a proven hardass bug-killing champion.

"Heroes one and all." He paused at his own joke. "I was coming to you two next. We'll need every one of us for the plan to succeed. If you two join Geiger here, he'll find you a nice spot where you can take shots to support the main assault." I looked at Weatherby who gripped his weapon tighter and seemed pleased to be included and not forgotten.

"Any questions?" Hendricks asked. When no one responded he continued. "Captain, this is your show now. We'll all have open comms, so try to keep the chatter down to business calls only. If Annie turns the lights off before opening the door, we'll get into position at the tunnel entrance. Once in position it's up to the captain when to begin."

He went around each of us individually—at least those not part of his original team fresh from the icebox—to make sure we all understood the plan before indicating to Williamson that he was now in command.

"NVGs on, people," he said curtly and then a little more unsure as he spoke to Annie directly for the first time. "Annie? Can you switch lights off and open the door?"

"Of course, Captain. Lights off in five, four three…" It took me a few seconds of reorientation to once again get used to the artificial view created by the goggles. I picked out the form of the captain standing by the door as it gave a barely audible metallic clink as the locks disengaged and squeaked slightly as it began opening.

Chapter 25

A Cry for Help

The goggles flared slightly as they adjusted to the increasing light levels the closer we got to the cavern. At a silent command from Williamson's hand we hinged them up and waited for a few minutes for our eyes to adjust to the light seeping through the mouth of the cave. My eyes must be worse than the others because I could hardly see my hand in front of my face when Williamson's voice whispered in all of our ears for us to start moving again. Putting one foot carefully in front of the other I moved forwards following the barely visible back of Jones in front of me.

As we entered the cave, Williamson went to each of us and whispered instructions as to where he wanted us to position ourselves. I found myself with my back to the wall of the cave where I had a decent enough view of the barricade.

Williamson silently formed his soldiers into two groups. He planned for them to use the sides—I think these guys called them flanks—leaving us in the middle ground clear as like a free fire zone. In the low light, which was getting better so I guessed my eyes were adjusting, I checked my weapon. With my limited experience that meant checking it had a magazine attached and reminding myself where the lever was so I could turn it from safe to fire. I didn't want a repeat of last time. I tensed and rested my finger on the lever when Williamson broadcast to us all in a whisper.

"Fire at will."

Hendricks, Jones and Geiger immediately began shooting controlled single shots toward the heads I could see looking over the barricade. They all ducked from view—at least the ones who weren't already dead—as soon as the first bullets were fired. Pushing the lever to take my weapon from 'no bang' to 'bang' mode, I raised it and looked down the sights to begin firing in the general direction of the barricade. I knew the chances of me hitting anything on purpose were remote but I understood the tactics of needing to keep our enemies' heads down to help the assault teams, so I kept a constant rate of fire up. We'd restocked with ammunition from the stores in the bunker so all of my magazines were full, and we carried plenty more in our packs so running out wasn't exactly my biggest worry.

The teams on both sides of the cavern were moving fast, alternating between crouching and firing and advancing in a well-choreographed display that distracted me. I'd seen no arrows, or anything else being fired or thrown at us, so my guess was that the defenders were too busy avoiding our incoming fire to be able to do anything else.

Now, I liked to consider myself a realist which most people saw as me having a real downer on everything, but this whole thing seemed to be happening much easier than I expected it to which told me that something had to go wrong sooner or later.

Karma is kind of a dick like that.

Tanaka ran at the head of his men through the dense forest, his desperate need to return to The Source pushing any thought of a

222

cautious approach aside as he did the low branches and foliage that blocked his path. Sixty warriors, breathing hard on the lung-bursting sprint, kept pace with him as he crashed recklessly through the forest intent on violence, driven by a bloodlust he hadn't experienced before.

Tanaka skidded to a stop when the sharp, concussive sounds of guns firing reached him through the trees. He knew he was less than half a mile from The Source, only a few minutes running at the pace he had set, and his mind raced for a moment before reaching a decision—the only one he knew he could take. He had no breath to spare but managed a hoarse cry of, "Come on, we can't let them escape," before setting off again as fast as his tiring legs could carry him.

When he cleared the trees surrounding The Source it was easy to assess the situation. His men were cowering behind the barricade, which he noticed with satisfaction had been constructed to a pleasing height, and continuous gunfire sounded from beyond it, coming from the cavern itself.

He may have been a vindictive and cruel leader, but a tactical fool he was not. He took only a few moments to decide what to do as he waited for the rest of his men to arrive. As soon as they emerged from the trees, sweat lathered and legs wobbling with fatigue, he began pushing them into position. He couldn't work out how many guns were firing, he just knew there was more than one.

"Archers stay here and pour arrows into the cavern, the rest of you to the wall with me." Running the last hundred yards to the barricade, the quickest of his warriors to recover their breath were already firing arrows in an arc over their heads.

Annie had positioned the drone so it covered The Source entrance. Its advanced optics were zoomed in on the immediate area surrounding it. When the first few arrows harmlessly buried themselves in the ground at the cavern entrance, Williamson seemed unconcerned and I guessed he'd expected some sort of resistance. But when more and more arrows began raining down he realized they weren't coming from the barricade but from a position beyond it. With the amount hitting the ground to either bury themselves deep in the soft earth or skidding along it as the arrowhead bounced off the many stones or rocks that littered the ground, he knew instantly that they came from more than the eighteen warriors they were expecting to fight.

"Annie. What's going on?" he asked, the urgency in his voice making it sound more like a command than a request.

"I don't know, no one on the barricade has used a bow. Hold while I reposition the camera." Seconds later she was back, her voice again displaying either despair or panic, it was hard to differentiate. "Tanaka has returned with in excess of fifty warriors. He has positioned…" She paused as she seemed to be counting. "Thirty-two of them back from the barricade and they are the ones firing the arrows." Another pause. "Studying the firing trajectories you have from all of your current positions, you will be unable to bring any fire to bear on them unless you can gain higher ground."

No one spoke for a few seconds as we all absorbed the information. All of us stopped firing and Williamson told his two groups to stop advancing any further by holding his hand in the air in the universal 'hold position' sign even I understood. It was only when a gunshot sounded from the barricade and a bullet ricocheted off the cavern ceiling that Hendricks shouted, taking command again. "Everyone withdraw. Back to the tunnel now."

Weatherby and I turned and fled. The others executed a more organized and calm retreat.

Gathering together in the tunnel I looked toward the small cave-like opening, starkly bright against the darkness of the cavern. Arrows still impacted the ground outside, but now our outgoing fire had stopped, the amount of incoming arrows had slowed down to just the occasional one embedding itself the dirt. The amount that had been fired in a short time though made the ground outside look like a medieval battlefield.

Weatherby's voice had more than a hint of panic as he stated the obvious. "We're trapped. We can't fight through that many."

Hendricks shot him a cold look. "There are always options. Let's not get our knickers in a twist just yet. Captain?"

Captain Williamson thought for a second. "Fall back. We have no advantage here and I don't want to lose anyone. Only a fool looks for a fair fight, and I ain't no fool."

"They won't run out of arrows," growled Harrison, supporting Williamson's decision not to break cover.

"Okay everyone, back to the bunker and close the door," Hendricks commanded, with a hint of exasperation in his voice. "Annie can you maintain overwatch please and inform us of any changes?"

"Affirmative," she replied softly.

Blinking in the brightness of the artificially illuminated control room, silence reigned for a few seconds as we all gathered our breath.

"We go back to the bunker," Williamson said as he inserted a fresh magazine into his rifle and pulled back the charging handle, "get some heavier weapons and blow the sons of bitches away." His men all nodded their agreement. They were all highly trained combat soldiers able to deal with any circumstance thrown at them, but with all their training and modern weapons they had been forced to retreat by enemies armed with bows and arrows. I could tell they didn't like it one bit, but I also worried that guys like that only knew one way to approach a problem. Show a hammer a nail, and the outcome is pretty obvious.

Hendricks shook his head. "We'll be in the same position and face losses. That or we risk another cave-in."

Harrison spoke next. "Find me a way to get to my warriors. I will bring them back and we will destroy them. Tanaka has declared war on my people, we must punish them for what they did to us."

"How many warriors do you have?" Hendricks asked.

Standing tall and proud, Harrison replied without hesitation, "Over two hundred. All ready to avenge families and friends killed when he attacked our home."

Annie spoke through speakers embedded in the wall of the chamber. "Harrison, you don't need to leave, we can contact them via Weber and the radio, do you want me to open the channel?"

"You beat me to it Annie, again," chuckled Hendricks. "Yes, open the channel please."

Harrison looked monetarily confused until he remembered the magic of the radio with which he had spoken to his people earlier. He then smiled and nodded.

"Comms open," Annie announced.

All eyes were on Hendricks as he called out loud, speaking to the air in the room. "Weber, Hendricks, how copy? Status and location."

After only a pause of a few seconds Weber's heavily accented voice responded through the speakers. "Hendricks, good to hear you. I vondered if you had forgotten about us? I am still at the Three

Hills. The people here are looking after me well." His voice changed to a low, deep laugh. "They are more than a little desperate to do something. Sitting around and vaiting is something these people are not good at."

"Good, because we have a job for you lot." Hendricks gave Weber an update of their situation and what he wanted them to do, telling him to get the radio set up so Harrison could talk to his people.

A few minutes later we all listened as Harrison talked out loud through the radio's inbuilt speaker to his people. He commanded the elders to call all warriors for duty and to head at best speed to The Source. Weber would accompany them and maintain communication via Annie to coordinate the attack once he had assessed and reported on the situation outside.

When all was agreed and the conversation ended, we found ourselves at a loose end in the complex. It would take over an hour for Harrison's people to get organized and make their way to us, so Hendricks told us all to eat and drink something from the supplies we had brought with us and get some rest.

As I was spooning chicken and noodles from the MRE I'd opened, and knowing that my body was still on high alert so rest wouldn't come easy, I decided on the only way I knew to relax my mind: to continue my work investigating and understanding the changes made to Charlie Annie's code by Kendall. Sitting in a chair with my laptop on my knees and Annie in my ear, the both of us worked through lines of code, identifying and discussing any changes we thought needed making. The soldiers seemed to inhale their meal, then maintained their weapons and reloaded magazines before those not on guard found a quiet corner and instantly fell asleep the way only military people seemed to be able to do.

Hendricks, Harrison, Jones, Tori and Geiger did the same, but instead of sleeping, sat quietly together talking between themselves. Weatherby chose to sit in a chair, detached from all of us, with his data pad held in his hand working on something.

It could have been a scene from any airport departure lounge anywhere in the world from before. People wasting time, sitting on chairs that just weren't comfortable enough until called for their flight to continue their journey. The difference was we were waiting for the call to go into battle.

Was it me or was I the only one who couldn't concentrate fully on what I was doing? My nerves were still on high alert and any movement or sudden noise from anyone around me made me jump like a balloon had burst by my ear.

All too soon Annie whispered in my ear, "Put your laptop away, David. The drone outside has detected Weber's wristband approaching. He should be here in ten minutes. I'll warn the others now."

Her voice came through the speakers passing on the same message without any tone to announce her presence.

"Annie, I meant to ask before. Why have you stopped using the bleep to indicate you're on- or offline?"

The laughter in my ear sounded genuine. "You noticed my experiment. I had calculated how long it would take anyone to notice, and you haven't disappointed me. I knew you would be first, most likely because you know my original programming the best, and you asked almost exactly in the middle of the time parameters my calculations dictated you would."

There was no point in telling her I'd noticed before as doubtless she would have an answer for that as well so I remained silent, an indication she should continue.

228

"The tones used to be my primary indication that I was available or not, but now everyone knows my voice I decided to omit it as, apart from not having a physical presence, I feel I am as much a part of the team as anyone else. More so in the fact I can communicate simultaneously with many people individually at the same time and perform numerous unique tasks. The tone, even though it only takes a zero-point-three-five seconds to sound, when they are cumulated together accounted for an average of eight-point-two-six minutes per day. I decided my time was better spent in meaningful communication and not playing noises in your ear when you know I am always there anyway. The only time I have used it is when the bleep would provide a quicker response in times of urgency or my memory would be better utilized on other tasks. The fact that it took you twelve hours thirty-six minutes to notice proves it was a useful experiment to undertake."

She paused and her voice then took on a more sheepish, quieter tone. "Did I do the right thing, David?"

I didn't know how to respond. It was another stage of her development into what she was becoming, and I couldn't even begin to imagine where that would end up.

"We'll talk about this later, young lady," I replied, adopting a fatherly like tone of seriousness. "You're still learning human interaction and we don't want you to run before you can walk."

Her response, intoned with a trace of humor, made me splutter with shock and more than a little embarrassment as to what she actually knew I had got up to with Cat in the pod not so long ago. "So are you, David. Maybe we can learn together. I will look forward to it."

Her voice became serious again. "Weber is on comms."

229

His voice, breathing heavily to betray the exertion he just undergone to get to us so quickly, came through the speakers.

"Ve are overlooking the cave now. It is as you described. The wall is crowded with men and there is a line of archers about fifty meters behind." He went silent for a second or two. "My proposal is ve work around to their rear and when you start firing at them from the cave ve attack. Just don't shoot us, okay?" he finished with a wry laugh.

Hendricks looked at Williamson who nodded and gave him the thumbs up.

"Good plan, nice and simple. We'll return to the cavern and when you're ready we'll begin sniping at the barricade. Good hunting, Weber."

"Ja, you too. See you soon."

Hendricks, walking toward the barricade, raised his voice. "Okay same drill as before. Captain Williamson is in command of the assault."

Amir and I, both holding our weapons a little more confidently, exchanged a nod.

Williamson addressed his men. "Okay boys, same as before. When we get to the wall pick your targets and stand by. If this goes down how I think it will, it's going to be a total melee beyond it, and we won't know who's a good guy or not. We need avoid any blue on blue so if in doubt don't shoot unless you're sure of the target."

"If they're running away can we take it they are the enemy, sir?" one of his men asked.

"My people will not be running," Harrison stated proudly, puffing his chest out. "If any do it will be the cowards from the Springs."

"If they're running away, son, you leave them alone. Unless you have a clear shot that is." The man nodded and muttered a noise of affirmation as we all moved toward the door, stepping over the bodies for hopefully the last time.

Chapter 26

Watch Your Back

Tanaka was staring in growing frustration at the entrance to The Source. The firing had ceased not long after his archers had sent volleys of arrows when he arrived, but since then nothing had happened. He hadn't dared send any of his men to investigate the cavern in private fear that they would refuse, so had spent the last hour doing his utmost to ensure their continued loyalty by telling them what they would do once they defeated the newcomers and took their weapons. Proudly showing everyone his new weapons, removing bullets from the magazine to explain how they worked by inventing the facts he didn't know, trying to prove they were nothing for brave warriors to fear. They were still many and the newcomers few and the next battle would be on their terms, thus rendering their weapons useless. Their arrows had forced them to retreat and would again until they were so few, they would beg for mercy.

The more he kept repeating it the more he began truly believing it himself.

One of his men shouted, "I think I saw movement," as he pointed toward The Source entrance and brought them all to their feet with weapons raised. Tanaka looked but couldn't discern anything different happening in the dark gloom of the cave; still, it was a warning he couldn't ignore.

"Archers get ready," he commanded. Turning back to the cave he could hear the wooden clatter of arrows being nocked and grunts as men drew back on strings. As his own eyes caught a vague alteration in the shape of the darkness ahead of him and he was about to call to his men to loose, the trunk of a tree beside his head splintered under an onslaught of bullets, making him stagger and fall. The archers, in need of no instructions, began pouring volley after volley toward The Source.

Roaring at his men to stand and fight as some were cowering from the withering fire, he kept stealing glances over the rough barrier.

When the firing stopped he experienced a moment of jubilation that once again their guns were useless, when a sudden keening roar of a multitude of voices screaming behind him made the blood in his veins turn to ice. Whirling around, his bowels loosened as the tree line erupted with what seemed like hundreds of men all running in his direction brandishing weapons.

They sliced into the unprotected archers, barely breaking step as blades and axes ripped through bodies leaving twitching corpses in their wake.

"Attack!" he screamed in desperation, raising his own weapon and depressing the trigger to send wild, unaimed bullets into the mass of running men and women. He cut a swath through them, stalling a small section of the attack which allowed his men, who had turned to meet the new threat, the opportunity to counter. Screaming their own cries Tanaka's men ran to meet them. Blades clashed on blades as the two forces collided. Screams and shouts of pain rang out as razor-sharp edges found their marks to cut through clothing, flesh and sinew.

The only men of the Springs not to attack were Tanaka and the few chosen as his personal bodyguard, who crowded around him using their own bodies as a shield no matter how tenuous his hold on the throne had become. In panicked desperation he stared at the field of fighting warriors being forced back, overwhelmed by the savagery and speed of the ambush they faced. His position was hopeless, and he knew it.

It was only when he turned and looked at the cave entrance that he saw with uncomprehending dismay the many men dressed as the newcomers—many more than he knew had entered The Source—running from it, all carrying weapons similar to his.

The coward in him took over. That voice of doubt belonging to the fearful child who possessed the necessary cruelty to be The Tanaka, but not the bravery or resilience to support it, yelled at him in terrified panic. He had no idea where the extra men had come from, but they were there and just about to reach the now undefended barricade.

"Run!" he whispered, the strength and volume of his voice abandoning him as fast as his courage had. He repeated the word, shrilly screaming it at the warriors closest to him. He shouldered through his men and started to run to the tree line as his bodyguards, momentarily stunned by his actions, watched him run until their own sense of self-preservation kicked in and they too took off after their illustrious and brave leader.

Williamson was the first at the barricade, leaping at it and clambering up and over it with ease. As he hit the ground, he raised his weapon and began searching for targets, his senses picking up the others as they jumped down beside him. Ahead of him lay the confusion of battle as two sides fought their vicious hand-to-hand combat either individually or in small groups. Bodies lay underneath the trampling horde writhing in agony or still in death, forgotten as their comrades fought for their own lives.

Not being able tell friend from foe, he and his men formed a semi-circle, using the barricade to protect their rear and stood or couched with weapons held ready scanning the melee in front of them through the sights of their rifles, fingers on triggers ready to fire at anyone that even raised a weapon in their direction.

Turning his head, he saw a small group break away and run for the trees swinging axes and machetes wildly at anyone near them. Smiling slightly as he remembered the conversation in the caves about only their enemies running away, he shifted his aim and muttered to himself, "Only cowards run." Then more loudly, "Eyes left. Six making a break for it." His finger squeezed the trigger and two fell before he was forced to pull up his gun as a small group of warriors fighting desperately blocked his sightline.

~

Tanaka, six paces ahead of his men, had almost reached the trees when bullets started zipping past his head. Crouching as low as he could without slowing down, he heard the meaty thwacks of bullets striking flesh and men crying out in pain. Tears of fear began pouring from his eyes and a high-pitched squeak of sheer, unadulterated terror sprang from his lips as he fell to the floor and scrambled the last few yards on all fours like an uncoordinated dog and threw himself behind the nearest tree to curl up in a trembling, crying ball. His remaining men, lost in their own terror, ran past him and crashed blindly through the undergrowth desperate to be anywhere but where they were right then.

In battle, a person's senses are at their ultimate height as the body absorbs and inputs as much information as it can about your surroundings. Your full concentration is on the person in front of you, trying to kill you as hard as you're trying to them, but subconsciously you're also taking in every unexpectedly insignificant facet of your surroundings.

Harrison, with Tori protecting his left side, was facing two men at the same time. His blades slashing at and deflecting the blows aimed at him whilst Tori swung her own blades at anyone that got close. The one on his right, overreaching as his swing hissed past his left shoulder, left the smallest of openings which Harrison took without hesitation. While his left arm swung toward the other man, making him pause his attack and giving him the fraction of a second he needed, his right arm shot straight out impaling the other one in the chest.

Even as Harrison pulled back the blade he knew it was a killing stroke; the man was out of the fight. He shifted his position and raised both blades once more before he felt it. The mood of the battle had changed; the pulse was different, like a point had been reached where some undetermined balance had been tipped in their favor.

Men were still screaming their battle cries, but beneath that he felt the hint of panic and desperation.

With a mighty roar that was heard by all, he smashed both his blades through the defenses of his one remaining opponent, seeing the fear flash in his eyes as the warrior foresaw his own death. His blow knocked his axe aside as if it was a stalk of wheat bent by the wind. Harrison's arms were a blur as he reversed his swing and, unleashing all his pent-up rage, powered both his machetes in a vicious downward arc that almost cut the man in two.

The men from the Springs, desperately trying to defend themselves, broke when Harrison's roar rolled across the battlefield. As soon as one turned, the dam broke and the remaining survivors turned and fled to run in all directions. Some fell as blades reached out to them as they passed, but mostly the men of Three Hills were momentarily disorientated by the battle ending, so allowed their fleeing enemies to push past them as if knowing they posed no more threat to them.

Williamson and his men, also surprised by the battle ending so suddenly, couldn't bring themselves to fire into the backs of the fleeing men.

A silence, only broken by the screams and whimpers of the injured and dying, washed across the battlefield. Men, blinking with shock and surprise to find themselves still alive stood silently and stared at the blood-soaked field and carnage that surrounded them. For a full minute no one spoke until Harrison raised his blood-covered machetes in the air and screamed in triumph, "Three Hills!"

His men all roared their reply and brandished their own weapons as they joined in. Their collective outpouring releasing the adrenaline and gut loosening terror that had powered their arms to beyond normal endurance and won the victory.

~

I was crouching with my weapon raised, sandwiched between Hendricks and Jones. Listening to the clashing of blades and roars of battle that was raging unseen beyond the barricade I was trying to work out what was happening. Were we winning? Or would Tanaka be leaping over the barricade to overpower us with an unstoppable tide of warriors our guns couldn't stop?

The silence, when it fell, was more terrifying than the noise of battle; it was so sudden. Hendricks muttered softly but loud enough for us all to hear.

"Hold your positions." I'd lowered my weapon slightly, as if removing it from my shoulder would increase my hearing, but when he gave his command I raised it again, my eyes flicking everywhere in panic searching for an enemy I couldn't see.

When Harrison's victory roar filled the air I literally jumped out of my skin in fright. If I had had my finger on the trigger of my rifle I'm pretty sure I would've involuntarily pulled it. I turned my head to look at Hendricks who, along with Geiger and Jones, had lowered their weapons. The stares of determination and concentration their faces had been filled with changed to smiles of jubilation.

"Ha…have…err, have we won?" I stammered uncertainly.

Hendricks smiled at me. "Looks that way, old chap." Still struggling with the strange phrases the he came out with which always took a few seconds to interpret I just nodded at him.

Before he moved Annie spoke into our earpieces. "The battle is over. Do you want casualty figures?"

Shaking his head, Hendricks replied, "The butcher's bill can come later." He held his hand out to me and pulled up from my crouching position. "Shall we join them?"

Standing next to him he glanced at my rifle and said softly, "Put the safety on, Anderson. I rather suspect it would be bad form to shoot anyone now." I looked at my rifle and guiltily noticed it was still set to full auto, so with a flick of my thumb I moved the switch to safe mode before lowering it on the sling that kept it attached to my body.

"Aw come on, man. I'm new to all this soldiering stuff. You have been doing it your entire life. Cut me some slack, will ya?" I replied, a little bit embarrassed at my rookie status being so obvious.

Hendricks put his hand on my back as we walked toward the barricade.

"I was, chap, I was. It's not a computer game now though, and we don't respawn or get extra lives, so gun safety is paramount no matter how experienced or not you are. But I will say this young man, you are exceeding mine or anyone's expectations on how you would act and behave when the chips are down. What with killing those bugs, especially that beautiful kick you did to protect your girl-friend, I'd take you out with me any time to fight them."

I automatically started to say, "She's not my…" until I realized with a pleasant shock that after the night we had shared in the pod together she more than likely was. He smiled at the wistful look that came over my face.

"Come on," he said, slapping me on the back and almost knocking me off my feet. "The sooner we get this mess sorted the sooner you can get back to her."

The field of slaughter that lay before me, once I had scrambled over the barricade, almost made me throw up the food I'd eaten not long ago. Bodies lay heaped together, each showing the horrific wounds caused by weapons.

Harrison and Hendricks took command of the field.

Harrison's warriors, following a command from him, began sifting through the bodies for any who still lived—Springs or Hills—following their leader's orders to bring them to the newcomers.

239

With aid kits spread before them, Williamson's men had set up a triage area where their battlefield medical training was put to full effect treating the wounded as best they could.

Annie was keeping a constant overhead surveillance, changing the drones that zipped overhead continually but was not communicating much with us on the ground. Hendricks had to ask Annie to land one of the drones so the people from the Three Hills could see it was not a demon or some devil of the sky. Every time one had flown over they'd all cowered from it or raised their weapons to try and smash it from the sky. Once Weatherby and Hendricks had shown and explained what they were, even though suspicious glances were cast toward the whirring machines, the work continued.

Amir had commented on Annie's silence and Annie, with a haughty tone to her voice, answered immediately. "Mister Weatherby, I am here but I do not need to keep reminding you of the fact when it is apparent that you are busy. It will only have the effect of slowing down the work you are doing. My point is proved by the fact that both you and David have now stopped what you are doing to merely have a conversation with me, which will only delay your departure time." I was amazed when she gave what seemed to be a sigh of exasperation before continuing.

"As it happens, in five minutes I was going to open up a communication channel between you two and Mister Hendricks to remind you that if you do not leave in the next thirty minutes you will not make it back to the compound before night falls. I do not need to remind you that even though it is highly unlikely due to the waning moon, The Swarm could still appear.

At the mention of night approaching and The Swarm I noticed Weatherby glancing around in panic as if expecting them to appear at any moment. When he noticed me staring at him he gave a small smile and shrug of apology. I was surprised, though, at my own re-action. The moment Annie mentioned it my first reaction, before I stopped myself, was to reach for my pistol in defense, and not fear, as Weatherby had shown.

Chapter 27

Complacency Kills

Tanaka lay under the cover of a huge fallen tree. He had, in panic, burrowed himself under it to escape any pursuit he had expected to be hot on his heels as he ran from the battle and abandoned the remains of his men to their fate. Paralyzed by fear he hadn't dared move for hours and had lain in a semi-comatose state as his brain tried and failed to comprehend what had happened. He knew he'd soiled himself at some stage but didn't care. So used to getting what he wanted merely because of his name and the fear it brought with it, defeat and humiliation was something he had never experienced before and he didn't know how to deal with it.

He swung between raging with quiet, vengeful anger at how he would bring death to any that defied him, to sobbing fits brought on by fear at the thought of leaving the safe hole he had dug himself into and having to meet his enemy. His mind, always unstable, was becoming truly unhinged.

It was only when the light coming through a small hole in the earth and branches he had used to cover his hiding place began to dim, that the fear of being outside the walls as night fell outweighed the fear of him being discovered. It forced him to dig his way out. Climbing unsteadily to his feet, he shambled off in the direction of his compound, jumping at every sound and expecting at any moment for an attacker to leap out at him from behind every tree. He continually stumbled and fell over as unseen tree roots in the growing dark caught him unawares. Holding his prized rifle out in front of him he screamed in shock every time he fell over, thinking he was being attacked by either a human or an animal.

The ground was soft, often muddy in places, from the torrential rain that fell regularly. Every time he fell in one of these places, his face, hands, clothes and his weapons became covered in a thick layer of it.

In the rapidly fading light he was forced to break into a run to cover the last mile before the land he held sway over in the day became the property of the night, and the terrors that it contained, even though logic and knowledge told him that The Swarm probably would not return for weeks. Forcefully trying to compose himself he made a vague attempt to brush off the worst of the mud and pieces of foliage that covered his clothes and exposed flesh as he stood before the closed gate and raised his fist. He banged on it, bellowing to be let in.

He stood expectantly, assuming that within moments one of his sentries would notice him and immediately open the gate, welcoming him inside with gratitude and deference. He smiled and began thinking of the long hot bath he would enjoy, mentally choosing which of his concubines he would grant the privilege of joining him to ease the stresses he had suffered during the day. Once refreshed, he would then call his loyal lieutenants for a war council so he could issue the orders for the attack that would wipe out both the newcomers and the traitors at the Three Springs.

Impatient and angry at the lack of immediate response, he banged harder on the gate with his fist and commanded once more for it to open. Eventually, a scared-sounding voice called from behind the gate. "Who…Who is it?"

"How *dare* you ask who I am," he screamed back, the rage building inside him. "Open the gates or you will be punished!"

He heard the man's voice call out that Tanaka was at the gate before the screeching sound of the locking bar being withdrawn drowned out his voice. The moment the gate started moving he kicked at it with his foot and forced his way through the widening gap. He aimed a kick at the gateman and berated him for being so slow but was surprised when, instead of cowering in fear, the man stood and stared silently at him. More stood behind him, their faces not showing the fear or respect he usually received, but instead open-faced and obvious hostility.

Uncertainty and fear built up once more in him. He needed to get his most trusted men around him, so he walked determinedly to his quarters. The crowd that had begun to gather in the open space in front of it parted as he stormed past, scowling at them as his mind raced. He could sense the hostility of the people but was too arrogant and blind to the self-belief in his own powers he couldn't understand *why*.

The fact that, in the last twenty-four hours, he had led his people twice to crushing defeats and had brutally at the cost of more of his people, ended a rebellion against his rule did not register in his unhinged mind to why they would still not unquestioningly follow him.

Most of the warriors had died either in the failed attacks at The Source or in fighting on both sides of the rebellion against him. The ones who had escaped the massacre when the warriors of Three Hills had smashed into their exposed rear brought back with them the story of how The Tanaka had fled the field, leaving them to their fate.

244

People openly began celebrating his hopeful demise and collectively they felt the weight the oppression that he had ruled by being lifted. No one had yet dared to even suggest they needed to find a new leader, but the more ambitious of the remaining men knew the time would come when those questions would be raised.

The cost of defiance was clearly on display; Byrne's mutilated body still swung in the town square where he had been hung by his feet as a reminder to everyone the cost of defying The Tanaka. The warriors, especially those that were marked as being loyal to their leader who had guarded the community when the others left, kept their hands on their weapons and a close eye on any they deemed a threat. No one knew where each other's loyalty ultimately lay.

Tanaka stopped on the veranda of his quarters and turned to face his people. Scanning the crowd he was shocked at how few there were. It was mainly the women, the too young or too old to fight, who stared at him. No more than twenty warriors were in the crowd.

"Where are my men?" he roared. "I want everyone here."

A hidden voice, that of a woman called back, the venom in her voice evident to all. "They're all dead. My husband and my two sons have not returned. Hardly any have."

He tried to find the woman who spoke without success, so he fixed his eye on a random woman in the throng to pretend he had and replied, "If they have died, they will be honored as heroes of the Springs when we win our final victory. Their sacrifice will not be for nothing."

"Victory?" another voice, this time male, spat back. "What victory? We have no warriors left."

He had never had his words questioned like this before. No one ever dared, as they knew to do so would bring harsh and immediate punishment upon them. His oratory skills were all about issuing

245

commands he expected to be obeyed immediately, not debating whether he was right or wrong.

Not knowing what else to say, he shouted back, "We have their weapons," as he raised the rifle up in the air and shook it triumphantly.

"You promised we would all have them," another hidden voice shouted from the other side of the throng. "Where are they? We can't fight these people with blades and arrows, not after they decimated us at the entrance to The Source."

"We won!" Tanaka screamed back, his voice high-pitched with rage, spittle flying from his lips as he continued his lies in desperation. "We made them retreat, they could not stand up to your power, we forced them back."

Another man pushed to the front of the crowd and faced Tanaka directly. "Won?" he asked, his voice mocking. "Won? It took me all night to get out of that hell hole. Only one in ten of us who entered returned, and you call that a victory?"

Tanaka could see a warrior he knew to be loyal, the man named Sanchez, who he had recently named as his captain, pushing through the crowd trying to reach the man.

Good, he thought to himself. *At least I have one loyal man left.*

Before Sanchez got to him the women surged around the man blocking Sanchez's efforts to reach him. Sanchez struck out at the women but they mocked him, baying and hitting him back.

Tanaka watched shocked as his loyal captain was mobbed by the women. Eventually he fought his way through the crowd and joined Tanaka on the veranda. He needed to end this gathering as he feared the few lone voices of dissent would soon multiply with each person that escaped punishment after speaking out as his mind sought desperately for an avenue of escape.

And then it came to him.

He stopped the rising noise by raising his hands and calling for quiet, trying to sound more placatory as he spoke. "My friends. I know we have all suffered and lost many—husbands, sons and brothers—but I promise you their sacrifice will be paid for with the blood of our enemies. He reached into his inner pocket and pulled out the object that had been kept secret from everyone for more generations than they could count.

"I will send The Swarm to kill them. The Three Hills were lucky last time and got their inner gate closed, but next time they won't be." He paused studying the crowd. At the mention of The Swarm he had gotten their attention again. Everyone now knew he had the power to control them. "We killed many of the newcomers at The Source," he lied. "When The Swarm breach their walls, they will not stop them this time." Lowering the beacon, he put it carefully, even though he knew it was useless, back into his pocket. The reverence with which he treated it was part of the show he knew he needed to put on to buy him some time, and he could see it was working.

"Now if you give me some time I can instruct The Swarm." Without waiting for a reply, he turned and strode into his quarters.

Pushing the door closed behind him he stood silently trying to calm his rising panic. His people had defied him, daring to openly question him in front of others, and he had been unable to stop it. The crowd had protected the one man brave enough to face him directly, a man he had previously thought of as one of his loyal followers, and it scared him.

A knock at the door made him jump and almost cry out in fear. He pulled his pistol from its holster and held it out in front of him.

The knock came again but this time he recognized the voice as Sanchez's. Hastily hiding the pistol behind his back, he took a moment to compose himself before telling him to enter.

An hour later he was feeling better. Two of his favorite concubines were sharing his large bath, letting their practiced hands run over his body as they soaped and massaged his tired muscles whilst another naked woman kept topping up the bath with buckets of warm water heated on the brazier situated in the corner of his sleeping quarters. His senses dulled from the heat; he was exhausted, and the attention he was receiving almost let him believe that everything was back to normal and that once he was refreshed and rested everything would continue as before.

More to show off and as a symbol of his power he kept the pistol on a small table by his tub. He had cleaned the mud and dirt from it earlier, ejecting the magazine to carefully clean and replace each bullet before pushing it back into position. He didn't know how to break the weapon down and clean it properly; if he had done so he would have seen the mud and dirt that was soiling the inner workings and cleaned it properly.

Oblivious to anything but the sensual pleasure he was experiencing, he was unaware of the looks of disgust and loathing the three women were continually exchanging when he wasn't looking.

A discreet tap at the window, indiscernible unless you were waiting for it, made the women go wide-eyed with fear and exchange a look that changed from worry to determination. They gave each other small nods of encouragement. The plan had been agreed and now they were essential to ensure its success. Buckets clanged together as the girl filled them with water. Noisily she put one down and filled another then rattled them against each other. She clumsily carried both to the brazier, apparently struggling under the combined weight. Tanaka grunted with disapproval. The two in the tub sensually moved in and began nuzzling and muttering what they wanted to do to him in his ear; they knew from bitter experience his depravities and what would get his full attention.

Groaning with anticipation and pleasure he didn't hear the muted cry from Sanchez, who had been guarding the chamber as his last remaining loyal dog. He'd been more interested in the serving woman who had recently entered bearing him a tray of food and drink, before she unexpectedly reacted to his lewd comments and sat on his lap allowing his hands to run all over her. His excitement built right until the moment she drove a hidden knife straight into his heart, with an unexpected crunching sound as the rough blade pierced the muscles between his ribs. Choking in wide-eyed shock, Sanchez died without making a sound that Tanaka could hear.

Her brother and her son, one of Tanaka's bastards she had given birth to years ago when she was a favorite of his before being relegated to a serving girl and pleasure thing for the inner circle of his men, had both died in the attack at The Source. She wanted revenge and she was getting it.

Tanaka heard the door to his chamber open and his senses, despite what was happening to him, shot to full alert. Nobody was allowed to enter his chamber when he was with his women, *nobody*. He pushed the girls off him. His hand searched for and grabbed the pistol from the table and he raised it toward the door. A woman stood in the doorway, a blood-covered knife in her hands, and she stopped in shock when she saw the gun pointed at her.

He saw the blood dripping from the knife and knew Sanchez was dead.

"You *bitch*," he roared, tightening his finger on the trigger.

Nothing happened. The gun didn't fire.

He pulled the trigger again and again unable to comprehend that it wasn't working. His mind raced as he looked at the now useless lump of metal in his hands. Slippery with soap he tried to stand, screaming in rage until the woman behind him placed a rope around his neck and using all her weight, pulled him back into the tub to pin him against its edge and cut his shouts off as he gagged, unable to suck in breath. Water splashed everywhere as his arms tried to reach behind him and his legs kicked out. The gun slipped from his hand and fell into the tub as the two women still in there with him jumped on him, trying to hold him down. He tried to call for his guards—for help—but the rope bit too deeply into his windpipe and all that emitted from his throat was a raspy croak as he fought for air.

No one in the compound reacted to the few screams of rage and shouts of women coming from Tanaka's quarters. They were used to them and had over the years learned to ignore whatever noise, no matter how upsetting, came from their leader's quarters.

Tanaka fought viciously against the three women trying to subdue him, fists connected with faces and legs kicked out as he fought for breath and tried to free himself, but the women were resolute in their actions. Punches didn't bother them as they had all been on the receiving end of one of his beatings more than once; bodies healed, they knew. It was their mental strength that kept them going.

As soon as they were deemed old enough they were selected from within the community and told they were being given the honor to serve their leader. Tanaka was always keeping an eye on the young girls that grew up under his protection and told his lieutenants which ones he wanted them to pick. Their parents knew what was going to happen and did their best to prepare their daughters for it. They could not, under pain of death, prevent it from happening and were forced to accept their child's fate. Being attractive and female was considered more of a curse than a blessing in the Springs.

For years they had endured continued abuse at the hands of their leader, and it had hardened their hearts. They were going to kill him, now that his power was weakened, or die trying.

Once she had recovered from the shock of not being shot the woman holding the knife still wet with Sanchez's blood rushed forwards. The naked figures in the bath were writhing and twisting too much for her to see what was going on. A backhand swing from Tanaka momentarily knocked one of the women off him and she saw her opportunity. Lunging forward she stabbed downwards with all her might and with a scream of fear and rage, thrust the knife into Tanaka's chest.

Convulsing with pain he bucked and knocked the other woman off him. His eyes wide with shock and disbelief he tried to grab the hilt of the knife sticking out of his chest. This only made the wound more ragged as his uncoordinated hands ineffectually tried to pull at it. The water in the tub quickly turned red as the life pumped from him, pouring out of the wound. His strength left him rapidly, and the girl holding the rope released her grip and stood up to watch his face.

Four pairs of eyes—eyes who had all seen and who had all suffered so much because of him—watched as his movements became weaker and more uncoordinated. His own eyes betrayed the realization that it was the people, the people who he had treated as mere property and not important enough to be counted for anything in the society he had perpetuated through his leadership, had done this to him. With a final barely audible gasp of, "You…bitches…" the last Tanaka to rule the Springs died, naked in a bathtub of water colored deep red with his own blood.

Chapter 28

Home Sweet Home

I shook Harrison and Tori's hands as our two groups prepared to depart. Weber and one of the new soldiers called Redford, who Captain Williamson said was their best medic, were going with Harrison and his people back to the Three Hills.

A few of the wounded were still critical and Harrison, after witnessing the apparent miracles they had performed in saving their lives, using equipment and knowledge lost to his people centuries before, gladly accepted the offer. Hendricks offered more of his people to help bolster their security as he could see most of his warriors were both wounded to a greater or lesser degree from the battle and were exhausted from the events of the day. Harrison insisted that they could look after themselves, especially now that what he calculated to be the bulk of Tanaka's warriors were either dead or still trapped inside the bunker.

He may've been too proud to accept the help of other warriors, but he gratefully accepted the offer of our medicines. His men needed it and the politician in him also knew that showing another benefit of what the newcomers could offer his people would probably inflate his standing and help the two communities in coming close together.

"Cat is asking if she can talk to you. Shall I connect you?" Annie asked in my ear. Instantly panicking about what I would say I stammered uncertainly, "Yeah sure, Annie, patch her through."

I spoke to Cat, fighting back the unexpected urge to cry when I told her the basics of what went down. I knew, scientifically at least, that my body was reacting to the downer of the adrenaline leaving my system, but knowledge didn't make the emotions any easier to deal with. I didn't even care if anyone else was listening when I told her I couldn't wait to see her again.

Five minutes later I rejoined Hendricks and the soldiers who were all checking their gear and doing a final sweep of the area to make sure nothing important was getting left behind. The last of Harrison's group were just leaving the clearing, and pairs of warriors carrying their more seriously injured on rudimentary stretchers disappeared from view as they entered the dense canopy of the surrounding forest.

"All okay, lover boy?" Hendricks asked, grinning at me.

Embarrassment flared on my face as again I wondered who'd actually been listening in on my recent conversation. I muttered a reply before turning and shrugging my own pack onto my shoulders.

"Annie?" called Hendricks. "Are we clear to depart?"

"Yes. I am now broadcasting on an open channel to save repetition. The drones have checked the route back to the base and it is clear. The pack of Dragons we encountered on our way here appear to have moved on and I cannot detect them, but please take care in case they evaded my surveillance. If you head southwest, I will give you further directions en route."

Knowing everyone would've had heard what she had said, Hendricks waved his arm in a circular motion above his head and pointed to the southwest corner of the clearing, calling to everyone around him. "You heard Doris; the route home is that way. Remain in formation and don't shoot anything unless I tell you to, as it will probably only piss them off and get you eaten." The new soldiers had all heard our story of the fight to escape from the Dragons in their nest and Annie had shown them via the screens in the bunker her footage of when we came across them on our way to The Source. From conversations they'd had with Harrison's warriors when working together after the battle, they all now had a healthy respect for the terrain around them and what it contained. Metallic clunks of weapons being charged rippled down the line of men.

"Doris?" Annie asked.

Hendricks laughed. "Sorry, Annie, it's what I called the sat nav in my car and it sort of slipped out. No disrespect intended."

"None taken, Jimmy. I detected the reaction your attempt at humor had amongst the men and understand why you did so. I will add it to my memory as it will help me further develop my study into how I should correctly address humans to achieve the most effective results."

"Comedy is all about timing not about analyzing every single word uttered," Hendricks muttered to me as we set out, holding his hand over the mic on his radio. "I'm going to make that girl laugh involuntarily if it's the last thing I do."

I was about to point out to him that Annie was *not* a girl, but a rapidly self-developing highly complex algorithm of code that had taken years, countless millions of lines of work and a vast memory and processer to develop. But I stopped myself as I guess I realized she was much more than that. *She*, hell, I didn't even program her to be any kind of gender and gave her a voice I liked which just *happened* to be female, didn't even exist in the physical sense of the word like we did.

She was omnipresent, always there monitoring probably far more than I realized. We relied on her to keep us safe, perhaps more so than the trained soldier-types whose job it was to do just that and so much more. Her influence was everywhere, and we couldn't function like we were without her.

That Hendricks had referred to her as 'that girl' kinda summed it up for me. Even though you couldn't see or touch her, she was as much a part of our community as any of us.

"If and when you do, Mister Hendricks," she said, demonstrating my point about omnipresence, "I will be the first to tell you, as I will consider that a major development in my evolution." She paused. "And if you think putting your hand over the microphone would stop me hearing you, you need bigger hands."

"Did you just tell a joke, Annie?" Hendricks laughed.

"Did I?" she immediately replied, this time with an element of surprise in her voice. "What I was simply informing you of was that your hand would need to be twenty-one-point-seven percent larger and have a minimum density fifteen-point-nine-five percent greater than current measurements to deaden a voice at the decibel level you emitted to be muffled enough to be inaudible to me."

"Annie, you just ruined it," I admonished her. "If you'd just said yes that would have been funny, but you went and ruined it by explaining your own joke."

"Okay, David," she replied sounding puzzled. "When I have spare capacity and am not actively monitoring you from three surveillance drones, while maintaining overwatch on the base and multiple other activities, I will dedicate some time to study this conversation further." Her voice changed again. "Now please continue your journey otherwise the battery life of the drones may fall below acceptable operational limits." Hendricks and I exchanged shrugs but

256

complied as we knew we'd involuntarily slowed down as we talked to her.

The moment I entered the forest the humidity increased dramatically and within a few hundred yards I was feeling like the out of shape computer programmer I was and not the bug killing, battle-hardened, steely-eyed tough guy I thought the experiences of the last days had made me.

Keeping my head down I concentrated on putting one foot in front of the other and not tripping over any of the roots, branches or other stuff that littered the path, as I tried to keep to the pace set by Geiger. Hours later concentrating too hard on just breathing I barely noticed the daylight increasing, and I bumped into Hendricks' back when he stopped as he emerged from the forest into the open area that surrounded our base.

The ones behind me spread out as they hit sunlight and the new arrivals stared at the metal walls of the circular compound. I noticed a distant figure standing on the walls raising an arm in welcome. Hendricks returned the wave with a smile, recognizing Nathalie even from that distance.

"Shall we go home, gents?" Hendricks asked politely. "I don't know about you, but I could kill for a cup of tea."

Williamson's bark of a laugh almost made me duck like there was more incoming. "Man, could you *be* any more British?"

Entering through the gates we were greeted by the entire community standing waiting for us with a few claps and a low cheer. Slightly disappointed at the lack of a hero's welcome after what we had been through, I remembered that, with everything else that had happened since, I had momentarily forgotten that three of our original group hadn't made it back.

Amir, who had been one of the first through the gates, took advantage of the near silence and spoke.

"In the last days our community has lost people we cared about." He spoke with a soft tone, deftly judging the mood of everyone. "The mission we all signed on for was one of rebuilding and repopulating our planet, our home. Those we lost came willingly, bringing their families with them in many cases, knowing the years of hard work and sacrifice that they would have to endure to ensure humanity's survival. They did *not* expect to land centuries later than we anticipated in the middle of such turmoil and trouble." He paused for breath and to pull a face of mixed concern and resolve. "I would ask for a minute of silence so we can all pay our respects to those no longer with us."

Saying no more he bowed his head and everyone followed suit.

A minute later he raised his head and thanked everyone with a humility I didn't know he possessed. I guessed, like me, he was more than a little tired.

Despite that tiredness which seemed to make even blinking hard, I realized that Amir had just played another power game by being the one to speak first and get everyone to follow his lead. I scanned faces to find Hendricks' but stopped when a hand touched my shoulder and made me turn.

"Hi there," Cat said, her soft, southern accent like music to my ears. Taking my hand, she led me toward a shelter that had been erected against the wall of a pod. Entering it I stopped and stared at the blankets on the large sleeping area made from a pair of inflatable mattresses. The shelter was lit with the soft glow from a few lanterns.

"Did you do this?" I stammered.

"Well, I thought if we wanted privacy this would be better than a pod," she said, taking my other hand in hers as she turned to face

258

me. "They were nice and private, but my back has only just recovered."

I went red with embarrassment and tried to hide it by grabbing her and clumsily attempted to kiss her. Pushing me away she laughed and theatrically held her hand to her nose. "Whoa there, killer. You need a shower first, despite what you northerners may think of us southern girls, we do like our men to smell better than a four-day old jockstrap." Pushing me to the door she told me she would go and get some food ready for when I had cleaned myself up.

Despite whatever I thought I may get up to that night, by the time Cat returned, I was sprawled over the bed, a towel around my waist, fast asleep.

Annie's whispered voice calling my name from a speaker hidden in the wall behind me slowly and reluctantly woke me in the morning. Opening an eye, I saw Cat lying asleep beside me, her long hair draped over her face. My heart missed a beat at how beautiful she looked, and I couldn't take my eyes off her.

"Annie," I groaned in a voice scare above a whisper, "five more minutes…"

Cat's eyes blinked slowly open as Annie replied, "Mister Weatherby has requested you attend a meeting in one hour."

"An hour?" I asked as I smiled at Cat. "*Way* more time than I need…" Annie's only response was to sound the down-tone which, unless I imagined it, sounded like she was rolling her eyes at me.

With my hair still sticking up all over the place an hour later I walked to where Hendricks and Amir were standing, both holding mugs of coffee in their hands. Hendricks gave me a wink as he handed another mug to me and I smiled back weakly knowing that he most likely knew what my new sleeping arrangements were.

"Gentlemen," Amir began, "I've only included the four of us at the moment as we hold all the answers we'll need." He glanced at Hendricks. "Can you give me your appraisal of our current security situation and ability to handle whatever may come at us?"

"It's good," Hendricks answered. "With the new defrostees our strength, as you know, has greatly increased. Coupled with the fact that Tanaka's army has been decimated, the only threat we should need to consider is another attack by The Swarm. Happily, Annie tells me that the moon is waning, and The Swarm tend only to emerge when it's full—that's backed up by Harrison and records Annie has retrieved from Charlie site—so we shouldn't need to worry about them for another few weeks. The only outward action I do recommend is to send a patrol to conduct reconnaissance at the Springs."

"Thank you, Hendricks," Weatherby said. "Security is your department, so please proceed as you wish." He turned to me. "David, I want to know what the full capabilities are of combining Annie with the Annie at Charlie site."

"Surely she can tell you that herself?" I asked. "You don't need me for that."

He smiled and shrugged his shoulders as if offering an amused apology. "I've already asked her and she told me to ask you."

"Annie, why do you need me?" I asked out loud.

"With the two of us I calculate we can answer the question quicker and more efficiently." I detected a tone of hesitation in her voice. "I have already told Mister Weatherby that when I add the memory and processing power of Charlie Annie my ability to operate on a wider scale will increase by a factor of four. But I…I…"

"Annie, you okay?" I asked quickly

"Yes, David," she replied smoothly, back to her normal voice again. "It is just that I think it would be best for you to check the programming I am writing and inserting into my subroutines. They are now proven against the memory and processing power we currently have but I am concerned about my rate of development when that capacity is increased. I may attempt to evolve faster than I can control. That could lead to small errors being missed which could generate unforeseen problems which may be too late to correct."

In the silence that followed I looked at the other two. Was I not the only one once more suddenly with a vision of robots and machines destroying the human race when its self-aware, all controlling computer, decided to eradicate them as the greatest threat to its own survival?

Seeing their faces, I was not.

"Annie," I said cautiously, "put everything in a sandbox and we'll go through it line by line, okay?"

Her voice when she responded sounded relieved. "Thank you, David. I would appreciate that."

"Sandbox?" Weatherby, still musing over what Annie had said, asked with an eyebrow raised in my direction.

"Literally a safe space where we can program things which, if they don't work, can't get out of the sandbox to mess with other systems."

They understood, and I left to find some breakfast before I went back down the rabbit hole with Annie.

Chapter 29

The King Is Dead

The four women of the Springs, now fully clothed, walked cautiously out onto the wide veranda of Tanaka's private terrace, unsure of what to do next. They'd just killed their leader, and no matter how cruel and vicious and hated by some he was, there would still be some loyal supporters amongst the community that surrounded them.

The night around them was full of the normal sounds that filled such a tightly packed community: a baby crying, immediately stopping as the child was comforted; a woman wailing in the distance, probably grieving the loss of a husband or child or maybe both; the soft call of sentries on the wall; the crackle of a log splitting in a fire. The night seemed normal, but it wasn't. The air was filled with an electric sense of tension and unease. It was imperceptible, but it was there, and anyone used to the normal sounds of the community would feel it.

"You, why are you there? Where is Sanchez?" a voice called to them from the darkness. The women froze in fear and clung together as a warrior emerged from the darkness.

It was the warrior who had spoken openly against The Tanaka the previous day. Getting closer he recognized the women and his voice lowered and softened. "Come on, girls, get back inside. If that bastard Sanchez finds you away from his master's chamber, you know what he'll do to y…" his words faded into nothing as he got close enough to see the blood on their hands.

The older woman, the one who had killed Sanchez stepped in front of the others, as if protecting them with her own body. They couldn't hide what they had done for much longer; the dawn would soon start lightening the eastern sky and the community would wake.

She knew the warrior. He had never been granted the honor of the inner circle, instead he lived with a wife and children in a small hut against the southern walls of the community. Even though he had been loyal to The Tanaka he had not been cruel and vindictive as others became when the power of their position grew larger than their morals.

"Sanchez is dead," the woman blurted out. "I killed him."

The warrior recoiled in shock at the words and hurriedly glanced around him to see who else was in earshot. Recovering quickly, he stepped closer to them.

"Then go and hide," he hissed in warning. "You cannot let The Tanaka find you."

He turned to walk away but stopped dead when the woman, with a steely edge to her voice, replied. "Tanaka is dead too. We killed him."

Not believing what he had heard he turned slowly and stared at them as he thought until, with a scream of alarm from all four women, he bounded up the stairs to the veranda and burst into Tanaka's quarters.

A minute later he emerged, white-faced with shock, to lean on the rail in silence for a long time as his mind raced. Eventually, his mind made up, he turned to the women. What had been done could not be undone, it was how to get the community to survive was the question.

"Go and wake the Elders," he ordered, reeling off a list of warriors he thought—*hoped*—he could trust. The elders did not hold as much influence as the ones at the Three Hills did, but they were still respected and honored members of the community. Tanaka did not refer to them much, but the lesser members of the community did, as to raise anything with their leader usually resulted in a punishment of one form or another. The elders provided a valuable buffer, often solving disputes and issues without trouble or bringing them to the attention of The Tanaka.

The Elders entered the bedchamber and stood looking at the man who had ruled them. They had all been community members a lot longer than the man who lay dead in his own bath with a knife sticking out of his chest. They all remembered The Tanaka that ruled before, and some of them the one before that. Indoctrinated in the culture they had lived under for hundreds of years, they were all loyal to the Springs. Some had once been part of the inner circle, before their advancing years caused them to be replaced. The current Tanaka preferred to surround himself with sycophantic followers and not ones who would, through experience gained during a long life serving and keeping the community safe, offer counter advice or question his decisions and orders.

"It is done," one of the Elders said quietly. "We must gather the people. Our strength has gone, wasted by the one lying dead in front of us. We cannot defend ourselves from the Three Hills, especially if what is said is true and they have forged an alliance with the newcomers; something *HE,*" the man spat, "refused to do in case he lost face. Our only avenue is peace, otherwise we face annihilation. We have a duty to protect the people of the Springs now more than ever."

With nods and murmurs of agreement from the others gathered around him, the elders filed from the room and walked onto the veranda.

The elder looked at the warrior who was standing below him surrounded by the ones who had answered his call.

"Sound the bell. Call the people."

The man approached the large triangle of metal that hung from a frame, picked up the steel rod leaning against it and, ringing it loudly, called the community to gather.

⁓

Hendricks chose to include all the new soldiers in the patrol to reconnoiter the Springs the next day. It would give them all a good opportunity to acclimate to the surroundings and, as most had not served together, to work on unit cohesion. Annie was providing drone coverage, her voice continually updating Hendricks on the terrain ahead and what it contained.

Two hours into the patrol Annie detected a concentration of wildlife ahead which on closer inspection proved to be a pack of Dragons and Hendricks decided to work into a position so everyone could observe them. Annie agreed eagerly to his proposal because she wanted to study them closely to aid her research. Hendricks wanted to show the soldiers what dangers they faced in the new world they were in, and also wanted to put his own fears to rest after the terror of having to fight them in the dark, dust-filled tunnel. His leg still hadn't healed fully when one had scraped its teeth down him.

Dr. Warren had inspected his wound, cleaning it thoroughly and redressing it, and had given him an injection of antibiotics declaring him lucky. The wound didn't seem infected and if it had been any deeper, he would probably have walked with a limp for the rest of his life, so long as he didn't lose his leg to infection.

The line of men crept stealthily up to the ridge that overlooked where the Dragons were located. Not knowing how good their senses were Hendricks had chosen a place to observe them that was over two hundred meters from their position. All trained in observation and concealment techniques, the soldiers blended into their environment and lay still. It would take a trained eye to spot them at a distance further than five meters, either that or a nose finely attuned to predation.

Fifteen pairs of eyes studied the pack through binoculars. Hendricks knew what he was going to see, but when the magnified sight filled his vision he gave an involuntary gasp. He heard others, either side of him, despite their training uttering gasps and low curses and he smiled wryly to himself.

Welcome to the thirtieth century boys, he thought to himself.

Over twenty Dragons of differing sizes were foraging through the forest floor below them, their long, scaly armor-covered bodies varied from ten feet long for the juveniles to over twenty-five for the largest adult and that didn't include the thick tail. Their legs were short but overtly powerful-looking, and Annie's earlier description of a Komodo dragon crossed with a saltwater crocodile was a fair description.

"I'm repositioning the drone to get close," Annie whispered in Hendricks' ear. "It will approach from the opposite direction so as not to reveal your position."

266

The faint whirring of the drone moving above the sparse canopy caused the Dragons to react. With a burst of speed faster than anyone could have thought possible for something so big, the largest ones crashed through the undergrowth, their legs a blur as they raced toward the alien noise and their heads searched everywhere to locate the unknown sound. The rest of them acted as a pack; smaller ones were pushed into the center of the group and a ring of protection was formed around them. Every Dragon was emitting growls and hisses that easily reached our position with the exception of five—the largest ones—which began climbing the bigger tress to try and get closer to the sound.

Annie was flying the drone about twenty feet above the largest Dragons, zipping around as she studied them from all angles.

The ones still on the ground had all spotted the drone and their heads followed it perfectly as it moved, rearing up and using their tails to push them further upwards as their snapping teeth-filled jaws made percussive noises.

"Note the behavior of the adult males," Annie said almost conversationally. "It appears that the lounge are adopting protecti—"

"The what?" Hendricks asked, interrupting her.

"The collective terminology for a group of lizards, which I suspect the Dragons most closely resemble, is a *lounge*."

"Can we say pack? That sounds like people would understand."

"We can, if you prefer, Mister Hendricks," Annie answered with such formality that it was obvious she was annoyed. "However, it would be incorrect."

One of the Dragons leaped from the tree it had climbed without hesitation, twisting its huge body as it followed the drone that darted to one side. Annie desperately steered it away but the thing caught it in its jaws and crashed to the ground with a thud that the men watching felt from their position.

"Anything falling from that kind of height has to be injured," Williamson hissed, but the Dragon leaped back up with the drone still trapped in its mighty jaws to charge around, swinging its head at trees and chomping down to smash the drone to pieces in a matter of seconds.

Wide-eyed with shock the men watched with terrified awe the display of pure power and animalistic aggression being played out before them.

"I'm...I'm blind now," Annie spoke urgently in Hendricks' ear. "Can you activate your body camera to enable me to continue monitoring?" Hendricks glanced at the others and could tell she was talking only to him, as though she was nervous or embarrassed.

Hendricks pulled the camera from its pouch and attached it to the mount on his webbing pointing his body toward the Dragon still chewing on parts of drone.

"Try and hold still," she commanded, not having the time for pleasantries.

Hendricks watched as the Dragon suddenly let out a louder roar, more of a screech of pain as it tossed its head from side to side desperately and opened its jaws wide like a snake to try and void itself of the thing it had destroyed.

"It's punctured the battery," Annie exclaimed in Hendricks ear.

"It's what?" Hendricks uttered, not quite understanding what he was seeing. His first thought when smoke started pouring from its jaws was that it was going to turn into a *real* dragon and start breathing fire. If it had, he was not sure that even he could have fought the urge that was raging within him to run away from such a hellish scene screaming in utter terror.

"The chemical reaction activated when the battery is compromised and exposed to atmosphere can cause a violently combustible effect," Annie tried to explain, but Hendricks was still staring at the scene below him, his eyes, usually calm, full of terror.

The rest of the pack—lounge—followed the still screeching Dragon as it thundered away through the undergrowth at a speed none of them had seen an animal move before and disappeared from view. Its harrowing, bone-chilling screech could be heard for a long time after it was lost from sight, but thankfully getting further away all the time.

Letting out a long breath, Hendricks rose to his knees and spoke with a sotto voice, trying to use comedy to ease his still jangling nerves. "I think you broke the drone, Annie."

"*I* didn't, the Dragon did," she replied in an annoyed tone. "I will, however, admit to underestimating the levels of aggression and problem-solving they displayed. When I have analyzed the data more, I will present my theories, but first I must deploy another drone to replace the one destroyed. I was detecting no other threats in the area, so to keep on timescale, if you continue on a bearing of zero-five-zero degrees it will be overhead in approximately ten minutes."

Hendricks looked at the men on either side of him, their faces also showing disbelief at what they had just witnessed.

"Welcome to the thirtieth century boys," he muttered again

Hendricks studied the walls of the settlement he had been to once before through his binoculars from the cover of the dense foliage that grew at the edge of the forest.

"Do you see what I see?" Annie asked.

"Yes, can you get a closer look?" Hendricks replied staring at a section of wall. Within seconds the replacement drone zipped over the cleared ground toward the gates and hovered still for a few seconds before gaining height and returning overhead.

"It's him," she said simply.

Hendricks signaled to the men to get ready and, with a final check of his equipment, stood up and walked into the open.

"Weapons down but stay alert," he said as the men formed up behind him, their weapons held low and eyes scanning everywhere.

A horn sounded from the walls as they approached, heads appearing on the walls and ducking from view. His body tensed ready for action when the gate fifty yards ahead of him began to open. He relaxed again when, instead of armed warriors, a group of older men stepped out from the shadow of the gate and walked toward them.

Stopping five paces apart the elderly man at the front held out his arms and said simply, "Welcome."

"Is that your work?" Hendricks asked, nodding his head toward the walls.

"No, not mine personally, but it is a symbol of our willingness to end the bitter conflict that we have suffered since our ancestors first woke from their long sleep. It is now time for peace. The war is over."

Hendricks raised his head and looked at the head of the last Tanaka, his unseeing eyes staring over what he had once ruled, fixed to a spike on top of the walls.

Epilogue

"Annie, have I got this right?" I asked, not quite believing what he had just worked out.

"Yes, David," Annie replied calmly. "If we want to control The Swarm, we must access Echo site Annie. I have studied all the data and records from Charlie Annie and now we have found the device Tanaka used to direct them I understand it more fully."

"Wait." I held my hands up. "Call Weatherby and Hendricks in here first, they need to hear this."

Under five minutes later the two stood in the small room Anderson had adopted as his office. The desk that took up most of the space was filled with screens and keypads linked together by a tangle of leads. "Annie, I'll explain what we've discovered, but please interrupt if I miss anything."

"If we want to control The Swarm, we need to get to Echo Site." I let that statement hang in the air for a while before continuing. "Eades created the origins of The Swarm but, following the asteroid impact where his region was hit by irradiated lumps of debris caused by the last-ditch nuclear strike attempt, his creation mutated and evolved rapidly. It became, over the course of a few years, what we see now." I looked at two blank faces I was on the verge of losing. "The science will take too long to explain, but it appears the hive queen that he developed controls all swarms globally."

271

"How?" Amir asked.

"Through VLF, very low frequency, that is," I explained unnecessarily as both knew what it meant. "The computer Tanaka used to control it was powered from Charlie site and the transmitter, the one he kept in his pocket, sent the coordinates to the transmitter built into the structure of the bunker."

"Yes," Amir cut in, "we installed it as a back up to send data transmissions to the other sites if primary means of communication failed."

I looked at him annoyed at my flow being interrupted. "If I may continue," I said staring at him. This was *my* meeting and not his. "The best guess is that the hive queen at Echo site receives it then gets relayed by, again we suspect following our study of the organic electronic devices in the captured bugs we dissected, VLF transmission to them. And then they just follow the instructions like lemmings."

"Can't we send our own signal?" Hendricks asked when I paused.

"Unfortunately not," I replied with a sigh. "Tanaka's device was uniquely programmed, and Annie can't replicate the code without accessing Echo Annie's memory, which she can't do until we reestablish the communication link, and that can only be done at Echo site."

"How far away is Echo site?" Hendricks' voice sounded tired as he knew it was a long way.

"Annie?" I asked.

"Echo site is four thousand six hundred and twenty-two miles from our current location," Annie said, this time her voice sounded apologetic.

"There's no way we can mount an expedition over that distance," Hendricks said dejectedly. "Just walking there would take years; it can't be done."

"David, may I?" asked Annie.

I nodded, grateful to let her take the lead. "I agree, Jimmy, until we know what the condition of the site is, the unknown dangers and supply issues involved means that to mount such an expedition is far beyond the capabilities we have." She paused as if knowing her next statement needed a little drama. "But I can reach the site in approximately twenty-two days."

"How?" Weatherby and Hendricks asked at the same time.

"In the bunker Mister Weatherby had secreted at Charlie site is a prototype drone. Its capabilities are far beyond the ones we are currently using. Due to its size and weight it was impractical to send to the ARC so was included in the inventory at the bunker. It's called a Long-Range Autonomous Reconnaissance Drone Aerial Surveillance System or, as I will refer to it by acronym to save time, LARDASS"

I interrupted with a childish but ultimately justified laugh as did the others.

"Lard-ass, Annie? Seriously?"

"I am glad that my attempt at humor was successful," she said without a trace of humor in her words. "The original designation for the prototype was the Long-Range Reconnaissance System, which the designers simply called LARS which is a name that was common in the twenty-first century in areas such as Denmark and Sweden. It is derived from the Roman or Latin name Laurenti—"

"Annie," I interrupted. "The point, please?"

"I apologize, the...*drone* is designed to covertly monitor and send back intelligence on insurgency groups in all theaters.

Developed to fly silently, it recharges via PV, that's photo-voltaic panels, and a small deployable wind turbine giving it the ability to remain on station indefinitely, tracking its targets as they move."

Weatherby interrupted Annie with more than a hint of pride in his voice. "The concept stemmed from severe losses special forces were suffering on covert reconnaissance missions in inhospitable theaters. The drone is capable of replicating most of their mission parameters with no danger to life. It ca—"

"Why twenty-two days?" interrupted Hendricks as he could see Weatherby was about to continue extolling the features of his wonder drone.

"If it flies at night and recharges during the day, I calculate that is the minimum flight time needed," she replied curtly. As if in reaction to her calculations being questioned when they should be taken as fact.

"Is it vulnerable to anything?" I asked.

"Only the electronic disruption prototype device designed and built by the same sub-division of Mister Weatherby's organization." Both mine and Hendricks' eyes turned to Amir, who shrugged.

"If you make bullets," he said unashamedly, "doesn't it make sense to make armor too?"

"My first summation," Annie continued as she ignored us, "was that Echo site was destroyed when the asteroid hit. I was not as independent as I am now and programmed only to observe the other sites when I passed overhead in space. "I understood my error when we studied the records when I brought the others out of cryostasis in the bunker; I assumed the crater at the site was from an asteroid impact, however, following our discoveries about Eades when we connected to Charlie Annie, I discovered a more likely probability."

"Which is?" Hendricks prompted.

"The site remained active for fifty years following the impact, until it was partially destroyed by a nuclear explosion. If you recall, I mentioned this when we were in the bunker. I do not know who fired the weapon, only that the blast radius and pattern fit the profile of a ground burst, low-yield tactical nuclear detonation. The fact that The Swarm is still being controlled by their hive queen intimates that she was not killed in the strike and was most likely located elsewhere. Until I can observe the site, I cannot answer anything else with certainty."

"How will you control the drone over such a distance?" Amir asked. I wasn't sure if he looked smug at finding a potential flaw in the plan.

"The ARC has just enough fuel for me to reposition it in a geostationary orbit over the route I have planned, and I will link my signal directly through the onboard array. The solar panels are still operational and will provide sufficient power to broadcast continual live feed which I will analyze and report on. I estimate that the decaying orbit the station is in will render the possibility of this plan unviable in seventy-nine days."

"So, you *have* thought of everything," Hendricks replied, looking at Weatherby's slightly sullen face. "When can you start?"

"As soon as the drone is unpacked, fully charged and checked over I can begin."

~

The sun was setting when the large, odd-shaped drone with its eight conical rotors that looked more like ice-cream cones than a drive

275

system, spun almost silently to lift it into the sky. The chameleon camouflage system as it was known with some obscure official reference being abandoned because it wasn't cool, instantly blended it into the surrounding environment to hide it from view.

"What Annie said got me thinking," Hendricks said to me casually. "If Echo site was targeted by a nuke, then the chances are it would be either the Russians or the Chinese. My question is, why would they still have an operational nuclear arsenal one hundred and fifty years after the impact? And why would they use it against Echo site?"

He put his hands on is hips and watched the darkening sky the drone had vanished into. I'd asked myself the same questions and more, but the conjecture always led me down a dark road. Better to wait until we have more data to start extrapolating, I told myself, but I still couldn't shake the feeling of dread. I sighed and answered Hendricks.

"I have a funny feeling we may not like what Annie finds there."

About the Authors

Devon C Ford is from the UK and lives in the Midlands. His career in public services started in his teens and has provided a wealth of experiences, both good and some very bad, which form the basis of the books ideas that cause regular insomnia.

Facebook: @decvoncfordofficial

Twitter: @DevonFordAuthor

Website: www.devoncford.com

Chris Harris was born in south Birmingham and proudly declares himself to be a true Brummie, born and bred.

He has a wife, three children and one grandchild, all of whom are very important to him and keep him very busy. His many interests include tennis, skiing, racquet ball, darts, and shooting. He's also been an avid reader throughout his life.

Facebook: @chrisharrisauthor

Website: www.chrisharrisauthor.co.uk

Lightning Source UK Ltd.
Milton Keynes UK
UKHW040626080520
362982UK00001B/93

9 781839 190209